Two Together

Anita L. Allee

Cover Painting Taken from Sunset Photo and silhouettes by the Author
Cover Painting: Mary King Hayden
Graphics Design Linda Hamilton at B & W Graphics

ISBN: 1-59196-852-6
Published in USA by InstantPublisher.com
PO Box 985, Collierville, TN 38027
800-259-2592

This is a work of fiction. Ultimate design, content, and editorial accuracy are the responsibility of the author. Some characters and events are based upon family memories. National leaders and battles are portrayed as they occurred.

Scripture references are paraphrased by the characters from the King James Version of the Bible.

Publisher' cataloging-in-publication
Allee, Anita L.

1. Civil War Missouri. 2. Northeast Missouri History
3. Palmyra Massacre 4. Vicksburg under siege
5. Christian Life-Fiction
Fiction-Title

Printed in the United States of America
by **Instant Publisher.com**
For information contact: anviallee@earthlink.net

Dedication:

This book is a salute to all the small towns and hamlets of the past that produced the grand and gentle citizens of our great nation of the United States of America. May her small towns and communities continue to uphold her heritage in the production of these fine Christian citizens of the world.

This book contains much about the Civil War or the War Between the States. This was a tragic time in America and still has its effects upon the nation.

May the nation stay the **United States of America** and may God continue to bless her.

Characters

Jonathan David Logan - father/adult Union Soldier
Amanda Bowles Logan - wife/mother
Florence Logan - Jonathan David Logan's sister

Second Generation:
Emma Louisa Logan - daughter
Matthew David Logan - son

Madisonville Community Neighbors:
Sarah Waddell - Neighbor Woman
Community Pastor - Rev. Wilson
Village Doctor - Dr. Marshall
Neighbor Girl - Faith Waddell
Village Storekeeper - Noah Liter
Storekeeper's Daughter - Matilda Liter
Talkative Town Matron - Maybelle Warner
Young Union Civil War Soldier - Billy McIntire
Young Civil War Soldier from Iron Mountain Country - Alcott
Matthew's Soldier Friend - Private Martin Anthony

- The Battle Hymn of the Republic was first used in February of 1862 and originally published in *The Atlantic.*
- Dream Quotes for JD Logan are taken from Public Civil War Military Records.
- Other quotes are taken from newspaper accounts or written to appear as authentic reports.
- The Wilson's Creek Courier and Ray family conversations and some names are fictitious.
- Information as to places and casualty numbers was censored in soldiers' letters home from battlefields.

TWO TOGETHER

Prologue 1862

An inhuman scream pierced the peaceful sleep of the fog-ridden night. Men lurched out of their bedrolls.

The strange cry lifted the hair on JD's neck. His men clutched their rifles in one hand. They searched with their eyes and crouched to roll their blankets.

Get out of here, screamed in their minds.

JD and his men were enshrouded in dense fog. He noted faint embers of the cook fires across the clearing. The drip-drip of moisture in the timber was the only sound.

Each listened.

Another sound came—

A moan?

Heatin' Up

During the late winter of 1858, tension rose in the communities before the national senatorial elections. The Illinois senator's race exemplified the discussions in the nation. There, incumbent Senator Stephen A. Douglas raised the issue of the defeated Missouri Compromise. He defiantly argued for *states' rights* or *states' sovereignty,* with new states enabled to make their own decisions on the possession of slaves.

Abraham Lincoln, from downstate Illinois, re-entered politics and became the spokesman for the newly emerged Republican Party. He became their chief leader in his home state. Lincoln uttered his *house divided* speech at Springfield on June 16 of that summer. He felt a nation could not endure, *half slave and half free.*

When Douglas spoke, July 9, at Chicago, he charged, "Lincoln attempts to stir up disunity in the nation."

Lincoln challenged Douglas to a series of debates in their home area. Seven debates were agreed upon to be held over the state.

Because the arguments involved their own state of Missouri, JD journeyed to Quincy, Illinois, to witness one of the debates on October 13, 1858. His son Matthew, and Madisonville leaders: Mr. Snedigar, Yates, Liter, Waddell, and Dr. Marshall, made the trip together on horseback or in the Doctor's carriage.

"There's the Mississippi River. Our ferry should cross just above Quincy, then we'll be on the Illinois side," JD explained to his son.

They passed a small island to the north and docked below the town. The group joined others and trudged up the hill to arrive at the crowded Washington Park. Hours would pass before the candidates' train puffed into town.

JD looked at Quincy.

The town is built on the eastern side of the Mississippi River on bluffs set above the river. The river spreads a mile or more across to the flood plains below Quincy and into Missouri. The states' boundaries lay right out there in the middle of the Mighty Mississippi.

JD stood and looked at the power of the river. He remembered times he had journeyed on its waters.

He turned to observe the men in the crowd.

They seem split. Some follow Lincoln's championing of the north and some Douglas' cause for opening the spread of slavery by offering each new state the chance to determine their own policies.

A few men, keep quiet and listen to all that transpires. For which side are these silent men? Like at home, both causes are represented.

The crowd grew more boisterous. Bottles of spirits passed amongst the men.

Our group is going to keep a clear head and hope to understand what will be said here.

The atmosphere became more and more buoyant as the afternoon wore on.

A short, ornate train, with a passenger car in its length, finally huffed into the station. A cheer went up. The men crowded near the rear of the cars, where a platform had been constructed for the debates.

Douglas was greeted with wild cheers. He acknowledged his fans, then spoke with the skill of a great orator. He wove a spell and held the crowds attention for the first hour with his contention *the citizenry has the authority of self-determination on slavery and other issues.*

JD looked around. *He's quite a magician with this crowd.*

When he finished, the crowd cheered with great enthusiasm.

Lincoln was given an hour and a half. He rose, tall and gaunt to scattered applause.

He's not impressive, but I don't place great importance on first appearances, it's the outcome that proves the man.

Lincoln spoke concisely. His body took on an animation of depth and seriousness during his speech. JD listened attentively as Lincoln laid out his premise in simple and sincere tones.

The man has something about him which draws me into his thought. He makes me dig deep. What I see is not always comfortable.

The crowd laughed boisterously at the home anecdotes Lincoln used to emphasize his points. He finished and seated himself much short of his hour and a half allowance.

Douglas rose and took the full half hour in reply. He attempted to counter any points made by Lincoln. The Senator finished to an ovation again.

This isn't much of a debate, these two speak alone, without contradiction or answers from the other. JD pondered what he heard.

The train departed soon after the end of the speeches The raucous crowd quickly dispersed.

JD and his companions discussed the debate while they journeyed back to Madisonville. There was a difference of opinion, even among this small group. Most felt Douglas far outshone Lincoln as a speaker.

"Lincoln offered more *meat* and common sense in his speech," Dr. Marshall commented.

JD agreed. Like everything else in the nation, *opinions varied.*

JD went home to mull over the thoughts offered in the debates. He discussed his thoughts with his family. He and Matthew told Amanda and Emma of Lincoln's thoughts.

"He wants to grant slaves the right to eat the bread of their own labors, while Douglas argues the slaves have *no rights*."

The family had an opinion, *a man has the right to his own earnings, be it bread or money.*

"I'd hate to work for nothing," Matthew said.

Strange Happenings

Most Sundays, fifteen year old Matthew liked to sit behind their neighbor Faith Waddell in church. He looked through the spider-web of her hair at the kerosene lamps mounted on the wall reflector.

I imagine she looks like the angels the preacher talks about. She and her sister have yellow hair that flies loose from their braids. It curls like a halo round their head and curls to their faces. It is like a piece of Grandma's lace, I can see through it.

Matthew and his sister, Emma, had been special friends to the sisters their entire lives and their friendships continued as the four grew into their teen years.

Matthew looked for Faith and her young dog at every opportunity while he worked on their farm next to the field of her family. He often called the big pup to him, in order to encourage Faith to the fence. The dog gave him an excuse to talk to her because she and the animal were inseparable since she received the little ball of fluff on her fourteenth birthday.

By the time Shep was ten months old, he looked wolfish and neared adult size and strength.

One day the pair played with a stick in their yard. Without warning, Shep turned on Faith and slashed her repeatedly on the arms. The dog leaped into her face. She fought him off, then turned her back and he ripped at her. She ran toward the house. Shep hung on, his fangs locked into her back.

She managed to get the outside door open and herself inside the house, with the snarling dog outside. She slammed the inside door quickly. He savagely attacked the outer door frame. A board bulged loose, he tugged frantically with his jaws.

Sarah heard her daughter's hysterical screams and discovered the girl in the kitchen covered with blood and emotionally whimpering.

"What happened?"

"Shep hurt me," Faith wailed.

Sarah took towels and applied pressure to some of Faith's deepest wounds.

She soothed Faith, "We must bathe you in soapy water to remove as much dirt as we can."

Faith trembled as she removed her torn and bloody clothing.

Her mother placed the wooden stave wash tub on the floor beside the cook stove. Sarah persuaded Faith to step into it. She mixed soap gel into warm water and poured it over Faith's body. She knew the water and soap stung terribly. She couldn't bring herself to scrub any deeper.

When Sarah judged the wounds to be as clean and free of debris and saliva as possible, she rinsed Faith and patted her with toweling. She wrapped the trembling girl in a blanket and treated her most serious wounds, some of which were bleeding again. She applied pressure and linen wraps.

"Faith, let's put your old flannel gown on you. We'll go see Dr. Marshall. You can put your light coat on to cover your gown."

"I don't want to go," Faith sniffed. Her teeth chattered.

" We have to do this, you may need some attention I can't give you."

Faith was very overcome emotionally with her whole

situation, but was reluctant to have anyone see her in this condition.

Her mother reassured her, "With your coat on, no one will think anything unusual. We'll have Dr. Marshall come to his extra examining room. We can stay out of sight of everyone else."

Dr. Marshall was appalled as he worked over Faith. The bites were ripped and jagged.

She is not only hurt physically, she is hurt emotionally.

Faith whimpered, "Why would my dog act this way? Shep and I are friends, I've fed and loved him from the day we got him from the Smiths."

The doctor poured in an anesthetizing ointment and poured chloroform on a soft cloth he placed over her nose. She resisted the sharp scent, but he soothed. When she relaxed, he continued to counsel her as he cleaned and stitched.

Sarah spoke softly and held her daughter's hands in her own as she turned her daughter into positions for the doctor's ministrations.

The wounds required seventy two stitches to close. Those on her right arm and her lower back, where she had turned to protect her face, were most serious.

Surely no friendly, hand-raised pup would do this. He must be rabid, Dr. Marshall thought.

When he finished, he drew Sarah aside. He instructed her privately and asked her to direct her family.

"You must confine this dog for ten days, if he has active rabies, he will die within that time, if he is healthy at the end of the ten days, he isn't mad. During this time don't come into contact with him or his waste. Take precautions to feed and care for him, without coming within his reach. You must do all these things for your family's protection. He could infect other animals too. Don't let cats or other dogs come around him. Do you understand the importance of this?"

Sarah caught her breath. "Do you mean he could have infected Sarah?"

"Yes, I'm sorry, but that could be the case. We won't know for a time." He patted her arm, "In the meantime, you must do as I've said. It all has to be done, regardless of how we feel about it."

Sarah composed herself under his steadying hand on her shoulder.

"Watch the dog for any symptoms and everyone stay away from him."

Dr. Marshall continued, "Watch Faith for a headache, fever, and swelling, or redness of the wounds. She may develop infection in any of these bites."

Dr Marshall turned aside. *And may go mad.*

He ushered Faith and her mother out the back door and spoke one final time.

"Give her one of these envelopes every six hours or so, if she has pain and if you have any problems with any of her wounds or wish to ask any questions, feel free to come and see me any time." He patted the girl's left hand, "Take care of yourself Faith."

Mother helped Faith into the buggy and went back to pay Dr. Marshall, who spoke to her quietly.

"Mrs. Waddell, don't let this be too much on Faith's mind. It's been a very sad thing for her. She needs to heal and not have lots of worries. As for her wounds, be careful she's not too active. She could tear out stitches and the wounds would end up worse. Dress the areas as I've directed and come back in four days. I'm going to send to Hannibal for a mad stone. If it is not loaned out at this time, we'll bind it on her worst wound and hope it can do its work."

"What is a mad stone?" Sarah asked.

Dr. Marshall looked down. "Some feel the mad stone will draw out the poison should the animal have hydrophobia. I'm not sure there is basis for their belief but we want to do everything we can to prevent more serious after-effects. I'll bring it to your house as soon as it comes, if I am able to secure its use."

"If the dog is mad, is there any assurance Faith is not already infected?"

"I'm very sorry, but there isn't anything I can do, other than attempt to prevent other infection and keep the wounds dressed and dry. I'll pray for the best, but watch her closely for any symptoms at all and let me know immediately if anything occurs."

"I will. Thank you, Doctor," her voice caught before she squared her shoulders.

Sarah fought to compose her face and thoughts when she walked to retrieve the anchor from in front of their buggy horse.

Both lost in thought, Sarah and Faith returned home. They were greeted by a frisky pup. Shep bounced around the buggy.

When Sarah helped her down, Faith avoided him. Her mother watched the dog but ignored his antics. She helped Faith into the house and settled her into bed.

Sarah dosed her daughter with the powder the Dr. had given them.

When Faith closed her eyes and her breathing deepened, Sarah went back outside. She took a spare tug chain from their light buggy harness, and cautiously hooked Shep to the clothesline. He had some freedom, but was far away from the back porch. The family could pass in and out of the house beyond his reach.

Two days later, Dr. Marshall arrived with the mad stone. He examined Faith's worst wounds and bound the stone to the largest place on the middle of her back.

"I think this place will give you less problems when you lay down on your side or sit in a chair. Mrs. Waddell, take this dressing off and wash the stone in lye soap once a day. After you dry it, put it back on as I've just done. By the time we remove the stitches, we should be able to see if it's doing its job."

"What will happen if it's working?" Faith's mother asked.

"It is said the stone will turn green if it is drawing out the infection. The washing may remove some of the color and then it can absorb more." The doctor closed his bag and went outside with Sarah.

They talked on the porch.

"Her wounds seem to be making good progress. Do you see anything different in her actions?" he asked.

"I can't see anything, other than she can't move too much without the wounds pulling and giving her pain. I've kept her mostly in bed or doing quiet things. She has peeled some potatoes and mended a couple of pair of socks. Mostly she sleeps. It seems hard for her when she remembers what her pet did. I try to keep her mind off him. She hasn't asked about him, but I see her gazing off into space when she thinks I'm not watching."

"Keep her mind occupied and continue to do what you are already doing. I'll check back in a day or so to see how she is progressing. Some of those minor wounds can soon have the stitches removed."

"Thank you, Doctor. Please continue to pray for us all."

"You know I will." He patted Sarah's shoulder and moved to his horse.

Matthew usually saw Faith each day. Sometimes his sightings were from a distance when they went about their chores, but at other times they worked together or side by side in the families' adjoining fields. He missed her for three days.

On the evening of the fourth day, his worry came to a head. He could stand her absence no longer.

"I'm going to return the shingle cutting tools to Mr. Waddell. Do you want to tell them anything?" he asked his mother and sister. The two ladies shook their heads.

He stepped toward the Waddell home on the pretext of looking for the man of the family.

When he walked up on the porch, Matthew caught a fleeting glimpse of Faith sitting in front of the window.

Faith couldn't miss his approach but left the window. She hurried out of his sight, then closed the door behind her.

Mrs. Waddell was slow to answer his knock. She didn't invite Matthew inside.

He was nervous and stood first on one foot and then the other.

"Is Faith here? I'd like to ask her something?" Matthew said.

"Matthew, Faith is indisposed. She'll be fine in a day or two. I'll tell her you called."

This confused Matthew even more.

"She isn't sick, is she?"

Mrs Waddell shook her head. "She isn't feeling her-self."

"Thank you." *I don't want to be rude but I really wanted to see her myself.* He turned to go.

He walked thoughtfully out to deliver the tools to Faith's father at the barn. He hung them in their place on the wall.

"Thanks Mr. Waddell for the use of your tools. I put a fresh edge on the shingle-blade for you and wiped a little grease on the metal part. That'll keep 'em from rusting if you don't use 'em for awhile." He turned to go and thought better of it, "I wanted to speak to Faith but she didn't seem to be available."

Mr. Waddell ducked his head for a moment.

"Matthew, I'm goin' to break a part of my daughter's confidence, but you must not say anything to her or anyone until she's ready to talk. She has injuries and is embarrassed about them. If we give her a little time, she'll be ready to talk about it before long. She went to the doctor three days ago.

Her pride is hurt and it will take a little longer. Be patient with her."

Matthew was more confused than ever, but Mr. Waddell chose to give him no further information.

For the next week, Faith's family pushed Shep's food to him and lifted his water bucket to and from its place with the prop pole from the clothesline.

The dog showed no further signs of illness and seemed his usual playful self. He ate well and begged to be loose. The ten days drew to a close.

Faith blamed herself, "I must have hurt him in some way to make him attack me. Surely he didn't mean to hurt me." She constantly mauled her thoughts for an explanation for the pet's behavior.

After two full weeks, she sat on the porch in the sun. Shep whined.

"Mother, can I turn Shep loose now?"

"His time is up, I suppose so, but be careful around him."

Faith reached to him, he licked her hand and whined, she stepped closer to give him his freedom. When she raised her arm to release the chain from the clothesline, he turned, leaped for her upraised arm, and clicked shut his jaws, *mostly on air.* His reactoin clipped her forearm, and drew blood from two deep abrasions. Faith reacted quickly and stepped back from the dog.

The chain was still about his neck. As she held her bloodied arm, he was brought up short. Shep lunged viciously toward her. He hit the end of his chain. It jerked him from his feet and he fell backwards. He gained his feet, lunged again, and made terrifying sounds as he struggled against his restraint.

Faith turned. She sobbed and ran back into the house. She shut the door firmly and leaned against it. She trembled and sank to the floor. She covered her face and whiimpered.

"Mo-ther, there is something wrong with Shep, he's crazy again, and at other times— ."

Her mother soothed, "I'm glad you weren't badly hurt again, but animals are not human, to be treated or confined in a safe place. We have to handle this before it goes any further, no matter how badly we feel about the outcome."

She ushered the girl to her room and calmed her.

When Sarah could leave Faith, she motioned her son to the back porch where they conversed quietly.

When Faith returned to the doctor the second time, her eleven year old brother, accepted his responsibility. Ivan took the rifle from behind the door and loaded it.

He threw Shep a piece of raw meat and walked quietly to stand behind the dog. He couldn't bear to look into the eyes of the big pup in a friendly mood. Ivan snapped off the safety and aimed just behind the right ear. His parents had always taught him, *You don't abuse God's creatures. When one must to be killed, it is done quickly and mercifully as possible.*

He closed down his thoughts of Shep as their friend and squeezed the trigger.

Ivan wrapped the dog in his old coat. The family had a special place under the apple tree where they had put the Old Grandma Kitty, Boots, and other pets over the years. He had buried the pet rooster there too, when the old bird died at an advanced age.

Faith returned from the doctor's office. She didn't ask what had happened to Shep. She had a logical answer, but not one her *heart* was ready to accept. She mourned Shep's good side, but feared the unexplained rage he showed toward her.

In a week and a half, Matthew saw Faith walking behind the milk cows.

He hollered over the fence, "Faith, sure good to see you out. We've missed you. Do you want to come over for popcorn and apples Saturday night? It'll be just the family this week."

Faith didn't approach any closer and avoided Matthew's eyes.

I'm surprised at her actions, she usually bubbles over to tell me the latest happenings.

Faith started the cows off and spoke over her shoulder.

"I can't come this week, I've got to finish a sewing job. Maybe I'll see you next week."

She dashed cold water on my relief at seeing her. She can't be too sick or she wouldn't be moving the cows. Matthew observed her going toward her family's barn.

She isn't walking very fast. He removed his straw hat and hit it against his leg. *I'm more mixed up than ever.*

Matthew searched for his sister as soon when he arrived at their house.

"Emma, why don't you go over to see Faith? She hasn't been out much all week and she wasn't herself when I saw her driving the cows today from their woods pasture. Maybe you can figure out what's wrong, but don't tell her I sent you. Maybe she's mad at us or something."

"I need to see her anyway. We've been working on a piece for the next church meeting and it's about time we finished our practice. I'll go after dinner today."

Emma arrived at the Waddell homestead at two in the afternoon. She rapped on the porch door as she usually did and walked in without waiting for a greeting.

Faith washed dishes, she quickly turned, then looked relieved when she saw Emma, but rolled her sleeves down over her wet wrists.

"Oh, you scared me. I guess I was gathering wool and wasn't thinking about anyone being here."

It's odd Faith turned her cuffs down without drying her hands. There are still dishes in the pan. Emma grabbed a dish towel.

"Let me help you there. We got finished early today.

We can practice our song for the meeting next weekend."

Emma saw her friend relax. *My brother was right, Faith isn't her usual self. Wonder what's going on?*

Faith looked at her friend, "Uh, Emma I need to tell you what happened to me. Something went wrong with Shep, I don't know what, but he turned and ripped my arm and back. I've been shocked and hurt by it and didn't want anyone to see my arm."

She rolled up her dress sleeve.

"It's healing, but I plan to keep it covered for awhile. I'm not ready to talk to everyone about it, but you can tell your family—they are all my friends. Matthew was here. I'm ashamed to say I hid from him. I made Mother answer the door and talk to him. She made an excuse for me. I'm really sorry I treated him that way." Faith was breathless.

Emma made soothing conversation to Faith; assured her the family would be concerned about her; and they all cared for her.

"You can tell Matthew what happened. Tell him I'm sorry I didn't tell him myself," Faith said.

Faith wore long sleeves most of the winter, she didn't want to explain her scars to everyone, afraid she'd break down from the scars left on her heart.

Gradually the scars on both receded and became an *unexplained episode.*

Joinin' Up

Seasons passed. The young people grew taller and the country grew more and more unstable.

As the weeks advanced into spring, JD read and thought more and more about Lincoln's attitudes. He became more and more impressed. Murmurs began of Lincoln running for President in 1860 on the Republican ticket.

Douglas had won the senatorial election in Illinois, but Lincoln became the leading Republican spokesman.

Along with everyone else in the country, JD stewed for the last year and a half. The country advanced more and more toward conflict over states' rights and the issue of slavery.

Lincoln was elected President in 1860 and inaugurated March 4 of 1861. Immediately states began to fall away as they seceded from the Union, *leaving a nation split asunder.*

JD had chewed on his decision for the past months.

I knew if trouble came, I must go defend my family and our country, the United States of America, it must stay together.

"Amanda, God will not allow me comfort to sit idly by and see this democracy go up in war. I feel compelled by the plight of the Negroes, they *must* be allowed the freedoms other Americans enjoy and this nation must be kept whole!"

A heavy cloud hung over the family. They absorbed JD's decision. He had mustered every week with the local Missouri State Militia group of neighbors. He went to New London and joined up with a locally raised group of Union soldiers.

I came into this with hope my actions and those of our loyal men will stop this turmoil and bring us all back together.

JD knew when he left some neighbors leaned toward the new Confederacy. Even some in his militia group had southern leanings. Their intention was to protect their own property, not defend the Union. Some river boat pilots quit rather than ferry Union troops and war material. Those in other occupations began to make decisions of loyalty.

It hadn't come down to a final decision in Ralls County, but the tides quickly swept that direction. There would be a parting of the ways for the two factions.

At New London, JD met Billy McIntire, a boy from near Madisonville. They began their war journey together.

JD had no military training, but he had worked under *discipline, his own and his father, Bailey's.* He set out to do a good job at anything he was commanded and to become an obedient soldier.

He found many of the first enlistees *indecisive and out for a lark.* Merry mix-ups occurred when any efforts were made at marching, setting up camp, or carrying out the most simple maneuvers. Their commanding officers, were sometimes militarily trained, these brought some order to the ranks.

The nation advanced toward battles and skirmishes while other local *boys* trained.

Secret Messages

JD could read and write a decent hand. As months flowed by, his officer requested him as scribe for the messages carried by the courier. JD's mind absorbed information, no matter how hard he *tried to forget* what he read..

These messages haunted him. At night the messages played through his mind.

The messages I read further convince me the cause of peace is hopeless and war is inevitable.

He lay down at midnight. Thoughts bounced into his mind. From St. Louis in May of 1861, warnings of common dangers to the citizenry. . . *appeal for your patriotism and sense of justice to exert all your moral power to avert them . . . Governor Fox's southern partisan. . . General Assembly of Missouri, the military bill, regarded as indirect secession ordinance.... This last item refers to Governor Claiborne Fox Jackson and Sterling Price's secessionist leanings and their actions to take Missouri out of the Union.*

This worries me tremendously, I know other Missourians who have northern sympathies. We are a divided people.

JD's mind quieted and he drifted toward sleep, when this message came into his mind: *No Government in the world would be entitled to respect such openly treasonable preparations,* referring to the establishment of secessionists preparations at Camp Jackson near St. Louis and the taking over of the Federal armory there.

I can't believe this can happen in Missouri, with the sentiment of which I'm aware.

I appreciated the actions of the Federal government attesting to the safety and protection of the law-abiding citizens of Missouri and to suppress all unlawful combinations of men, whether formed under pretext of military organizations or otherwise.

I pray, Amanda and the citizens of the state will be protected and safe. Things can get out of hand quickly, if cool heads don't stay in control and serve as a calming influence on the communities. I transcribed this message, "Secessionists have captured fifteen thousand pounds of lead at Lebanon, Missouri, and shipped seventeen kegs of powder by mail to a prominent secessionist."

Union Soldiers are placed at various places in the state where there are threats of hostility. I'm pleased with those at Hannibal, within twenty miles of Madisonville, as one of these placements. I'm not sure if that calms my fears or adds to them. If the forces are necessary, it may mean the war situation has become more serious in my home area, but if a preventive, I approve.

I copied, "Home Guards were authorized for settlement of "the very great excitement has lately pervaded the community." This added to his fears.

I participate in investigations to obtain information as to violations of laws, report rebellion, or acts of oppression by secessionists. I become paralyzed with fear for my family as I see normal, indistinguishable, citizens turn to unlawful acts in their zeal.

JD relayed a message to General Lyon that instructed enlistment of loyal citizens of Missouri to volunteer, without pay, as home guard, and arms to be distributed to these groups.

I witness much disarray in the organization of the local citizenry. I can see problems in determining loyalty among these from my own experience at home.

Armed boats were placed above and below Boonville with patrols to keep surveillance over ferry boats and others navigating the Missouri River, "preventing usage as transport for hostile troops or other illegitimate traffic."

That area is a hotbed of rebel sentiment and southern aristocratic slave owners along the river banks.

More evidence came, the affairs of the state of Missouri became more explosive each day. "Five hundred muskets and other heavier armaments were confiscated" from a shipment bound from New Orleans to St. Louis and Camp Jackson, shipped as *Marble. It has to be disloyal for them to attempt to fool those in charge by using false statements as to contents.*

The District Judge was not found suitable to try this case because of questionable loyalty.

It is rumored the Governor shipped powder and ammunition to my area and around Hannibal to arm his loyal followers. The rumor extends to dispersal of the armaments to be used "against President Lincoln's invading army. The latter "invading army" points to Billy and I."

Hannibal particularly jumped out at JD *Only twenty miles from Madisonville and my family.*

He transcribed: Newspapers, *inflammatory voices, instigating rebellion* are to be closed and Federal troops placed on the Hannibal and St. Joseph Railroad.

This rail line runs through my home area. I'm more and more concerned for my family's safety.

May 8th shipment of arms from Baton Rouge.

Some dispatches raised J.D's hopes, others dashed them to bits. One especially alarming message came May 11th, 1861. *General Lyon was appointed over the area of St. Louis. He captured Fort Jackson May, 10, and claimed those stores for the Federal Government in a bloodless victory. When he marched the 635 to 1000 disloyal prisoners through a section of St. Louis, a mob scene occurred after shots were fired by both sides. Twenty eight civilians and soldiers were killed. With this action, "War is officially declared in Missouri."*

I wish I could relay messages and copy reports without absorbing any of the forthcoming information. Lord, help me keep all this in proper prospective and rely on You for guidance and protection of my family and our nation.

Wilson's Creek

"I've been transferred to General Lyon's command. We're to start for Little Rock soon," JD told a courier, "I won't see you again soon."

They were drawn off from the Missouri River to the Springfield areas, by reported Confederate troop movements.

A Quincy, Illinois, regiment was sent from St. Louis, down the Iron Mountain Railroad to Ironton, Missouri, to join the troops from there to keep the southeastern part of the state, toward St. Louis open, and keep the Federal Arsenal safe.

In Lyon's corps, during the heat of the summer of 1861, JD found the men very independent, they obeyed only as it suited them. It soon became evident to the commanders there must be discipline and subordination of thought, if the soldiers were to function. Reorganization occurred, with the selection of men of leadership to command groups of soldiers. JD Logan became a line officer.

He was now a foot soldier and assigned thirty men to whip into shape. He found three men of substance in his ranks, who refused to take orders. When they refused to march to Jefferson City, he had them disarmed and placed under arrest. These, quickly reconsidered and were placed back in the ranks with an *improved* attitude and knowledge of their mission.

When JD and his men trained, they were ordered to march toward Springfield, where they found flooding waters and a lack of expected stores. His men couldn't travel on empty stomachs, or fight with no supplies. Soldiers with three month enlistments came up for release, some of these determined to leave and returned home. Wages weren't paid, frustration reigned in the ranks, JD included, but he kept his own counsel.

"It pleases me Colonel U.S. Grant, Twenty-First Illinois Volunteers has been assigned to command at Mexico, Missouri for much of the territory of northeast Missouri. This is getting closer to home and includes the Hannibal-St. Joseph Railroad. I'll place my faith in the protection of our home area upon Grant's authority and soldiers," JD said to Billy McIntire as they rested by the campfire. "I hope he's got enough men who are willing to soldier. That's a big area he's supposed to cover."

JD was directed to send out patrols and scouting parties to keep himself informed of all matters in his jurisdiction. He was to supply information to insure the peace of the countryside.

"Sending us back and forth across central Missouri, below the Missouri River has given us drill practice and we've become soldiers," Billy concluded.

They crossed the Missouri and Osage Rivers by the *meanest ferries ever invented.* The men were wet, hungry, and exhausted from the march.

General Lyon received word of eight hundred secessionists. He prepared to send soldiers to capture and disperse this band. Then more urgent word came from Colonel

Sigel near Springfield of 1500 enemy gathered near there. Southerner leaders of Missouri, Governor Jackson and General McCulloch commanded this larger, gathering army.

Lyon had a special dislike for Governor Jackson, he had fought him at Boonville and sought to catch the exiled state officials as they fled south. Lyon followed Jackson to Florence, Missouri, but the exiles outran him.

JD and his men were involved in this fruitless chase.

It appears a pro-union governor will be appointed by a state convention which declared all the offices vacanted when Jackson left Jefferson City. Senator Frank Blair has had a hand in these new developments with a direct connection to Lincoln's cabinet.

General Lyon hurried his column to meet Sigel's request.

Before going far, they received a courier who told of Sigel's defeat and the fleeing of Jackson. After these words, the column was allowed more humane marching conditions, with time for rest and food.

Word came the Confederates gathered at Cowskin Prairie in greater numbers than expected. Southern sympathizer Price's Missouri State Guard, was joined by General McCulloch's, and Pearce with Brigadier General McBride's armies. The southern strength increased daily in southwest and central Missouri. This build up must be curtailed very soon.

General Fremont, still in command of Missouri, failed to supply Lyon's army, but instead concentrated on the Mississippi River corridor. He ignored his other armies despite pleas for men and equipment.

Lyon's army, with Little Rock, Arkansas, as their objective, outran their supplies. They were short of shoes and ammunition. The men were disheartened.

"Withdraw until resupplied," Lyon relayed to his smaller bands, as they camped near Springfield, August 6, 1861. JD and his men rested as they waited. Sore footed, they could not march effectively without shoes.

The southern army of 12,000 were ill equipped and poorly organized, but followed behind Lyon's northern army to within ten miles of Springfield. The rotund, white-haired Price, inspired his army, but his southern men were so eager to hit the enemy, in order to speed the planned attack, Price deferred to McCulloch's command of the collected armies.

Southern Brigadier General Benjamin McCulloch and his command camped ten miles south of Springfield on a creek winding through a wooded and pastoral area of small farms.

On August 9, McCulloch prepared to attack, but an all-day rain hindered them. He cancelled the attack. The men went into camp to prepare meals and rest for the day. All seemed secure, even the pickets rested. Confidence reigned with the larger southern army.

Lyon gathered his aides and field commanders after darkness.

"Retreat, now, will be fatal. We will attack at dawn and then retreat quickly to our supply lines. Franz Sigel's artillery will open at dawn to clear the sleeping Confederates in their camp on Wilson's Creek. The shoes have arrived from Rolla, you've had one day's rest during the rain and we're ready. Prepare your men."

The plans were laid out to field officers. "Sigel will attack from one side of the triangle with his artillery, cavalry and infantry; my main forces will lead a charge on another side, and Sturgis on the other."

JD took aside his men,"We're to follow Lyon into battle. Prepare your equipment and yourself tonight. We hit before daylight tomorrow."

JD's men nervously prepared for their first real battle.

Before daylight, a courier came across an open pasture before the firing was to begin. He met two small children on an old work horse. The courier stopped long enough to speak to the children.

"Where are you going? There's going to be a battle here any minute!"

"We're bringin' in the cows," replied the little boy.

"Well, you get back home, quick. This won't be a safe place for you. Hurry, go!"

"This is our pasture, you can't come here," the little boy was fearful but stood his ground.

"Son, in a battle, we go where we can. Now get. Quick!" The courier pulled the children's old horse around and headed him for home with a slap on the rump with his bridle reins.

The soldier turned to look over his shoulder as he galloped on. The children bounced along on the old horse's back, with no control of the reins, or direction. He noticed the horse was hard-mouthed and older than the two children combined. The courier could tell that those little ones would arrive home, because the old horse was *in control.*

He raced on to deliver his own message.

At the quietest hour of the night, just before dawn, Sigel opened fire. He was in place and on time, as planned.

The children's horse galloped into the front yard, as artillery sounded in the distance. Their father hit the front porch and questioned the two.

As soon as the artillery ended, Lyon and Sturgis advanced to take advantage of the camp's confusion. They maneuvered to begin close combat and held positions to prevent the escape of any southerners from their sides of the triangle.

Back at the Ray house, the children yelled to their father, "Poppa, a man in a blue coat said there was gonna be a battle in our pasture and he made ole Ben come home. I don't know what that noise is, but it scares me," the little boy breathlessly told his father.

The children's poppa stepped back up on the porch, then climbed the railing. He looked into the distance. He could make out the flashes of the battle beginning in the hollow of the woods below the house on Wilson's Creek.

He scooped the children off the old horse. With a child in each arm, he raced into the house. His wife ascended the cellar steps with breakfast meat.

"What's that noise?" she asked.

He shoved the children to the top of the cellar steps.

"There's a battle in our front pasture. Take the young'ns to the cellar and stay there. I'll put the door down. Don't come out, no matter what. Here's the candle."

"Aren't you comin'?"

"Not now, I'll be out here watchin'. If it gets close, I'll be along. I love you all." He lowered the door and covered it with a braided rug.

The little family heard the sound of boots go across the cabin floor and then the scrape of a chair on the porch. The noise of the rocker sounded in the eerie light of the cellar.

Marie was scared, but soothed her children.

"Is Poppa rockin'?"

"Yes, he's lookin' over the farm." The soothing sound of the rocking chair reassured them over the rumble and shake of the earth. Dust sifted from the floor above their hiding place. She began to tell the children's favorite story of Jonah in the belly of the whale.

"Let's pretend we're Jonah. Play like we're in that whale's belly. I'd sit down and rest if we were in the whale's belly. What would you do?"

Poppa Ray heard slight murmurs from the cellar, but he thought, *This is better than tears or cries of fear.*

The courier rode into the area where he'd left General Lyon to find a bedlam of soldiers moving forward toward the southern camp. From astride his horse, he could see Confederate fires being extinguished and the dark forms of men attempting to get themselves outfitted to meet the oncoming tide.

JD and his men spread at arm's length. They quickly flowed toward the confused enemy. By the time JDs men cleared those in their own front ranks, rifle fire was being returned. The element of surprise was now ended and the battle began in earnest.

Union's Sigel met stiff resistence from hard-core Arkansas, Louisiana, Texas, and Missouri troops formed with McCulloch. Sigel pulled back in confusion. He left all but one of his artillery pieces. His batteries turned tail and galloped back along the Springfield Road.

Sigel and his men were routed, but sent no information to his commander General Lyon.

Lyon attempted to rally his men to victory. A bullet took off the general's hat and creased his scalp. Blood ran into Lyon's face and down his thigh. In the thick of the fight, JD saw him take a shot as the general's foot jerked.

The next time JD looked for Lyon, the general's horse was dead and Lyon limped to the rear.

"I fear the day is lost," JD heard him mutter, as he passed.

Lord, don't let that be a prediction of the outcome . JD uttered his own prayer between loading and firing.

Lyon and Sturgis sheared off to regroup. JD's posi-tion was over-run and he found himself, with his men, down and scattered, or in retreat. He hunkered down behind a fallen log in enemy-held territory. He had the opportunity to shoot into the backs of those in gray uniforms who passed him by, but didn't. One man turned back, but when another soldier looked to the rear, JD feigned death, knowing he could lose his life or his freedom at any moment.

Daylight came. The two armies could now see each other. They walked up, fired and reloaded. The carnage was severe. One soldier would call it *reciprocal murder.*

Missouri boy stood toe to toe with Missouri boy and slugged it out.

At the Ray house, the farmer rocked on his front porch. He had the *only front row seat* to the battle being waged on his property, and that of his neighbors. The noise had become too loud for him to hear his family in the cellar.

Lyon rallied his men and returned. As the enemy retreated over JD's position, he rose and joined his own ranks. Lyon lacked reinforcements or support from Sigel, and was blasted off the field. Firing deafened the soldiers. Smoke burned their eyes and they choked, unable to distinguish friend or foe.

The farmer went below to join his family when the armies shrouded in smoke surrounded his home.

Maria was alarmed by the noises but attempted to keep the children occupied and her fear at bay.

During a lull on the battlefield, JD looked around and saw ghoulish faces with mouths full of papers from the cartridges and dissolved gun powder ran off everyone's chins. He was sure he looked the same. He took a drink of water from his canteen and washed his mouth out, then poured water into his hand and washed his face.

He felt better, whether he looked it or not.

"Here they come again! My gun is cool and loaded. Get ready men!" he ordered.

Lyon saw Sigel's colors coming and was relieved. "The artillery is advancing. Now we'll get some relief."

He secured a second mount and swung his hand. The men followed. Lyon led the point of soldiers penetrating the enemy lines. The artillery opened fire, *not on the southern enemy, but upon Lyon's own soldiers.*

The soldiers advancing toward them were not friend, but foe, captors of Sigel's abandoned artillery and colors. Their uniforms were similar to the First Iowa Volunteers' and Lyon was totally fooled, until they were almost amongst his soldiers. The red bearded, bare-headed savior of St. Louis, General Lyon fell dead, with a bullet through his heart.

The routed soldiers of the north fell back. They scrabbled through Springfield, and continued scrambling toward Rolla. They left their fallen commander on the field, along with almost 1200 other northern casualties, and a like number of southerners.

Exhausted and disorganized, the southern soldiers did not pursue the defeated northern army's retreat.

The Ray family adults ventured out of their cellar when the smoke cleared. Their crops lay in ruins and bodies were strewn as the smoke cleared.

Ray turned to his wife, "Keep the children in the house today. I'm going out to clean up."

When Southern President Davis received word at his office of their victory, he ordered McCulloch to Arkansas in deference to Missouri's neutrality. He did not wish to alienate this important border state by any adverse circumstance of occupation. He awaited the secessionist legislature's actions to bring Missouri into his fold. He hoped for a political victory with exiled Governor Claiborne Fox Jackson rather than on battle fields.

At a distance, Southern's Price followed the Federal retreat and left some soldiers to occupy Springfield. General Price felt he had shown his superiority to the northern defenders. He hoped they would go home, lick their wounds, and never come against him again. Some were Missourians, he did not wish to give an undue hardship to his fellow Missourians and soldiers from other states. He had once been their governor, *perhaps in the future?*

JD and his northern troops walked dejectedly along Sigel's route toward Rolla. They were hungry, footsore and demoralized.

The overall northern commander of the district, General John Fremont, finally placed importance on the Missouri countryside and turned from his main goal of conquest of the Mississippi River. He sent five regiments to

Rolla and begged for soldiers from Illinois, Ohio, Indiana, and Wisconsin to join his Missouri soldiers to secure Missouri for the Union.

Sigel had been second in command to Lyon. Despite his defection and the animosity of those who felt he had abandoned them at Wilson's Creek. *Militarily,* they followed him toward Rolla. All but Sigel's own, followed as an army of vagabonds.

Rather than an accepted military march, alternating positions fore and aft, with protection around the vulnerable equipment and supplies, the German Sigel continued at the head of his army. The line of march strung so long some soldiers did not reach camp and safety until midnight; went to bed hungry; only to be called out to repeat the *disheartening yesterday, today.* JD and his command suffered with the others.

The officers became disgusted with Sigel's conduct and the plight of their men. They demanded the equal-ranking, Colonel Sturgis, be given command. The German Sigel yielded to Sturgis on the grounds he personally had no commission. The complaint was signed by all but Sigel's field officers.

JD had survived the four hour battle and the march toward Rolla. He mulled over their situation during the next few days.

We blues fled back toward St. Louis. I am humiliated to be running from the ones we had hoped to beat. We hoped to end the war right there. I guess we were all being idealistic, now we know it will take more than one battle. So many killed. Those I saw on the battlefield. Even the trees were mowed down.

The Rebs aren't following us like we expected. Why didn't they follow up on their victory? We're baffled, but I'm grateful. Four hours — over twelve hundred men out, in only four hours! I hope and pray, my family never hears those casualties. We are demoralized after Wilson's Creek. We weren't ready for the kind of thing we encountered. Not one of us had any idea that two armies would stand face to face like that. I never saw anything like it and hardly any of our soldiers had seen any kind of war, other than some minor skirmishes before this battle.

After his exhaustion lessened, JD settled to write a letter to his family at home.

I'll have to tell the family enough to satisfy them and to match the news they receive, but I won't tell it all. They can't help, they'd only worry. I'll mention the men and other things, hopefully that will be enough.

I'll. get down to the business of my letter. I can't solve our problems now and guess I won't try.

JD scratched the words in parenthesis, to censor any secrets that might help the Confederates, if they found his Union letter.

(Near Rolla, Missouri,) August 15, 1861

Dear Amanda,

I'm fine and Billy McIntire is near by. Billy has stayed with me since we joined up together. He comes from a few miles west of Madisonville, even though I'd never met him before we enlisted.

We have pulled back from Springfield (to near Rolla, Missouri on the Springfield Road) and are resting now.

Let me fill you in on what happened to we three Madisonville soldiers when we joined up. Billy McIntire, Clancy Yates, and I, joined up at New London. We were sent to Jefferson Barracks at St. Louis. We got an enlistment bounty, so you'll find a few dollars enclosed in this letter. This is all I had left after we got outfitted. The regiment preferred we have some items that were more uniform than those we came with, so I traded the squirrel rifle, for a rifle at the armory. I'm sure this rifle is more accurate, but I'd gotten accustomed to the old gal. I tried to send her home, but was unable to find anyone coming your way. I figured with the two guns you had, and the pistol, maybe we needed the money more, so I traded her in.

We went by barges from St. Louis to Jefferson City and docked at a landing below and east of the capitol. The capitol is on a hill top and cattle grazed on the lawn. I had expected a more citified look, but it fit we Missouri country boys.

From there we went overland to Springfield, (but after the Wilson's Creek Battle, we went back to Springfield again and then here to Rolla). Our group will join Samuel R. Curtis' Army of the South West. Doesn't it sound grand? (We'll go into the SW part of the state as) we're following a group of Confederates.

They tell us if we're successful in the campaign, we can save Missouri for the Union. At Wilson's Creek, near Springfield. I saw Missouri boys fight Missouri boys. Some of the southern boys called it Oak Hill. The northern and southern reports contain different names for the same battles.

JD sat looking into the fire and remembered the past days.

When our boys broke and ran I was so ashamed, confused. We weren't able to retreat in an orderly manner. We lost many supplies and munitions. We can't afford a rout like that often or we won't have an army left.

I've learned we were outnumbered almost two to one at Wilson's Creek. It's difficult for an army of one half, or any half to battle an enemy.

JD continued his letter to the family,

Matthew, we had an occurrence you might find interesting. We were very thirsty during one march and stumbled upon a spring in a shallow creek, we used a short piece of hollow tree, scooped gravel up to the base and tiled up the spring to raise the spring's outflow above the level of the creek water. The fresh water flowed from the top of the hollow log. It made a fine drinking spot for the troops as they passed the place. We all took time to fill our canteens. Yankee Ingenuity is a wonderful thing and we bring it into use often.

We will be out of contact much of the time. Don't worry if you don't hear often. I'll keep adding to my letter and post when I can.

Amanda, take care of yourself, Emma, Matthew and Mother. I love you all and hope after this campaign it will all be over and we can return home to peace.

I'm glad I was able to get the crops fairly well along before I left. With Mr. Wasson, Matthew should be able to get winter supplies laid-in for the stock and for the house. The fire wood we had left from last winter should last till January and by then, Matthew and Mr. Wasson should be able to cut more from timber we had down along the creek. It should be cured and burn well by now.

Be careful and look out for yourselves, there are Rebels in your part of the state. Many seem to be around here also. They shouldn't bother you this winter unless it's some hoodlum who is too cowardly to join up.

Amanda, I've folded this on a separate sheet of paper. Tell our children what you think they need to know.

I've heard of incidents of Bushwhackers and criminals from both sides threatening farm families, over the whole state. Keep some supplies hidden, and keep that old corral fence in the wood lot in repair, as a safeguard. I'm glad we taught ole Tennessee to lead. If you have to take her there, you can do it quietly. You sure don't want to lose the milk cow, if you can avoid it. You know our good neighbors. You can depend on them. Stick together if there is any sign of trouble.

Don't let Matthew do anything foolish. Being the man of the house might go to his head if any trouble arises. Better for you all to slip out and to the neighbors' or into the woods, rather than face something alone. Plan a few hiding places and be familiar with where each may go. Don't reveal yourselves until you can scout out visitors.

Loyal neighbors should be able to warn you of anyone on the Salt River road before they get near. Trouble-makers wouldn't know their way from the prairie, unless they are local people. There are well-traveled trails to the mill near Madisonville. Some might find those and investigate to determine why so many pass your way with heavily loaded wagons. The mill may draw hooligans seeking to steal feed and supplies. Again, be very careful. Keep everyone close to home and work together. Always have others around and in sight of each other, especially if you are outside, or in the woods.

J. D. ended his letter to the family:

We've heard Gov. Jackson tried to admit Missouri to the Confederacy, but surely he knows he wasn't speaking for all of us. He is now out of power in exile. We heard he is in Arkansas and former Gov. Gamble has been appointed governor of Missouri. He's a good and loyal man.

We have received reinforcements and are to march (up the River toward Kansas City) shortly.

Take Care of Yourselves, Love, Paw

September 15 and further, 1861:

(As you've probably heard by now, we went from battles along the Missouri River, to Lexington, Missouri and are now headed toward Arkansas. We're kind of hanging around the border right now and biding our time.)

I've remembered an interesting occurrence in the battle of Wilson's Creek. There was a fallen enemy battle flag laying between the two lines of enemy for a long while. A young mounted soldier rode between the lines during a lull. We supposed he intended to surrender, no one fired. When he was within twenty yards of the fallen flag, he spurred his horse and alighted on the side away from us; he picked up the flag and sped back to his lines. The flag sported a Texas Lone

Star as it's crest. We didn't fire as he retreated, we admired his courage.

I heard after the battle, a half dozen wounded Union soldiers gathered around Lyon's body under a small blackjack oak tree.

When word of Lyon's death reached the Rebel lines, Confederate General Rains drew his sword and threatened to kill anyone who touched the General's body. Later the Confederates carried his body to Springfield and turned it over to Union citizens for final arrangements.

There is still honor among soldiers.

At (Sugar) Creek, (Benton County, Arkansas,) Feb. 18, 1862

We moved into Confederate territory by going into (Arkansas) today. We heard General Price has joined McCulloch. Horses and some of our soldiers had problems in (Benton) County (Arkansas,) at (Dunagin's) Farm in early February, but don't worry about us, we're having no problems.

We were amused when we heard General Asboath placed a Union flag at the Court House in Fayetteville, Arkansas on the 23rd, even if it didn't stay long. That is deep within Confederate Territory. We are dug in watching the (Springfield and Fayetteville) roads. We expect to see S. troops any day, but it's been relatively quiet and we've been able to grind flour at the (Osage) Mills and replenish our supplies.

We heard Gen. Fremont lost his command and has been replaced by Gen. David Hunter.

March 10, 1862 (Pea Ridge,) Arkansas

Dear Amanda, Family and Neighbors,

I'll tell you some of the more exciting parts of this month, so you can keep up with what we're doing.

(At Pea Ridge, surrounding the Elk Horn Tavern,) we

placed ourselves in formation March 6th. The ridge formed a horseshoe around the valley fields. I couldn't help but admire the area when we looked out over the valley. The ridge was beautiful and had white granite out-croppings.

To our surprise, we discovered Confederates at our rear and faced about. Col. (Davis') arrival to help our division, saved the day for us. Our Missouri men captured the Dallas Battery.

The whole battle took parts of three days. I have thought about it and we've talked about the battles. I realize the fall of some of their greatest officers and our persistence turned the tide of the battle and assured our victory. The battle was hard fought, but we are safe and victorious!

JD tore off the last part of his letter and let the pages curl in their campfire. The message had stated:

After securing the area, most of the living and wounded moved out. We left many dead to be buried at Pea Ridge near the Elk Horn Tavern. I could never have imagined how it looked afterwards. Having viewed Wilson's Creek toward the end of the battle and helping with the wounded earlier, I shouldn't have been shocked, but I suppose I never could become accustomed to the battlefield after a battle.

He didn't write he'd picked up several caps from the battlefield with holes and remnants of soldiers on them.

JD started a clean page.

The most appalling news was the Confederate Congress admitted Missouri to the Confederacy. Let southern governments try to enforce that decree!

They tell us we've saved Missouri for the Union and for that I am grateful, but I am sad about the losses on both sides and know the repercussions will be felt by families for years to come.

JD stopped to pray. *Oh God, that it could have been brought to peace without the loss of life and limb. I'm sorry, help me, as I must not write this, but we are filled with the deeds that are just past.*

JD continued with his letter:

I am well and feel I will go through this war safely. Keep safe at home. I haven't heard from you for three months, but trust our mail will now catch up with us.

Things appear more peaceful, as we return to secured Union territory in Missouri.

Tell Little Phil Calvert we fought Indians at (Pea Ridge). They were Cherokees from Oklahoma on the Rebel side and their battle cries were worse than Rebel yells, if that's possible.

JD thought to himself, *I shall hear Rebel yells in my sleep all my remaining days. I'll never again allow a child of mine or a grandchild, to learn to scream like that, even in play.*

He again wrote:

I guess you noticed, we are now with an official Missouri regiment. Our MSM was absorbed some months ago into this larger group.

Love, Paw (JD Logan)

JD wrote for catharsis. He ripped off the following information: *bodies stacked like firewood or posts...laid out side by side for burial parties...burial parties advanced searching for wounded among those thought dead...interred together...bodies stripped of useable items...and on...and on...*

His letter continued: *On the governmental front, the War Department placed, Major General McClellan in command of the state of Missouri under the Military Department of Ohio, Illinois, and portions of Western Pennsylvania and Virginia. McClellen replaced General Fremont and his huge ineffective entourage of aides. As I wrote earlier, General Hunter is over the smaller area of which we are part.*

A Pledge of Allegiance

When Amanda went to the store in Madisonville, she overheard loud voices.

John Dickerson shouted, "They made me sign this blamed thing and it makes me mad! I don't know why they singled me out. There are others around here who have said how they feel. They took action on it too," yelled John.

Amanda observed his irate face. He waved his hand, in which he held a piece of paper. He showed the official looking paper to anyone who would examine it. Amanda intended to mind her own business, but John shoved the pages under her nose.

"Mrs. Logan, what do you think of this? Is this fair?" Amanda drew back a bit.

"Well, John, I really can't say, as I don't know what these papers say."

"Here, just read 'em," said the red-faced John.

Amanda took the papers. She found they were an oath of allegiance. She read silently:

"Oath of Allegiance

No. 589 John W. Dickerson Oath

Citizen Files Oct 19, 1862, Ralls County, Missouri

I, John W. Dickerson, County of Ralls, State of Missouri, do solemnly swear I will support, protect and defend the Constitution and Government of the United States against all enemies, whether domestic or foreign: I will bear true faith, allegiance and loyalty to the same, any ordinance, resolution or law of any State convention or Legislature to the contrary notwithstanding; and, further, I will well and faithfully perform all the duties which may be required of me by the laws of the United States. And I take this oath freely and voluntarily, without any mental reservation or evasion whatsoever, with a

full and clear understanding that death, or other punishment by the judgment of a Military Commission, will be the penalty for the violation of this, my solemn oath and parole of honor. And I also swear under no consideration will I go beyond the military liens of the United States forces. Subscribed and sworn to before me, this 29th day of October 1862
C.W. Parks Signed: John W. Dickerson
(seal) James Davis
Pro Mar Jeff City MO
No oath to be administered except by order or with the knowledge and said Commanding Officer or Provost Marshal"

Amanda noted the signatures of local witnesses and officials on the document, along with the instructions for copies with the signatures; and other legal requirements.

I can understand the reason behind such a document, as John has recruited and promoted for the Confederate side of this conflict. I know he is sincere in his viewpoint, even though I disagree. I don't wish to alienate him. He is a little older than my children, but he has been involved in the community. I can't help being familiar with his views on the subject of slavery, state's rights, and independent thinking.

John is one of the few young men his age who remains in the community, most are in the service of one army or the other. He may have recruited and been more active than I know.

"I'm sorry John you had to sign this, you must be irritated by that necessity," soothed Amanda.

"You're d_____ right, I'm irritated! I'm sorry Ma'am, I just got carried away there a minute," apologized John.

Amanda was indecisive as to what to say next, she shot a little prayer toward heaven before she replied. *He may take offense at anything I say.*

"Well, John if there is anything I can do, let me know. I'll pray on it and maybe I can think of something that would be helpful."

Strangely, John seemed soothed by her answer.

The men continued a heated discussion, some for the oath, others against it. Amanda shopped as quickly as she could and left the store.

I don't wish to be drawn into any arguments as to which side of the conflict is right. It's better for us not to alienate others more than necessary. The neighbors know where JD is and that's enough knowledge for them.

In his heart, John knew how Mrs. Logan felt. She was on the opposite side, but she was a good woman and he respected her as a wise Christian.

Amanda's prayer had reached God and rebounded back down into the spirit of John and made a small alteration in his attitude. His anger cooled by several degrees.

Later, Amanda heard John was forced to sign a second oath, as the government renewed the oaths on record, at intervals, or if officials felt there had been an unproved violation of the oath. She read the second oath when the form was published in *The Republican* newspaper out of Hannibal.

The oath is similar in thought to the first, but a little different in form. The main differences are in the stated forfeiture of property and monetary penalties for the breaking of the oath. Each oath becomes more restrictive as conflict progresses.

I know posted bonds are very financially prohibitive to most farmers and business men in our area. Some are required to pay ten thousand dollars. I can understand the necessity for some kind of strong deterrent when one with southern sentiment resides in the midst of northern territory and sympathizers. It creates a hot bed of anger, but it is the law and there for good reasons.

Later, I overheard talk at the store, while I waited for the clerk to add my purchases. Some have broken their oath in battle zones and faced immediate death, forfeiture of the bond, or seizure of their posted property. Thus far, all have been paroled or released when they signed a new and more strict oath.

Men are being caught with as many as three oaths in their possession. I've heard most are quick to place the papers in secure places and don't carry the documents on their person, if they intend to actively participate in things related to the war. Some change their name with each oath they sign. I see lists of oaths posted on the post office wall of the store. I avoid reading the lists, because I don't want to know who is included.

I feel the oath system is a source of fraud. The system has alienated some who were originally for our northern position. To them, it seems an invasion within their lives with little evidence being required to prove their disloyalty and bring about imprisonments or forfeiture.

I know families in the war zones are being penalized, when one of their own family members from the enemy side, come by for a visit and a meal. The military, considers this aiding the enemy. No association with the enemy is allowed. With both sides being American, often both sides represented in the same family. They look the same. It is difficult for anyone to recognize the enemy.

When a suspect, loyal to the south, leaves the family and goes south, an assessment may be placed upon their property or family. I hear this process can be legally protested and if disproved, the assessment removed from the family.

In our local community where people are well-known for generations, the families sense to which side other families lean in their political persuasion.

Some neighbors seem to enjoy turning in others, even on the basis of rumors and some of those have no validity.

As time passed, Amanda thought back on the martial laws imposed upon the citizens of Missouri by General Fremont in August of 1861.

Temporary detention could be imposed if a citizen was suspected. The matter was handled locally by military commissioners or referred to St. Louis. I found in the paper, where Fremont was rebuked when most of his martial laws were revoked. Many of the citizens of Missouri were extremely loyal to the Union, despite the fact they came from southern states originally. The martial laws grated on the nerves of most of the state's citizens and actually did more harm than good.

Other Goin's On

Amanda considered the rumors in the neighborhood.

I heard about another young man, Nathan Smith. He was placed in Grateot Street Prison in St. Louis. His brother bragged he escaped from this insecure place by disguising himself as a Negro laborer. The brother said, other prisoners went through the cellars or over the rooftops of Christian Brothers Academy. There are others among the local civilians, who are southern in their politics. They enjoy the lucrative rewards of arranged escapes. It is said a more secure prison at Alton, Illinois, will prevent such.

Many Missouri preachers are banned. At Hannibal, the Catholic church refused to raise an American flag over their church. There is a martial order, flags must be flown over all Public Buildings. Arguments are offered by church folk who feel their buildings are not public, but rather the house of God and exempt from civil order.

Clergy can not perform marriages, unless they take a provisional government test oath as a prerequisite.

I believe it is best, for the citizens desiring marriage, to marry in a church. These government orders seem to disfavor church weddings, or make them difficult for many.

On the other hand, I have heard of preachers who use

their pulpits and standing in a community, to expound on various political issues. It is a difficult decision and one our community has not yet faced.

At the quilting bee on Thursday afternoon, the ladies discussed the problems in their local communities.

Amanda shook her head and held her needle's eye to the light.

"I declare, running this country takes the wisdom of Solomon. I would be the first to admit I don't possess that wisdom. Let's pray for those who have the task, may God grant them His wisdom."

A dilemma was presented to all.

One Sentry

JD ordered his men, "We are in enemy territory, keep quiet, but lay along the banks. Watch for any traffic up or down the river. If you see anything, come back to this oak snag and report. We need information on an enemy troop which will be by in the late hours of the afternoon. You've got three hours to spend until dark, then we move out to the southwest. If you aren't here when we need to move, we'll go without you. Try to catch up as soon as you can. Questions?"

No one spoke.

The five JD ordered out, spread and quietly moved in the direction of their assignments.

The remaining twenty three men settled in for a three-hour reprieve from marching. Most dozed where they lay.

They were on the Arkansas River, in rough terrain of the western bluffs.

One of those sent out was Corporal Alcott, from Missouri's Pilot Knob country. He was known as a good woodsman and able to move without being seen.

He moved to high ground and sought a good vantage point where he could recline at a bend in the River, with a view for several miles in either direction. He moved quietly, when— *Is that a foot sticking out from under that bush?*

He crouched quickly. Silently he knelt behind a gooseberry bush and attempted to see more clearly. His effort revealed nothing more. He waited quietly. Alcott looked down and placed his knee on a pile of leaves. He didn't want to leave tracks, or be off balance if he had to lunge or hold the position for a long while. He waited — the foot did not move. He listened — no sound. He knew the boot could be *a cast off, a dead body, or a live person. Enemy or friend?* It had no distinguishing characteristics other than a hole in the sole.

Alcott moved his eyes to the left, right, up into the trees, then down toward the boot. No signs of others or anything out of place.

I can see the river, but I need a better view to carry out my duty.

After what seemed like thirty minutes with no movement of the boot, Alcott's leg cramped. He shifted carefully for relief. He decided to observe to a different angle. He crept away, carefully watching where he put his feet and hands. Still, he saw no movement and no better view. He returned to his original sighting and moved to the right. Still no view.

He was about to decide he looked at a body or a discard. He heard a snort, then a snore and the boot turned over. It settled after several twitches and he heard a gentle sigh.

I don't want to kill a friend. I can't see if it's an enemy. I have only an hour and a half left to watch the River. A shot might bring others and a scuffle might make noise. I could creep up and knife, or throttle the man. I don't know.

He crept to another point, one hundred and fifty yards down the river, but kept his eyes on the point where he had seen the boot and quietly checked out his new site.

Alcott spent another hour and a half in silence. Then

he moved off to the south west to rendezvous with his company.

Around the fire that night, he told JD of his experience.

"I saw a boot, under a bush. After I scouted fer about a hour, I couldn't tell who he was, so I crawled to another spot to watch the river."

"You probably did the right thing, under *those* circumstances. Retreat may have been the better part of valor," JD laughed.

No one ever knew if the boot belonged to friend or enemy — probably a shirker. They didn't see evidence it mattered.

Two soldiers survived a few more hours and no problems came from Alcott's chance sighting.

Home Fires

There was a feeling of disquiet in Grandma Logan's heart. She wanted the family always in view.

She, Maw, Emma, and Matthew settled in for a time of caring for themselves and the farm. Each performed their tasks in a subdued manner. It was constantly on their minds. JD, *their son, husband, and father,* would not be home tonight. He wouldn't be around for supper, nor be there in the morning when they got out of bed, or Sunday to go to church, or at Christmas to celebrate with them.

They were very busy. They each had more work to do than usual, but their lives took on less structure. Each felt the need to be more in the others' presence. Amanda felt more protective. Matthew felt the heavy load of being the man of the family and making decisions. He conferred with Amanda, or Mr. Wasson, as they went about the farm work.

Mr. Wasson had worked with JD so long, he said he

could almost read J.D's mind, even though JD wasn't present. The old man expressed his reluctance to make final decisions alone.

Amanda, Matthew, Emma, and Mr. Wasson established the habit of conferring over morning coffee at the breakfast table. Here, they made decisions for the day's work, the care ofthe livestock, the farming operation, and attempted to solve their daily problems. They established a comfortable routine and liked the thoughts they shared. They ended their sessions each day with a prayer for JD, the country, and themselves.

Grandma Logan remained in her home. Matthew or Emma stayed at night. The elderly woman continued the routine she had established when she returned from Kentucky after her husband, Bailey's death..

She suggested, "Soon, I may move over with Amanda and my grandchildren. We would use less wood and supplies than both households."

As the weather grew cooler in the fall, Grandma stayed more and more at Amanda's home with her family. Matthew stayed in her house some nights, but he ate with the family at Maw's.

Winter closed in. The family settled down to repairs on farm tools. They split wood, and cared for their animals. Some days, ice had to be chopped for the livestock that ran loose in the pastures. The smaller group of stock gathered near the barn or around the hay ricks during most of the day, for protection and forage.

Life settled into a pleasant a routine, *if* the family could only forget, *a part of the family is gone from home for the winter and involved in war.*

Amanda prepared for Christmas as if the whole family were home. *I think it best to keep a regular routine. It will make us all feel more secure.*

The Circuit Rider came for a short visit the day before

Christmas. He held special prayer meetings for the families and those away from home.

Amanda went to bed that evening with a special feeling of loneliness. She found herself arising at night to sit by the window and watch the moonlight. She wondered about JD

Does he have enough warm clothes and food?

She sat wrapped in a blanket in the rocking chair, with her feet up in the blanket. Fat snowflakes began to fall and the world became beautiful, clean white, and new.

I wish the world could be cleansed as easily.

Lord, make things right in this world. Change people so they do the right thing. Help us all to know what is right. Thank you Lord, for taking care of us all. Be with JD and keep him safe. Be with all the fathers, sons, and husbands tonight, and for as long as they have to be gone from home. Help the leaders to get this thing over with as quickly and safely as possible. Give them the knowledge and the character they need to do the Christian things. Be with us all in our decisions and keep us safe now, and this next year. Thank you for my children, Grandma Logan, and our good health. Be with JD, keep him well and comfortable this winter and the others too. Bring them home safely. Thank you Lord, Amen.

She crawled into her cold bed.

At four, she arose to put a log on the fire, she looked out as she passed the window and the moon sparkled on the snow. Moon rays touched the window as she looked.

I feel God reach for me. I sense His special blessing. I have a feeling of peace and acceptance, because the world is in God's hands.

Spring

Warmer weather found Matthew spending more and more time at Grandma Logan's house. He tended to the tasks at her farm, with daily visits to care for farm chores at home. He and Mr. Wasson planted the crops he and his Paw had discussed before Paw went to the war.

Matthew looked at the fields from the bluff above the creek.

I sure miss Paw. Wish I could see him now. I know he'd like to stand up here and look at the crops. We used to walk out every Sunday afternoon and look over the weekly changes. I miss that. Wish I could talk to him for a few minutes and give him a hug. I'd like for him to give me a big hug too. He would take me in his arms when I was little and say, "Squeeze me as much as you love me," and I'd squeeze and grunt and say, "This is how big I love you." I'd like to do that now. Sometimes I'd like to be a little boy again. I could ride on his foot as he walked along, or ride the horsey when he sat in his chair at night. Sometimes, he'd lay down on the floor and lift his foot straight up with me laying with my stomach on his foot. Those things were so much fun. I'd like to tell him I love him right now.

I'd better get busy, or I'll be crying like a baby.

He ran down the path to the creek and splashed across to start hoeing weeds again.

I have a hard time keeping my mind on my work when I don't have to think what I am doing. I miss Paw — I want to go to war—I like Faith and don't know what to do about that—

I feel like a snake with a too tight skin. I can't handle my feelings by crawling out of my skin. I don't know what my problem is, or what I need to do.

Letters Home

JD drowsed around his campfire. *Wish I could write Amanda about our experiences today. I would write her:*
Dear Amanda,

We toured an eastern battlefield, President Lincoln came to our front lines. I didn't talk directly to him, but what I saw put the fear in me! Mr. Lincoln can be seen in a crowd, even from a distance. He's tall and thin. He wore a top hat and made him even more conspicuous. I was afraid a sharpshooter might aim at the president. He met with our generals. It crossed my mind what havoc a cannon ball lobbed into their midst could wreck.

We need his cool head and kindness. His job weighs heavily upon him, but he has the faith to carry it as well as any man I know. People make fun of him, but I feel a brilliance, even more than when I saw him at Quincy, in the summer of '58, at the debates.

I probably can't write this because someone may read it and get an idea would be tragic for the nation. We are in the northeast. I think chances of any southern soldier reading it would be very rare as there aren't many southerners between Amanda and I. My letter will go under guard with the army courier straight to St. Louis and then to the provost marshal at Hannibal. The only unguarded part of the journey, will be between Hannibal and Madisonville.

J.D started the letter he'd actually place in the mail.
Undated Letter Home from Eastern Civil War Battlefield.

Billy and I are well. We're tired, as we usually are. We move around so much it is hard to get rested. The weather has cleared and there is promise of a good crop in the area where we are bivouacked.

Our group feels better with the sun shining so we can dry out. You would laugh as we have become real laundresses. It's very trying to get our clothes cleaned up. This is the first time we've been really dry for three months.

Coughs and colds are clearing and we've found a few early plants to add to our stew pots. We boiled some sassafras for tea to get our blood flowing. We were able to get sugar. The tea really was good. It made me remember when I was a boy and Grandma made us drink tea in the spring to purify our blood. Even more than the tea, I enjoyed the greens. We had a little sugar and grease, so we sprinkled it on some green sorrel leaves and rolled them. It sure tasted good. We are like a bunch of cows craving something green after the winter. Even the tiresome old beans tasted better with a few greens and some bacon grease.

As soon as it warms, we seemed to improve and our teeth tightened up. There's nothing worse than trying to eat hard food with sore teeth, especially when we march and don't have time to use our stew pots.

Pray the Lord will keep Mr. Lincoln and our nation safe. I pray for you all there.

James Brown will be sent home for medical leave. He is to report back as soon as he recovers. You can send messages by him, unless he is assigned elsewhere.

Kiss everyone for me. I love you.
God Bless You, Paw
JD Logan

JD failed to get back in time to catch James Brown before his neighbor started for home. He put the letter into his jacket's inside pocket until he could find the next mail going toward home.

One Month Later*:*

I didn't mail this at the time I wrote it, but thought you might find it interesting, even if it is old. I never want to take any chances of the enemy capturing us or my letters. All the circumstances change. Surely no danger will come from any information in this letter by now.

We're still well and about to move again.

Love, JD

Cape Girardeau, Missouri

Dear Amanda, I have much more time than usual, as there are twenty three of us with dysentery and we've had to stay in camp near Cape Girardeau, Missouri, for almost two and a half weeks. I'll catch you up on life here so far.

I'm one of the few married men at this camp and I'm much older than many of the fellows. Some call me Paw. Guess my seriousness and dedication to God cause them to think of me as an old man. I am able to help them. You'd be surprised at the things they ask me. I have to be careful to show no expression. Sometimes I want to laugh at their innocence and other times I want to cry for them and their experiences from home, and some of the horrors they have seen in the war. No one should witness some of the things we all see.

You remember I wrote you about Bruce, the young fellow who wasn't aware of the world. He walked into a gunner mule during shelling and got kicked on the hand. The mule was frightened. It reared and struggled. I would have thought he could hear and see its struggles. His hand is crushed and it appears to me he will be disabled for a long while. He is a hazard to us all. We had to watch out for him. We hated to have him beside or behind us. It's safer for us, he recuperates elsewhere and may be sent home.

I've come to admire the Dutchmen in our army. Most of them come from the St. Louis and Belleville, Illinois, area. They are clean around camp and stand like rocks during battle. The officers have had some training in the Prussian Army and have a greater degree of discipline than many of the officers we've had without previous military service. At times, we have trouble understanding them. In the heat of battle, we have one officer who reverts to German. He felt responsible for the death of two men at Wilson's Creek because they went the opposite way than he intended. He yelled his command in German. This incident made him very quiet and Van Bruener, his commanding officer, had to speak with him. When the Dutchman realized he was the best we had available, he got hold of himself and has made a special effort to use understandable English since.

Our first two surgeons were old and continuously ill. Now we are without medical attention, other than what we give each other. Many of our home cures work as well as those of the doctors.

Since I'm the old man, I've become the unofficial father, spiritual, and medical leader of our little group. Even the officers send information through me. Guess I'm the unofficial chaplain.

Tell Matthew, his commander says to take care of Amanda, Mother, and Emma for me.

When we are quiet and have time like the past several weeks, I miss you all much more.

Some of these boys aren't much older than Matthew. I pray this will be over before he is eighteen and comes. Many of the boys are Emma's age. I'd hate for her to go through what they've experienced

I didn't write earlier, because I needed to see the outcome, but I picked up Billy McIntire in the field three weeks ago. He had his arm blown off and was wounded in the neck. I held him while they cauterized his arm. As I held him, I couldn't help but think it felt like Matthew even though his face is older. I could close my eyes and feel Matthew in my arms. Hug our boy for me.

(Private to Amanda) Please, forbid Matthew's coming to the war until he is at least seventeen years old. It is my hope you can hold him off until he is eighteen, but I know he is eager to enter the war.

I stayed with Billy until they loaded him into a flat

wagon with others and took him to town. I don't think he knew much after the first few hours. Later he was taken into St. Louis, where he can get the best care in this part of the state. I've heard he feels much better and will be sent home as soon as he is able to travel. There will have to be someone coming your direction to escort him.

I'd hate to be twenty years old and have no arm, but there are worse things.

JD thought about the next and didn't write it. He had found it was cleansing to say it in his mind.

Yesterday, a twenty six year old man hung himself with a tent rope. He had dysentery and was ill for almost six months, he got discouraged and gave up. Some of the other men envied him his courage, or lack thereof. I wish I'd been able to talk to him earlier. I cut him down, but it was too late. We had no idea he had this in mind. He had been very quiet of late. I should have tried to draw him out.

JD picked up his pen and wrote: *Our spirits aren't very high, I hope we soon get back to work, it helps us to get our minds on other things. Don't worry, I am doing fine. God willing, I'll do what I can for my country and for God and for these boys, as long as He chooses to keep me here.*

Physically, we are improved, the water is cleaner, we're on high ground, so have plenty of fresh air. We've been eating mild food and that, with the water has helped the dysentery more than any medicine we've been issued. I think we'll soon move out. I don't know where yet, but the rumor is we go south from here. Send my mail to St. Louis. It will be forwarded to me wherever we are at the moment.

Three days later a new army surgeon came through the camp and sent twenty of the men home for medical leave, JD included.

He traveled up the river on a steamer. The Captain of the steamer landed JD with a small row boat and an oarsman, at the mouth of the Salt River. JD walked the fifteen miles home for a twenty day leave in the bosom of his family.

JD's leave did wonders for him and for his family. He spent the time loving them while he visited. He continued his attempts to convince Matthew he was needed at home and must stay to help his mother care for the family and Grandma Logan's farm a bit longer.

Before JD left, he led the family in prayers and did something else that would prove invaluable. He helped them prepare a buried, storage pit for winter vegetables and other foods behind the smoke house. He and Matthew dug below the frost line and lined the pit with clean straw from the wheat field. They carefully filled the pit with vegetables wrapped in hemp sacks. JD placed two gold pieces in a tobacco tin below the food. He covered the pit with a board and six inches of soil. They carefully tamped back the sod. It was difficult to tell there had been a disturbance. JD and Matthew heaped several sticks of wood and sawdust atop the cache for camouflage.

"Don't open this until you need it. There may come a time this winter when you are glad you have some things stored away. If you don't use it till after February, you'll need to open and use it, so it won't spoil," JD instructed.

When JD took leave from his family, he spent an especially long while with his mother. He had a strange feeling it might be the last time he'd see her on this earth. He absorbed her peace and serenity when he hugged her in farewell.

Amanda saw him to his horse. She had a hard time letting his hand go for the last time. The women stood in the yard as JD rode away with Matthew.

Amanda watched them go. *Despite all our pleading, Matthew will take the same trail before much longer.*

Their son rode with his father as far as the Mississippi River at the mouth of the Salt River. Matthew observed as his father hailed and boarded a steamer, which would return him to his regiment by way of St. Louis, Missouri, the railroad through Rolla and a supply wagon headed southwest.

Matthew returned to the Madisonville farm, riding their draft mare, Dolly and leading Dan. His father's departure made him more restless then ever.

Soon I must follow my father's footprints and join up.

Matthew planned on the way home for when he'd enter the army.

Maybe I'll go to St. Louis and join there. That would be far enough away from home the recruiters wouldn't know me, couldn't check with Maw about my age. I could rub a little coal soot into my face to make myself look a bit more bearded and maybe there are some other ways.

Threshing

Threshing grain was normally a pleasant community diversion from the seriousness of war. The scarce threshers pulled into the first farm in the small neighborhood. All remaining neighbors came to exchange labor.

Neighbors brought their teams and wagons with hay racks at the ends. These served as the bundle wagons, transporting the bundles of grain stalks from the field to the threshing floor.

The bundles of grain were tossed on to the threshing floor. Oxen and mules trampled the stalks of grain to separate the grain from the straw and chaff. Stackers threw the straw and chaff into the air. The heavier grain fell at their feet while the chaff blew away in the wind. The straw landed on top and was forked to the building rick for winter feed and bedding. The chaff stuck to the sweaty workers.

The neighborhood women gathered to prepare the noon meal.

At the completion of each day, the men made a mass exodus to the creek. They striped and plunged into the depths to wash away perspiration and debris from their hot and dirty workday.

"This is a whole lot better than Smith's dirty old stock pond."

"It's plumb heavenly."

"Say, did you hear about the new invention up at the United States Fair in Chicago. It's called a Rumely Separator. It won a prize. Maybe we'll get one of those someday."

" Sure would make our work easier."

"I'm not spending good money on some newfangled contraption! Couldn't afford it if I wanted to."

" I'll be too old for this in a year or so. I ain't going to keep this up much longer."

"Maybe them guy'll get home from the war."

"Shore hope so. I'm about tuckered in and I can't do this much longer."

"Matthew, heard you say you're going off soon, that true?"

"I aim to," Matthew replied.

"What yah gonna do about your farm when you leave?" the old man asked.

"We haven't crossed that bridge yet," he replied.

Matthew wiped his chest with his wadded shirt and pulled the damp shirt back on.

The other men dragged themselves out of the cool water and donned their clothing.

"I feel better. Think I can make it to the wagon now and go back up the hill. I'm hitting out for home, this is enough of this for me this year," old man Calvert said.

At the end of the several days and completion of threshing in one neighborhood, the crew passed to the next farm and the process was shared. The families contributed again.

Matthew and Mr. Wasson were the only workmen at the Logan farm. The pair worked for four weeks straight, going from farm to farm. They shared the work, paying those who would soon help them.

When the threshing crew arrived at the Logan farm, it was a jubilant day. The Logans didn't have a large crop, but they would have flour for bread and seed for the next season.

Being short of help, Emma served as water girl.

One of the men present was Lee, a known neighborhood bully and four years older than Emma. He attempted to get her attention all morning. He generally made himself obnoxious to all those present.

Finally he got mean and called Emma a name in front of some other men. The men looked away in embarrassment, but no one came to her aid.

Emma retreated from the group.

She patted Pal as she passed him where he lay under the trestle tables. The faithful dog and protector for years, had made many trip to and from the field that day, trying to kill every mouse Matthew turned up under the bundles. The dog had stopped by the creek for a drink and flopped down near the trestle tables in the shade of the house to rest.

Lee didn't let up, he sought Emma out privately at noon. He grabbed her arm above the elbow as she passed.

She'd had enough "Leave me alone, can't you just leave me alone?"

Pal heard Emma's raised voice and rushed around the house to her aid.

The dog planted himself between Lee and Emma. He curled back his lip and bared his fangs. A low rumble sounded in his deep chest.

Lee snatched up a hammer left from constructing the sawhorse tables. He raised the hammer and threatened Pal and Emma. Pal leaped toward Lee.

The bully stumbled and dropped the hammer. Pal advanced and stood his ground between Lee and the hammer.

"Stay, Pal,"Emma said.

"Wait till I get you away from your dog, I'll show you, you don't want me to leave you alone! You don't know what you're missin'," Lee spewed at Emma. During this speech, he had moved backward a few steps, he turned and retreated. He looked over his shoulder to see Pal's reaction.

Emma trembled, "Good Boy!" She patted and hugged Pal.

Going by the well, she rinsed the wash pan and pumped it full of water. She wet her hands and bought them to her face. She went in the back door of the house and busied herself with the cook stove to hide her nervousness.

Maw and Aunt Florence were occupied. They didn't notice, but Grandma didn't work as hard anymore and she kept her eyes open.

I wonder why Emma didn't eat much dinner when the women ate after the men went back to the field? She's very quiet and stayed close to the fence by the house all afternoon. Hope she didn't get too much sun today.

Emma was careful to give water to the men as they came in with their wagons, but she didn't go beyond the yard fence with her water bucket and cups.

Pal *moused* and helped Matthew.

The crew finished the threshing by evening and the neighbors pulled out for another year. There were thanks and farewells all around, and generally a jovial feeling between the men.

"Be careful of your grain. There's some bushwhackers around. They sometimes follow close behind our threshers," one of the crew warned.

"Thank you, all," Matthew doffed his hat. "That's good advice. We'll get on it."

With the threshing done, all the farm families could move on to other farm tasks and the remaining men in the community could stay home for a time.

Matthew planned for this to be his last season at home. He would leave before they threshed again. The next week, he puttered around the barn. He stored the equipment and grain for the winter and attempted to make grain boxes varmint proof and difficult to find. He cleaned up all clutter around the barns, before the cold weather.

Pal assisted.

One of the last boards Matthew lifted had a rat run. When he lifted the board, he got his hand on the confined rat. It clamped long yellowed teeth into the back of Matthew's hand.

The young man flung his hand. then pulled on the tail, but the rat hung on. Matthew held his hand down. Pal clamped his powerful jaws around the mid-section of the rodent. The little animal collapsed. Pal snatched it up and gave a bone snapping shake.

Matthew wiped the blood from his hand. He went to the pump, soap and rinsed the teeth marks with cool water.

Matthew called Pal to him and knelt down to hug the old dog.

"Pal, you're such a good ole friend. Thanks again, you're always there."

Amanda looked out to see Matthew come to the well and wash, then he hugged Pal. Her heart swelled with pride.

I wish JD could have been here to see how grown up and wonderful our children are.

Amanda put the last few things away in the kitchen and carried the small lamp to her room. Emma had quietly gone to her room early tonight.

I guess she was tired too.

Amanda dressed for bed and climbed on the edge. She opened her Bible to the story of Gideon threshing. He hid in the wine press to keep the enemy from stealing his grain.

Why did I read that part tonight?

Amanda shivered. She turned to the twenty-third Psalm and recited it with her eyes closed. She blew out the light and lay down. She prayed for JD, her family in Missouri, and Kentucky, for Mr. Lincoln, and for both nations. It had been a terribly long day. Amanda drifted off to sleep before she finished her prayers.

She didn't know Emma lay awake, brooding.

Unexpected Visitors

Amanda missed JD even more after he'd been home. She dreamed of his return, longed for him, her heart ached inside.

She awoke with her pillow crushed against her face and hot with her tears. She felt more empty than all the time he'd been gone from home.

Life is not easy during war. Women and children suffer too.

Two weeks after the threshing, they had scant news from Mr. Wasson, of an execution on September 25, 1862, south of Macon, Missouri.

After taking an oath not to fight the Union, eleven men had been caught for the third time.

"It was understood others would be dealt with in like manner, if they repeated the offense of disloyalty to the Union," Mr. Wasson reported from the *Missouri Republican* newspaper article.

"There is constant surveillance and an occasional skirmish in an attempt to keep the Confederates in line in northern Missouri. Execution just might do the job," Mr. Wasson assumed, aloud.

There were no battles in Madisonville, even though many of their men were gone to war. A few who remained, carried out old grudges and assumed slights, some were *bullies* and took advantage of the situation of the war. Other opportunists passed through and wrecked havoc. Bush-whackers and deserters used war as an excuse to pillage. They allowed free rein to their baser natures. Under normal conditions, most would have been kept in check by the goodness, strength, and unity of the community.

Amanda was cleaning the floor in the kitchen, when six unkempt, mounted men rode into her farm yard. She stepped to the front porch. Pal barked a warning and advanced on the horses.

The leader struck and bashed in the dog's head with his rifle butt.

Pal fell dead on the spot. His blood spilled into the land he had protected so well and long.

Amanda started toward the old dog.

"Kill those chickens, we're hungry!" the leader demanded in a loud voice.

"Hear me, I said get us some food!" He rode closer and flicked his whip inches from Amanda's face where she stood in shock over Pal's body.

Amanda knew Biddy's chicks weren't old enough for fryers, but she found five of the eight. She didn't tell the Sergeant three were missing. With unshed tears in her eyes, she prepared to dress the chickens for the men's meal.

The men, wore mismatched pieces of blue and gray uniforms. They poured into her kitchen and soiled her freshly mopped floors. They took the freshly baked bread from where it lay cooling on a towel. The scruffy bunch broke great hunks off. The men slathered the bread with fresh butter from the churn. They crammed great mouthfuls into their faces.

They ripped the curtain from in front of the cupboard. All edible items followed the bread in quick order.

Amanda considered tossing boiling water onto the men, when she prepared to scald the chickens for picking but reconsidered when she thought of their numbers.

The leader eyed her. "Woman, don't even think it. I can read your mind and it ain't nice. If you ain't nice, I ain't gonna be nice!"

Amanda's imagination worked overtime as the rabble scraped and ripped items in her house. She couldn't see what they destroyed as they rummaged through her home.

When Amanda had finished scalding and picking the chickens, she prepared the five fryers and the hen. After she cut up the chicken, she dredged the pieces in flour and started frying chicken in her largest skillet.

"Ain't you got nothin' bigger? We need to hurry."

Amanda got out her iron stew pot, put in a gallon of lard, and placed it on the wood cook stove. She fired the stove hotter and began to flour the rest of the chicken. She opened jars of green beans one of the men brought from the cellar and put those in her boiler pot. She made corn bread as another instructed.

"Make coffee!"

Amanda put the remains of ground coffee and parched corn into her speckled coffee pot.

Another man appeared from the springhouse with the morning's milk. They rustled around for her scarce sugar supply or any other seasonings she might have.

The rough men carried most of the extra food and seasoning to their saddle bags. They left only enough on the table for their meal.

Three of the soldiers went outside.

I hear them banging around in the barn and buildings. They are carrying a few items to their saddle bags. I see them place grain in their horse's feed bags. I know the horses are getting a skimpy meal. We only had a scant peck of corn, a gallon of wheat left for seed, and some oats we saved for the chickens.

When the food was prepared, they pulled out *her* chairs, sat at *her* table, and demanded to be served.

She placed all the food on the table and stepped back to go out the door.

"Stay here where I can see you," the sergeant grunted.

When they finished, she saw the men take her kitchen supplies. They dumped the remaining flour on the floor with the corn meal, and any other food they couldn't carry.

She watched as one of the soldiers stirred it with his dirty boot. She saw their leader start to unfasten his pants, she turned and went quietly to the sitting room and sat down on the settee. She held herself rigidly in control to keep from screaming. She cringed when she heard their dirty laugh — then all was quiet. The humiliation of this invasion of her home was too much to bear. She hoped they would stop at what they'd already done.

She heard their noisy leave-taking outside the house and walked back to the kitchen. The smell of urine permeated the air.

"They spoiled the rest of our food supplies!"

Too disappointed, tears sprang to her eyes and she turned to look out the window. Pal lay dead in the front yard.

"I have to dispose of him, before Emma and Matthew see their friend. I must move, or I'll break down. I need to stay strong for my family, they've already been through enough tragedy in their young lives." She talked to herself in an attempt to remain calm.

Numbly Amanda shoveled the ruined flour and meal into the wood box with the ash shovel and the broom, before she went outside to drag Pal away.

She began to plan.

The remaining chickens can eat the spoiled meal this winter. We can't let it go to waste.

She took Pal to the creek, where he had cooled his tired feet and drank during the hot summer.

"I don't have time to bury you properly, but the creek will carry you away. I don't want my children to have the unpleasant memory of seeing your body in the front yard. So long, ole Pal."

She talked to herself as she did the necessary tasks. *Later, I'll tell Grandma, Emma, and Matthew what happened and the sacrifice Pal made for us. We'll always remember him.*

Do even the pets have to sacrifice in war? It seems so. Biddy and most of her chicks are gone and Pal's gone; Nuisance the pet pig has been gone for months, bringing in a small amount of cash; the Tennessee cow and Black, the driving horse, have been taken by— who knows?

At least they didn't find the two gold pieces, the potatoes, carrots, and turnips buried in the ground. It was good JD had enough forethought to know we might be raided and would need to preserve something. I can probably buy flour and meal for the winter with a gold piece.

I didn't believe anyone would bother our home. We'll have to be very cautious. I want my children close today. Dear Lord, help us all to stay alive and well.

If— When, JD comes home, I'll feel a lot safer. I must keep busy and get on with living. My family has to do the best we can with what we have. I need to remember all the things I'm grateful for. My family was gone today, or Matthew might have felt the need to be protective. Emma is safe from those lewd stares and maybe worse. We have the remaining three pullets; the Tennessee cow's heifer has a calf in the woods corra;, the work mares Pete and Dolly are somewhere working in the woods with Matthew; Pete is in foal with her fifth colt to the neighbor's horse; and— I'm exhausted!

She sank in the shade on the back porch step. Tears silently flowed down her face.

Their diminished livestock would assure they could spend more time inside during the cold winter months and not have to venture out often, to tend to the animals.

Palmyra Massacre
October 18, 1862

Amanda read the Hannibal paper which told of a local Palmyra citizen.

"LOCAL RESIDENT ABDUCTED. Mr. Andrew Allsman, is a highly respected and well known citizen of Palmyra. Being aged, he cannot actively participate in combat but serves the provost-marshal's office. He is widely acquainted in the community and provides information and guidance.

W.R. Strachan, Provost-Marshal, General District of Northeast Missouri, backs the recent order given by General McNeil."

The message was reduced to the bare facts of the order: "It is reported, ten imprisoned Confederates, illegally sworn into the service of the southern army, are to be executed if Mr. Allsman is not returned by the end of ten days.

It was rumored the vocal old loyalist has been murdered near Shelbyville, but no remains have been discovered.

Colonel Porter's wife, is known to reside in nearby Lewis County. A written duplicate of the notice has been dispatched to her.

Colonel Porter is known to be in northern Missouri. It is assumed he has received the notice of the planned execution if Mr. Allsman is not returned promptly.

Many of the Confederates were captured near Kirksville. They were reported to be members of Colonel Joseph C. Porter's Army."

Due to the delay in information, the final grisly outcome was included in the same edition of the Hannibal paper.

"October 18, 1862. Shortly after Noon, Ten Southern Men Executed. The ten were alleged to have perjured themselves after taking the oath of allegiance and were previously pardoned on their parole of honor. The above offenses carry the penalty of death but seldom has that outcome been ordered.

Community citizens visited the prisoners during the evening. Prominent Union citizens added their voices in a plea to prevent the executions. Five prisoners were brought from Hannibal to round out the number required by the Provost Marshall.

General McNeil read the sentence for the 10 o'clock execution the next morning.

Reverend James S. Green of Palmyra, and others, offered spiritual counsel during the night.

It is believed a family man, W.S. Humphrey was spared the following morning and a twenty year old, Hiriam T. Smith was chosen to take his place. Provost Marshall Colonel W.R. Strachan came to the prison to read the edict to Smith.

At about 11am, three government wagons drove to the jail. A sufficient guard accompanied the wagons bearing rough board coffins. The condemned were seated upon their coffins and escorted east to Main Street. The cortege turned south and then east to the Hannibal Road. Throwing down the fences, they turned north and entered the fairgrounds. On the east side of the amphitheater, they paused for consummation of the scene.

The ten coffins were removed and placed in a row, forming a line north and south.

Thirty soldiers of the second Missouri Militia from Ralls, Lewis, and Scotland Counties were drawn up in a single line, north and south, and facing the coffins. Twenty had live bullets, ten rifles carried blanks. Twelve feet separated the doomed men from their executioners with reserves flanked on each end.

Reverend R.M. Rhodes offered prayer upon the condemned kneeling men. Each prisoner took his seat upon the foot of his coffin, most remained firm. They faced their executioners.

Captain Thomas A. Sidner, of Monroe County, was elegantly attired in a black suit with a white vest. Some said it had been meant as his future wedding suit. His long hair cascaded over his shoulders.

The others were attired in common community vestment of their arrest.

Provost Marshal General, Colonel Strachan and Rev. Rhodes shook hands with the condemned.

Out of range, approximately one hundred witnesses quieted.

Dead silence reigned.

The officer in command gave the order, "Ready, aim, fire." The discharges, were not simultaneous. Two of the condemned fell dead upon their coffins. Captain Sidner sprang forward with his head toward the soldiers and face up, also dead. The other seven were dispatched by reserves using revolvers."

Quotes were included from the participants: "The safety of the people is the supreme law. . . only by striking the deepest terror in them can they be taught to observe the obligation of humanity and of law. . . It was a slaughter ground, one of the women sobbed to this reporter."

"Those in sympathy with the executed men called it "*The Palmyra Massacre*."

"The ten southern men were executed by a firing squad at the Palmyra Fair Grounds on October 18, 1862."

Condemnation roared through the countryside from both factions. The *Butcher of Palmyra* resounded from the throats of the southern faction.

Opposition papers put out a different slant. "Innocent men murdered in Palmyra Massacre. These men were not involved with the arrest of Andrew Allsman. Many had alibis.

Only several of these condemned were actively engaged in war. It was rumored General McNiel first intended to execute prominent southern citizens ofPalmyra but instead condemned without evidence or trial, prisoners from the jail. Five prisoners were taken from Hannibal to round out the demanded number.

General Strachen was in attendance, McNiel was not present at the execution.

It is believed General Porter had ridden into northeast Missouri to recruit disillusioned citizens who were threatened with being forced to fight for the Federal Government. Some report Colonel Porter did not receive the order of execution and had no knowledge of a problem until after the execution.

This order further takes eligible fighting men into one camp or the other."

In an attempt to justify the harsh punishment, The Palmyra Courier quoted justification for the executions: "The madness of rebellion has become so deeply seated, ordinary methods of cure are inadequate."

William R. Strachan, Provost Marshal at Palmyra was quoted, ". . . here in Missouri, our Government commenced by extending toward the rebels in our midst every kindness."

In northeast Missouri, no longer would General McNeil be censored at headquarters for his "leniency toward the local disloyal citizenry." It appeared to the Union military presence that severe punishment would be required to prevent further blood shed amongst the loyal citizens of Palmyra. Other citizens were enraged and would require more blood *because of* the execution.

Colonel Porter was believed to have been at Florida. Not a great distance from the Logan farm.

Amanda didn't know if the men she encountered were from this group. *I have no way to identify them or bring them to justice. I don't know if they favored one side or the other. They wore dirty and ragged pieces of both uniforms.*

When Amanda went to the store, news of another tragic event at Madisonville took the attention of the local folk, as well as the usual battlefield news. Those present related the event with great drama.

"Anthony Benton Suttons, had ridden out to join Porter's Southern Brigade."

"Halt! the abolitionists ordered."

"The young rebs attempted to spur away instead of stopping. Shots were fired. Anthony Sutton fell from his horse. He died right there on the spot from a bullet wound."

"Nobody knows for sure who fired the mortal shot, but Thomas Suttons, his younger brother was in the abolitionists' party."

Rumors abounded, *no tombstone would be placed at the head of Anthony's grave in the Madisonville Cemetery*.

His family was divided. Their remaining son was in a northern group.

"Since his brother is alive, the family wishes to keep their remaining son in the family," one woman commented.

Discord and separation occurred even within local families.

When President Lincoln was asked to settle agitation over Missouri, he admonished Missourian citizens "to leave one another alone."

New Teacher

"Maw, Billy McIntire is coming home," Matthew shouted.

The Logans took special interest because JD had written about the fellow. The two men had spent time together marching and on several battlefields. The family wanted to hear about JD directly from one who had served with him.

Billy came home. He dragged his bone-weary, unhealthy body back to his hometown of Madisonville and virtually collapsed upon himself. He looked nothing like the little Billy Boy some neighbors remembered. He had one arm off at the shoulder and was thin as a snake. His face showed the ravages of not having enough to eat and the remnants of an infection when he lost his arm and had the side blown out of his neck.

Never believing he'd live, the army surgeons did the best they could. They cauterized his shattered stub and patched up his neck. *Live he did* and now he'd gotten himself back to the place of his birth. What was to be done with him now?

Amanda thought he looked like Ole Mr. Johnson before he died from consumption.

Oh, God, please don't let this young man die after all he's been through. He's had enough suffering for a whole lifetime. JD started him home to us, give us the opportunity to take care of him now. Give him some peace and make his life better from here on out.

The townspeople expected Billy to curl up and die. He had that look about him and very little left to put anything back into his life. His family was all gone. He'd only had an old Granny and she faded gradually away when he left early in the war. She didn't have much to live for after her Billy Boy left. They buried her in the Liter Cemetery the next spring when her body went to join her already departed spirit.

Billy had no family and no place to go. He moved into Maybelle Warner's second house, out back where she did her canning. She hadn't had anyone with her for two years and she was afraid to live alone.

Amanda remembered Maybelle said she had an old blunderbuss shotgun under her bed for protection, but this would be a lot more company than an old shotgun, probably safer for everyone involved. Maybelle wasn't known for her calm demeanor in times of stress and no one wanted to cross a hysterical female in times of duress.

Maybelle couldn't do enough for Billy. She fed him enough milk to make him slosh when he walked. She baked fresh bread every other day and heaped her table with all the good food she could find. Maybelle had a little money stashed and she didn't use it sparingly when it came to Billy.

Amanda couldn't believe her eyes when she next saw Maybelle and Billy. They both looked healthier. They had a spark in their eyes and a lilt to their voices. Billy reveled in all the attention Maybelle heaped upon him.

Maybelle crowed, "I feel more useful than I have in years. I have a job to do, I'm goin' to fatten up that young man and make his life better."

Amanda believed her from the looks of them both. Tender care and good food were just what Billy had always needed, and he needed it more than ever now .

He often dropped by Amanda's to tell the family of things JD had done. He hadn't known the family before he went to war, but because he knew JD, he felt he now knew the family. They welcomed and included him in family events and he came often. He showed some special interest toward Emma, even though she looked upon him as a family friend but didn't encourage him.

In the following months with renewed energy, Billy looked around Madisonville and saw young children with nothing to do. They roamed around the town getting into everyone's hair and generally causing a *ruckus.* With most of the men gone, their mothers and older children were busy trying to put bread on their tables. There weren't many hours left in the women's days to devote to anything additional for their children.

Billy had a good mind and began to think he could be of help to these families. *I always liked learning. Grandma was a good teacher. I think I could teach like she did and help these younger children. A one-armed man isn't able to do an able-bodied man's work, but I still have a mind and this is one thing I know I can do to help everyone.*

The more I think about it, the more I am convinced this is what I should do.

Billy made the decision, then committed himself to finding a suitable place for the school. He walked around, checked out the buildings in Madisonville.

The blacksmith shop has too many tools and is dangerous, even if it isn't open much. The old Smith is too frail to work the bellows and do the heavy work. The store front is full. It is a meeting place for the women when they come to shop and catch up on the news. Too much distraction there. The barns are too drafty and Maybelle's house has too much fancy furniture and breakable bric-a-brac.

Billy walked behind the buildings to check out-buildings. He noticed Noah Liter's Store had the largest back room and there were two outhouses out back. He went to Preacher Wilson and visited with him about the school.

"You know, there are a whole passel of young ones running around here getting into mischief. You think I could start a school in the afternoons? It would keep them out of everyone's way. I need to help Miss Maybelle in the mornings, but we could have a few lessons after we finish our chores. I think it would be good for us all. I don't like to see these young ones who can't read or do their sums. What do you think?"

"Do you have a place?" the preacher asked.

"Well, I was thinking of asking Noah Liter about the back room of his store. I could clean it out and store the plow and farm tools on boards, or in the beams of his loft. I think his back room would work out very well and he has two outhouses out back. What do you think, Brother Wilson?"

"I think you have a grand idea. I'll go with you to ask him and I'll help you move that plow, if he's agreeable."

Preacher Wilson continued as they walked toward the store, "If he'll let you use the storeroom, we can round up the benches we use for church. Those benches are mighty tall. We might have to put little benches under them for the children's short legs, but I've seen it done. Say, I'm getting excited about this venture, let's ask Mr. Liter, right now!"

The two men found Noah dusting his shelves. Shelves more and more bare, as the war wore on and supplies became scarce. Mr. Liter seemed a little bored, to Preacher Wilson.

"Mr. Liter, how'd you like to do a good deed for the community and get your storeroom cleaned up at the same time?" the pastor asked.

Noah was taken back, he didn't realize his storeroom needed cleaning. He couldn't decide whether to be offended or curious. Knowing it came from the Preacher, he gave him the benefit of the doubt.

"What do you have in mind?"

The two men excitedly relayed their thoughts on a school for the younger children.

"I've got two smaller ones of my own. I think it would be a wonderful idea. It will get my children out from under foot and they'd learn something too. I need little people who can add sales and receipts so I can start teaching them store keeping. I'm all for it. Let me go tell my wife," he said, as he started up the stairs to their living quarters over the store.

The two men below exchanged smug looks.

"Preacher, I think we got a job to do," Billy smiled.

Sure enough, they did. Mrs. Liter, Matilda, and the children scrambled down to give their vote of approval.

They all went to work to ready the back room in record time and had it ready by the next Monday at 12:30 in the afternoon.

Mr. Liter rounded up four slates from his store shelves, a box of slate pencils, two primers, six number two pencils and a few sheets of grocery paper.

It wasn't much for a brand new school, enthusiastic pupils, and a nervous new teacher, but the children hadn't been to school before. They didn't know what was required in the way of *conduct, or supplies*. The youngsters were so excited they couldn't stay on the benches. They checked out each bench to see if it was better than the others.

"Find a place which fits you, stay seated, and we'll start school," Billy directed..

With the new teacher's encouragement they finally settled on their favorite spot.

Preacher Wilson was present. He led the pupils in reciting the Lord's Prayer. Billy talked about the stars and stripes in the American flag.

I gave my arm for this flag, and we're going to remember the Union, even if I find a southern dissenter somewhere in the midst of these squirming youngsters.

Preacher Wilson stayed all the first afternoon.

A body didn't have to look far, to find storekeeper Liter, or Maybelle. They stayed out of the room, but didn't miss a sound. Mothers shopped a little extra too.

"Call me Mr. Billy, because Mr. McIntire is too much trouble to say," Billy explained his title to the children.

"Do any of you read or do numbers?" he asked. Two children held up their hands that they could read a little. No one seemed to be able to do any arithmetic.

The children varied in ages from five to ten years of age, but for today, Billy started them all together in the first primer. He would divide them into classes in a few days.

Billy took one of the slates and a slate pencil. He had no eraser, but used a new handkerchief. He wrote the first three letters of the alphabet. He filled the whole slate with the large letters.

"A is for apple, B is for boy, and C is for cat. These are the first letters of the alphabet and the first letter of these words."

An hour later, Billy said, "We'll have a play time that is called *recess,* for thirty minutes, then we'll have another lesson on numbers."

The children hurried to the outhouses as Billy

reminded them they could read some words.

"This house says *men* and the one on the left says *women.*" The children had previously come to the store with their parents, so each knew the appropriate small building.

When everyone had their turn, Billy produced a ball made from strips from Maybelle's rug scraps. They would play a new game called *Ante Over.*

Billy explained the rules. He selected two teams, placing the larger girls on opposite teams. He divided the larger boys equally and placed the smaller boys and girls on the teams in equal numbers. Each team had five players.

"Fanny's team go on the west side of the building, and Jenny's team will go on the east side, face the building, and we'll let Fanny toss the ball over. Jenny's team will try to catch the ball. If someone catches it, the whole team will run around the building and throw the ball at a team member on the other team. If the ball hits anyone, they are then on Jenny's team. If Jenny's team misses the ball when it comes over the roof, then they will toss the ball over the roof and the other team will do as I just said. I know you've got questions, but we'll start and learn as we go. Toss the ball over Fanny.

"Don't forget *Jenny's team,* try to catch the ball and get members from the other side. Here we go."

The children made mistakes but all had a rollicking good time and they groaned when Mr. Billy said it was time to return to their benches and do an arithmetic lesson. The rest of the afternoon passed quickly.

The children found the lessons such a novelty the afternoon passed much *too quickly.* School was dismissed at 4:30.

After the children left, Preacher Wilson and Billy discussed the day.

"Great job, Billy. I think things went exceptionally well. Most of these children haven't been in school before and they fell right in line."

"Thank you, Rev. Wilson, I couldn't have done it without you. Your support—" Billy choked, "has truly blessed me."

"I'll come tomorrow. If you wish, we can divide the children and I'll help with one of the classes," said Preacher Wilson.

More pupils came on Tuesday and through the next several weeks. The pattern for the school day had been established and two main groups were determined, even though the ages within each class varied. One class worked on their benches, or with Preacher Wilson, while the other worked with Billy, then the procedure was reversed.

As in all one room school houses, the pupils profited by the closeness of the storeroom schoolhouse. The less advanced classes served as review for the others.

This is very satisfying work, Billy thought.

Preacher Wilson and Maybelle commented to each other, on how happy Billy looked and how his health had continued to improve with each new day.

On Monday of the fourth week, a man slammed the door open against the wall and stalked up the aisle toward the teacher's desk.

"No d___ Yankee's gonna teach my brats!"

Preacher Wilson headed the irate man off and took him outside.

Mr. Billy said, "Let's continue with our work. Brother Wilson will take care of any problem."

Outside, Preacher Wilson addressed the stranger, "What's the problem?"

"My woman sent our young'uns without my permssion. She knew I'd never agree to a Yankee school teacher. He'll turn their minds from what I want for them."

Rev. Wilson spoke, "Do you mean politics?"

"Yes, blasted it!"

"Billy has not mentioned the war in these three weeks. When the children come in here, they can leave that behind them. That would be good for all of us. The only mention he's ever made that even hinted at the war, was he had his arm blown off, but not to pay any attention, he could do most

things without it. He talked to me. He wanted them to feel comfortable with any returned veteran. They don't even notice his lack of an arm now."

"I'll have to see it to believe it," the man spluttered.

"If you'll stay quiet, you can go back in and listen. I'll pull the bench back and you can sit by the door. If you must interrupt, I'll have to ask you to leave. You have already disturbed our afternoon arithmetic lesson. Do you want your children to be left out and ignorant?"

"Guess not."

"Billy's a good teacher. Let's go back inside." Reverend Wilson opened the door. He smiled at Billy and the children, "This is Mr. Watts, we'll sit back here. Go on with the lesson, we don't mean to interrupt."

After fifteen minutes, Watts became so engrossed he forgot to scowl.

After the children left, Billy came to introduce himself.

"I'm Billy McIntire. I'm always pleased to meet the parents of my pupils."

"Watts here. I'll be watching."

"You're welcome to come anytime, but I pray you'll allow your children to keep coming. We're making remarkable progress."

"I'll come, and I'll be quiet, unless you bring in your Yankee drivel, then I'll tear this whole school apart."

"The children don't need any more turmoil in their lives, we're strictly in the business of learning to read, write, and do arithmetic."

"We'll see." The man walked out the door and called his two sons to follow.

Reverend Wilson let out a breath. "He'll be fine after a few days. He needs to see for himself you're not teaching his children to be Yankees."

"I hope I am teaching them to be good Americans."

"I know, just keep on doing what you're doing. You've done a wonderful job thus far. Don't let him get you worried." He patted Billy on the back.

Later, the preacher said, "Maybelle, Billy explained to the pupils how he lost his arm and got the scar in his neck. Billy said to them, he wanted to tell them about his arm, so they wouldn't wonder or be afraid of him because he looked a little different. He explained he was the same person, even though he lacked an arm. He showed them his remaining arm was getting stronger and he could do many of the things other men can do."

"The pupils no longer seem to notice he has only one arm or that he wears a beard covering the scars left on his neck where he was wounded in battle. I think this has been good for them. Others will return from the war and they might as well get used to differences now. They love Billy and the whole experience of school is good for all of us, including me," Preacher Wilson said. "The Watts' father came the other day, even he's convinced Billy is doing a good job."

"I can't agree more," Maybelle said. "I see Billy bloom under your love, the children, and his work. I take a little credit too. Billy has a valuable place here in Madisonville. He is filling that place. Anyone can see by the children's faces they all feel we are accomplishing something important."

As an added benefit, Billy had met Miss Matilda Liter, the storekeeper's daughter. She showed more and more interest in helping Billy with his school project and he showed more interest in helping her, with *out-of-school* projects, with her family's complete approval.

They all came to know this young man in unusual circumstances. They liked what they saw and heard.

<u>Strange Time for Makin' Meat</u>
Arkansas Battlefield

An inhuman scream pierced the peaceful sleep of the fog-ridden night. Men lurched out of their bedrolls.

Unsure what he'd heard, the cry lifted the hair on JD's neck. His men clutched their rifles in one hand, searched with their eyes. They crouched to roll their blankets.

Let's get out of here screamed in their minds.

Enshrouded in the dense fog, he noted faint embers of the cook fires across the clearing. The drip-drip of moisture in the timber was the only sound.

Each listened.

Another sound came— *A moan?*

"I'm not sure what's out there, but it sounds like a wounded man," JD rose and summoned his closest soldiers, "You and you, you two, you and you, and you there, spread out and go to our sentries. The fog is so thick you can't see. Sound-off when you get out fifty yards. If you don't see anything unusual, come back. We don't want anyone lost out there."

The men grabbed their hats and arms, splitting off into the four wedges.

JD paced back and forth in the clearing between the fires. A light breeze stirred the fog into tendrils.

Ten minutes passed, JD heard the searching soldiers speak. The quiet, disembodied voices carried eerily through the fog. All seemed well with the men. Their sounds started back toward the fire.

"You there? I can't find the clearin'," a soldier complained.

"To your left, we're here," JD directed.

Each of the four groups reported their sentry had seen nothing. One on the right had heard a noise, but he was unable to identify the source.

"I 'spect it's just a mountain lion, he maybe roamed by our camp and wanted to let us know he was there. I've heard 'em back home."

"We'll check around the area at dawn, it will be much easier to see when this fog disappears. If we wander around out there now, we might get someone shot or stumble on the enemy. Keep alert, but get some sleep," JD instructed.

They threw more wood on the fires. There was a slight lessening of the darkness in the clearing.

JD flipped his blanket over his shoulder to keep out the damp.

The camp is unusually quiet. The men are not sleeping. They're awake, listening. We all imagine we hear the sounds of battle and death as we lay in our bedrolls.

Most arose earlier than usual and grumbled less.

After breakfast, the regiment split and searched the surrounding timber for any signs of the night prowler.

"Sir, over here!"

JD went toward the voice and found a group of men gathered around a mound on the ground. The men separated. A fresh corpse lay in the leaves. JD could see one shoulder had been blown away in an earlier injury, but the blood and flesh appeared fresh. He squatted, examined what remained of the soldier dressed in scraps of ragged gray.

"Move the men out, then send me our surgeon," JD ordered his sergeant. "I'll pick up four men for a burial detail, after I speak with him."

JD inspected the surrounding ground for clues to the mutilated corpse. Surgeon Smith materialized and the two conferred.

"Some animal ate on this man while he was still alive. I expect that was the noise we heard last night, when the animal got him. We didn't know he was here because of the fog, so we couldn't help," the surgeon spoke softly.

"Yes , it appears that way," JD agreed. "The ground is scuffed."

"I'd advise you to keep this quiet. You have some green kids who will leap at their shadow, even before this thing happened," the surgeon suggested.

JD was reluctant to keep information from his men, but in this case, he felt Dr. Smith's advise was correct. He wrapped the body in a blanket before he called over the burial party to complete their job.

For the next two weeks, as his men scouted the area, three versions came into the ranks of a big male hog, with four-inch yellow tusks, stalking the soldiers.

"One tusk is broken off jagged. He's wicked and has a mean lookin' gash in his snout. One soldier had to climb a tree to get away from him. The hog kept right after him until others came and ran him off."

JD's worst fears came true. Rumors flew about the hog and mutilated bodies. The men knew the cause of the scream in the night, but it didn't make them any more comfortable.

It seemed to JD the hog struck when he caught someone alone or the men spread over a wide area. Then he crept up on them and made a strike.

"He's going to get somebody hurt bad! We gotta do somethin' about him, before he gets one of us! I don't mean to tell you, I know what a riled hog can do when he's tryin' to get away, much less one bent on gettin' someone," one soldier argued.

"A hog can rip you comin' and goin," yelled another.

"He's been eatin' raw meat and is lookin' for more. Ya know hogs'll kill small animals. We've seen 'em eat snake like candy."

"He don't seem ta care if we're alive or dead when he goes after us."

"Men, I'm ordering the next person who sees the hog to kill him before he gets one of us. He'll make good flavorin' whether we're able to eat the meat or not," JD's General ordered.

"What if he's mad?" came from the ranks.

"More reason to get rid of him! They tell me rabid meat, *cooked*, is safe to eat. We'll depend on it. Go get them Rebel boys and the hog too!" General Dowell shouted.

JD's men were reluctant to voice their fears, but murmured of *eyes on their backs, a chill, and crawling flesh*.

Not seeing the hog, brought more fear than actual sightings. They felt foolish in their fear. Many had no first hand knowledge of hogs, making their imaginings worse, spurred on by comrades' hog stories. The evidence among the mutilated corpses of the slain was ominous over the next weeks.

From where they lay on either side of the road, JD could hear cannon fire in the distance. The air was a dispersed blue from the drifting smoke. JD reclined behind a broken tree that provided a barrier from the road. His company exected a Rebel advance from the south. While alertly comfortable, he lazed away the afternoon chewing on a twig. He struggled to stay awake.

He became uneasy.

Did I hear something? I have an eerie, distinct impression I am being watched. If I haven't been seen, movement will draw attention.

Slowly he turned his head and his heart lurched. The gaunt, long-legged, three hundred pounds of hog tested the air, attempted to locate the scent of his next prey.

Preservation thoughts flashed through JD's head.

My pistol and rifle are laying ready, pointed toward the road to hit the patrol. If I reach for either, or move my rifle in a three-quarter circle, I'll have to shoot with my off-hand. I'm not a great shot with my left hand, it would be awkward.

My pistol is beside my right hand, is it heavy enough to do the job? Can I do it fast enough?

The gray patrol is expected along the road at any minute.

If the hog gets to me, I'll make too much noise, or if the hog turns away wounded, it might get someone else. I have no choice, and I have a direct order. I have to shoot the hog with the pistol and hope to give myself time to get the rifle ready.

The distant sounds of battle faded as JD concentrated on this life-threatening decision. He slowly raised the pistol. The boar zeroed in on JD's scent and moved forward, slowly, step by step with the tusked snout raised.

Three steps closer. The hog had a predator's stealth in the menacing silence of his advance.

JD saw the light glint in the hog's left eye as the brute swung his head from side to side, testing the air currents. The intent manner of the hog's motions threatened.

JD made up his mind. *When the hog swings his head back, I'll take out the light in the left eye.*

He took a slow steady breath and controlled his body. The right eye appeared at it's fullest ark. The head swung back to the left. JD caught the glint of the eye looking straight at him. He fired.

The instant after he fired, he saw the *glint* had vanished. An empty socket stared from the left side of the hog's head. JD stepped closer to the downed tree and grabbed for his rifle, while he waited for the powder and smoke to clear.

The hog jerked and let out a short high-pitched squeal. Crazed, he charged.

JD's rifle up and already aimed, he fired as the hog charged into him. He heard a solid *whack.*

The hog lost control of his front legs and skidded into JD slamming him over the tree trunk. JD's head hung on the far side.

As his rifle flew out of his hands, JD was helpless. He could no longer see the hog's head. He wasn't sure of the outcome of his shot.

With a gurgle, the boar tossed his head, slashed with his ragged tusk one last time and lay still. JD's felt a harsh jerk, his trousers and his right calf gave under the onslaught.

JD rolled his head up and to his left, twisting down on his good leg. Both legs felt numb and wobbly.

"You— blamed ole hog— you almost— broke my back!" JD lay against the trunk, tried to feel his legs and get his breath.

He heard a slight noise to his right and jerked his head. *More hogs? No, I see blue around an elm tree.*

"You there, Sir?" Private Tubbs asked in a soft voice.

"Yeah, come— over here and stick this— ole hog. Quick, be sure he's dead!" JD doubled up from pain and slid off the tree trunk.

"*How*— do I stick him?" tentatively asked the Private.

"Right there on the side— of his neck, slash deep and quick— to bleed him out, just in case he's playing 'possum. Make certain he's dead!"

The Private acted as if he was going to tickle the hog under the chin.

"Don't be so cautious— you might just *wake him up!* Slash— Hard!" JD rattled.

Private Tubbs fearfully positioned the knife with the point at the side of the hog's neck, below the ear. He gave a mighty plunge and ripped downward. Blood sprayed in a hot wave onto Private Tubbs.

As if he'd touched a white-hot iron, Tubbs jerked his hand back. The knife flew out of his hand and disappeared into the dry leaves. The young man leaped away from the hog and looked as if he was fearful the hog might strike out at him. He gasped and wiped down the front of his tunic.

JD waited a minute, there was no movement from the hog. "You did it— Here take this— neckerchief and tie off my leg."

"Sir, is—is that *your* blood on your leg?"

" 'Fraid so, but I'm tough— if you'll just get at it—wrap this up," he breathed, his first *easy* breath in five minutes.

Private Tubbs tied off the wound with JD's scarf.

"Thanks. Now— could you help me sit down over against that tree? I gotta rest a minute." JD waited a few seconds, then soothed, "We'll try to get some— fresh meat— skinned out of this tough ole hog. "

Private Tubbs rolled his shoulder under his officer's arm and almost bodily lifted him.

JD's legs were still numb below his waist, but his back was starting to hurt.

Surely this pain means my back isn't broken.

Tubbs eased him down against the tree.

JD grunted with the exertion and curled over into a ball, with his head between his knees. The pain in his back ached dully, but the knife in his leg caught his breath. He felt very weak, even though he was beginning to breathe more easily.

I mustn't let the kid know how much trouble we might be in.

"Keep down as much as you can behind this log and see if you can— real quiet, roll the hog onto his back. That'll make him easier to work on," JD cautioned. His head cleared.

"What do you mean, work on him?" Private Tubbs stammered, "I don't see anything to be done with him."

JD could tell the kid had never done any butchering before. This whole job was going to be rough and they had to be quiet.

"Like I said, don't be cautious, put your weight behind it— take him by a front and hind leg on the same side and roll him up there. We need what meat we can salvage from this ole brute. Keep it quiet and low, that patrol may come yet."

"I completely forgot about those Rebs. Uh—Maybe

we better not do this right now," the private offered.

"You start, I'm not quite up to it yet, but I'll be better in a few minutes," JD's prospective cleared. His commanding voice returned. He paused..

I need to soothe Private Tubbs, settle him down. He spoke quietly. "You gotta do it son, we just can't do without any food we can find and this is a lot of it."

J.D's sharp ears detected a rustle across the road. He didn't know where his rifle had fallen. He snatched up Private Tubbs' rifle and quickly looked down the barrel. He searched for a target to go with the sound.

"You fellars awright over thar?"

JD recognized the voice of one of the Iron Mountain Missouri boys.

"Alcott, crawl on your belly to the bend in the road, look both ways. If you don't see anyone coming, high tail it across the road real low and come over here. We need you, but keep it quiet."

A slight rustle told JD, Alcott followed his instructions. He looked down the road in one direction from the bend, but couldn't see the other. They waited a minute, five minutes. Still no Alcott.

"I'm surprised more soldiers didn't come to my shots," JD said.

Something rustled directly in front of him, behind Tubbs. "Alcott, we're in front of you."

Alcott hadn't taken any chances, now he stepped from behind Tubbs' tree.

"Good gravy, what's that yah got thar? Looks big as a elephant."

"Tubbs has done a good job, but help him butcher out some hog meat. Keep it low and quiet, we don't want any Rebel Patrol down our necks eatin' our supper."

JD looked around. He became aware the sound of cannon fire had distanced and the air had cleared. The battle moved south, out of their terrain.

Alcott began to work with the skill of a man who had done this job before. The country boy opened the belly with a neat swipe of his honed, razor-sharp knife and rolled the innards out on the ground. He worked carefully, to prevent contamination of the meat. Alcott rolled back the skin from the hind quarter, but couldn't cut through the tough ole boar's breast bone.

He peeled out the hams and the loin meat, not severing the connection and kept the hide spread out between the leaves and the meat.

"Sir, we'll have ter wait 'til somebody comes with a' ax or hatchet to cut this here breast bone, this ole boy is too tough to do with justa knife. If I had a rock, I might could drive the knife through it, but that'd make noise, we gotta worry about the patrol."

"You're doin' a good job. You've got the best part almost out." JD hesitated, "If worst comes to worst, we may have to leave part of it right here." He watched as Alcott continued to work.

"Take this ground cloth and lay the hams and loin on it. We'll wrap it up and have it ready to pack out."

"We won't be able to cook it on this here side of the road, because of the wind direction. We'd be sure to bring in them hungry Rebs. Maybe could we wait till dark, skedaddle across the road, over that yon rise and out about five-hun'red yards, then build us a fa'ar? We'ns'll be able to cook a little toni'ht and smoke a little in the coals. That way, we'll have fresh meat now and a little in the mornin'."

"Sir, are you going to be able to walk on your leg?" Private Tubbs said, when he checked JD's injured leg.

"We'll worry about that after we finish looking for this patrol." JD attempted confidence. He noted his leg had quit bleeding, but the scarf was soaked through. He began to move his legs to see how they worked. He was stiffening, sitting doubled over in pain.

It seems everything works. Oh, how I hurt! I must be going to make it.

"If some of our boys come along afore dark, we'll get them to work on the front quarters of this 'ere hawg," Alcott said, as he continued to trim up the hams, saving every morsel of fat and flesh from the inside of the skin.

"The boys are hungry for meat, they won't be too picky or ask too many questions. We've all had to eat a few things we didn't want to know about, it tastes better not knowing," JD said.

He relieved his stiffened body. His back ached and his leg wound knifed him with each movement. He drifted back to shooting the hog.

"When word gets around, the men will be relieved to hear the hog has been eliminated. We've had several difficult weeks around here, now we'll have only *one enemy* to worry about." Tubbs observed.

"What, Oh, I'm sorry, what did you say, Tubbs?" JD asked.

"Sir, do you think that Rebel patrol is still comin'?"

"We'll stay quiet and keep behind this log, to be covered, but I think the odds are getting less they'll show. Keep Watch though."

In another quarter hour, Alcott finished with the hind quarters and moved toward the shoulders of the ole boar.

JD kept his own counsel.

The head is the part I'm not crazy about seeing. I remember the heads at home, after they were stripped for head cheese or head meat. There was always those naked, lidless eyes staring back at me no matter where I stood. Private Tubbs is making a point of not watching the hog butchering.

Tubbs moved closer to the road and concentrated on the bend up the road.

"It's all too hoggy for my tastes. I'll just wait 'til it's in the stew pot and try not to think about it. I'm glad my job is to watch for the enemy patrol, it keeps my mind and my eyes away from the gruesome sights behind me," muttered Private Tubbs, as if he needed to offer an explanation but didn't want anyone to hear him.

A horse appeared around the upper bend.

"Shhh, it may be an advance patrol for the grays," hissed JD, as the three reacted when they heard a rider coming.

"Hey, it's one of ours! What do you suppose he's doing there on this road?" whispered Private Tubbs.

"Watch him a few steps and see if he's running from somebody," whispered JD "No, he looks fine. Tubbs, step up there and ask him what's going on."

Private Tubbs stepped up just before the rider broke even with their hiding place. The rider spurred his horse to the right and jerked up the cocked pistol in his hand. The horse skittered and almost slid down the embankment, keeping the rider from getting off a shot, while he struggled to control his mount and keep his seat.

"Blast you, why don't you identify yourself before you step out in front of a body? You're liable to get shot!"

"Sorry," Tubbs apologized, "We couldn't see who you were until you got close."

"That patrol went around us on Telegraph Road and they won't be comin' through here. Every blasted one of 'em got away!" the courier groused.

"Our line officer is wounded back here and we've got some fresh meat. Can you tell us where some of our boys are? We need some help?" Private Tubbs asked.

"Yeah, they're comin' right behind me, I'm pickin' them up as I come along. Some should be here in a few minutes, you can commandeer them." The courier reined his horse from the side of the road. "I almost forgot, our Captain wants everyone to find a campground away from the road and bed down for the night. Be prepared to move south at dawn."

As he started ahead, the courier remembered, "How

bad is your officer? "

"Mostly, he needs to be cleaned up and his leg sewed. I don't think he's got any broken bones. He can walk, but he's gonna be stiff and won't march for a few days."

"I'll send a wagon back from up ahead, they're supposed to be only about a quarter of a mile down the road. Get on about the business of findin' a campground and keep it quiet," the rider spoke as he turned away.

Ten minutes later, a wagon arrived. Alcott and Tubbs hailed the driver and loaded JD into the back. They heaped the ground cloth full of the hind quarters of pork into the back beside JD.

"Hey, gimme your ax, I gotta job to do here," Alcott said to the wagon driver before he started away.

"Whatta you need it for? I gotta job to do too," muttered the driver.

"Han' it here and I'll give you somethin' you'ns'll like," Alcott stated emphatically, with a show of humor.

"Better make it good and quick, I ain't waitin' long", said the drive. He spit over the wheel.

Fifteen yards off the road, Alcott took three swings with solid *thunks* and stepped back to hand the driver the bloody head of the ole boar.

The driver swore ungratefully, but didn't hesitate to lay the head on the seat by his hip. He knew hog's head had good meat along the jowls, cheek, and there was a whole brain to be scrambled up for a quick supper.

The drover waited a bit more patiently as Alcott took two more whacks, to open the chest cavity on the boar. He wiped the ax on the leaves and handed it to the driver.

"Many thanks fer yer time. Hope you have a good supper," Alcott said.

He went back to the hog, as the wagon shuddered off to the south. He'd sent the main part of the hog with JD, but there was plenty here for him and his mess mates.

" Hey, Alcott, you cook that hog *real* good—

Did you hear?" JD yelled from thirty-yards up the road.

"Yeah, I gotch'ya Sir, but don't ferget you got the biggest part, you have yer cooks do the same."

"Sure. Alcott and Tubbs?" JD's voice had a little hesitation, "Thanks for all you did."

The wagon rumbled away over the rutted road.

Alcott skinned out the shoulders and the neck, laying the meat inside the hide. He removed the liver and the organ meats from the entrails and packaged the whole lot by rolling the hide up into a bundle, hair side out. He stepped out into the road, as his mess mates came abreast. It was getting dusky dark and the boys could see his enlarged pack.

"What you got there?" Jerry thumped Alcott on the pack. "Eeh, it feels all sticky and hairy."

"Well boys, we're gonna eat high on the hawg toni't!" Alcott laughed.

"Really? Boy, I'm starved, I may just eat it raw, hide and all."

Alcott was stern as he replied, "No, I don't think ya will this 'un." He softened his words with, "This ole boy's too ole and tough ter eat raw. We'ens'll get him a little tender by mornin', but I have the liver in here, we'ens can get it ready as soon as we'ens can get settled and get a fawr goin'."

"You know, even liver sounds good. Why don't Jim and me hoof it on up the way and get a fire going? Turn off a couple of hun'red yards on your right. We'll go up that little draw we passed on the way down. You know by the creek? We'll go over that little rise so we'll be out of sight and hearin' of the road. See you in a few minutes. Hurry it up, I'm hungry. Come on Jim, bet I can beat you!"

"Won't those boys ever grow up? Sounds like ten y'ar olds, et must be great to be youn'," Alcott tiredly shook his head.

"How old are you? I thought you weren't far from our ages?" Private Tubbs commented.

"I'm twenty-three, but I feel about ninety 'rite now. I can't wait to get some of this here meat in me, maybe that'll perk me up."

"I think it might help us all. Come on, the private said, "Let's move it," he shoved others ahead of him.

"My mouth is watering, even though I know what we're goin' to eat tonight," Alcott added.

Word was passed among the ranks, "The b'ar is dead, long live those who ate him."

JD suffered in the wagon as they bumped along to reach the field hospital. Their progress was hampered by troops and wounded from a nearby battle. The Reb patrol they'd watched for, had surprised another Union Regiment across the river.

I can feel the vibration of cannon, and smell the latent smoke, there's a constant hum from the river.

Casualties poured in. JD came in to the hospital at the same time. He was shuffled to the rear of the line, behind those needing immediate attention.

At the field hospital, time folded back for JD as he lay in the fever of infection, exposed to the sun.

He quickly became unable to determine fact from fever hallucinations. He remembered floating in constant pain and heat, with a searing pain in his leg and then, not much else.

He had no way to know a well-meaning, wounded, but recovering soldier, looked at his leg and used a home remedy. The soldier could see the surgeons were not going to get to JD in time. Amputation would be required to save him, if they waited any longer.

The soldier hobbled about gathering wood ashes from the cook fires around the rim of the field hospital. He poured spring water through the ashes, collected the run-off lye, and strained it through his last intact shirt tail. Holes came and he moved his shirt to another intact spot. He wasn't sure what strength he wanted for the lye solution. He boiled it, cooled the acid water, and mixed in boiled spring water. He took a risk and slid his little finger into the solution. It felt hot and then stung, but it wasn't an immediate burn. He hoped it was the strength he needed to cauterize the semi-conscious soldier's wound. He looked toward heaven and concentrated on hitting the wound with the small stream of lye solution directly into the wound in JD's leg.

JD jerked, but retained no memory of his treatment, it merely faded into his continual wall of pain, as another torment.

The soldier came by the next day and looked at JD's leg. The necrotic flesh in the wound was seared as white as raw meat placed on a metal spit. Some of the lye had run out of the festering gash to blister the back of the leg where the excess flowed down. The soldier turned JD, rinsed the wound and the blistered area with clean water. He attempted to feed the patient, then left him again, one of many laid out in the sun of the field during the day and the exposure of the night.

JD was sure he was home, until he felt the ground beneath his blanket. He was disappointed he wasn't in his feather bed at home with his family. He thought he could remember riding the Ohio and Mississippi Rivers as a little boy when his family went to Missouri.

In five days, JD began to have lucid moments without fever, and made steady progress. The recovering soldier had poured liquids down JD while he was the most ill, and now brought him broth and bread. JD began to gain strength and others pooled their efforts in cooking for a wounded group. Those well enough to cook, formed their own mess arrangements and also cared for some too ill to care for themselves.

JD's *soldier angel* moved on before JD was lucid enough to be aware of him as an individual. He had a vague recollection of someone bandaging his leg and trying to get him to drink. No particular face or identity came to his mind.

JD soon remembered why he was at the field hospital. He had an abundance of time to think.

Alcott, is sure a dependable fellow. His language is amusing, so hill-country with his over yon , we'ens and fur piece.

That hog I killed. Soldiers hardly ever admit to eating someone's woodsy pig crop fattened on acorns, but free-range grazing of hogs is not profitable for farmers when an army of hungry men advance through the countryside with loaded weapons. I hope my family's pork production is doing better in Missouri.

Hometown Happenings

JD wasn't privy to everything which occurred far from his field hospital. Missouri presented a strange mix of northern and southern sentiment. Retaliation continued to plague the defenseless.

In his local home township, neighbors and passers-by preyed upon each other. Past and imagined grievances were still being settled by petty or large acts against each other. The taking of a pig, or the disappearance of crops, and criminal acts some wished to perpetrate upon the helpless or unaware continued unabated. Bullies and opportunists showed their *real* character and low moral fiber during these hard times. Women, children and old people were left to fend for themselves.

Back in Madisonville, Missouri, Maybelle had Billy McIntire and Preacher Wilson to talk over the latest news, but she couldn't wait to tell the women of the neighborhood what she'd heard.

She walked over to Amanda's place.

"Amanda, did you hear about Mr. Coleman? Saturday last, six men came to his home. He was half-shaved because he was needin' to go into town. They called him out. I guess he thought they needed to do business with him, so they said he toweled off his face and told his wife he'd be right back."

"They said when Lucy looked outside, the six men had her husband at gun point and his hands were behind his back. She ran outside, then she noticed the men had cloth over the lower part of their faces and their hats were pulled way down so she couldn't even see their eyes.

One man said, 'We're taking your man down the road apiece.'"

"I'll go get his coat. Wait a minute," Lucy pleaded.

"He won't need his coat where he's goin'!"

"Don't nary a soul stick his nose out that door or window for thirty minutes or we'll blow it off!" He yelled at her, "Do you hear me?" He raised his voice for those inside to get his message, "You kids too, stay inside, every soul of you!" and he fired his pistol into the air.

Maybelle hadn't had this big a tale for years and she was making the most of it.

"The neighbors said Mr. Coleman said, 'Wife, do as they say. Take care of the kids and I'll be back soon.'"

"They said the men took Mr. Coleman around a bend in the road and his family couldn't see no more. After about an hour, when he didn't come back, little Joseph went down the road to see where they had gone. He found his daddy hanging from a big oak tree, *dead*! They said the family cut him down, but they couldn't do nothin' with him, he was cold-stone dead. They said all the family helped dig a grave and buried him. The Colemans were so scared they didn't go nowhere for days and they didn't tell nobody."

Amanda was trying to get a word in edgeways to soothe Maybelle and inquire after Mrs. Coleman's welfare.

"They said, Preacher Wilson come along and the family was so upset, and acted so strange, he finally drug it out of them." Maybelle continued, "They told him the whole story and showed him the grave. The Preacher said a few words over the grave, then he went to Aunt Sally's and told her she was needed to go help Lucy Coleman. Aunt Sally went up there and she stayed a week nursing and tending to that family. She said, 'They's just beside themselves!' Ain't it awful?"

"And, oh yes, Little Joseph kinda let it slip he peeped out the window. He told Billy he saw a big roan horse with a black mane and tail and a blazed face. The boy said it was the same horse that fought with all the other horses at the threshing last year. The horse's owner got mad during threshing and told Mr. Coleman he had a big mouth and he'd best keep it shet, or he'd get what no good Yankee devils got in this part of the country!"

"You remember who that was don't you? I'm not sure of his name, but everybody seems to remember him. Lucy won't tell nobody who the men were. She tries to act like she don't know, but I think she does. She must be awful scared. I guess we all better be scared. There's not enough men around here to protect us from anybody or anything, nomore."

"Amanda, you got a gun? Nobody better come around my place unannounced, or he'll be gettin' a load of buck shot. That'll stop 'em. Course Billy knows where it is and he knows how to shoot, but sometimes he's at the school and not around."

"Wish I could come and see you more, or we lived closer together. It would be safer for us all, if we all lived in town, so we could help each other. You be careful and we'll try to do the same."

Maybelle continued, "This Coleman deal, it has me scared. I wish some more of the men were home and not traipsin' around fightin' battles and gettin' killed. It really ain't very considerate of them to leave us alone like this. I need some woman to talk to once in a while. Come my way, next time you go to the village store. I just miss our big meetin's and get togethers, I can't wait till the men get home!"

Maybelle's information upset Amanda. It called back

unpleasant memories of her own experience with the destructive strangers who came by their place.

I am grateful they did no bodily harm to any of the family. I've always known it could have been worse, but this makes me realize it even more. I haven't told anyone but my family of my personal attack.

"Maybelle, let's pray for the family. All right, just bow your head and pray with me. Oh Lord, protect us all and help people to get along. Bring peace between us. Stop those who hurt others. Settle our differences and let life get back to normal. Thank you Lord, for protecting my family and most of the community. Lord bless Lucy and hers. Calm our fears and let us know what's best for us to do for each other. Bring our families back together. Continue to carry us in Your arms through whatever may come, precious Jesus. Amen."

Eyes

"Grandma, I don't like to be around Lee. He makes me feel undressed. There's somethin' behind his eyes that makes me feel—*crawly*. Why doesn't he leave me alone? I've told him often enough," Emma commented to Grandma Logan.

Grandma Logan quilted with Emma, while Amanda peeled potatoes.

Amanda didn't have to make an attempt to eavesdrop in order to overhear the conversation. She sat quietly, not wishing to interrupt the disclosure.

"Emma, your Grandfather would say some men had a *mean eye.* He would say the eye is a window on the soul and Grandpa judged men by what he saw in that window."

Grandma took time to complete another square and Emma sighed. She thought Grandma had forgotten their conversation and her problem wasn't solved. The sigh seemed to prod Grandma and she continued.

"That's the way your Grandpa judged horseflesh too. No matter how wonderful the outside looked, he said a *mean-eyed* horse was never to be relied on. There was some predictability to horses, even if a person couldn't put himself into the mind of the animal. Your Grandpa said there were horses *and men,* who are not to be trusted. When in their presence, be they horse, or man, *keep your guard up and keep your distance.* Ole Pete is in that category of unreliable. You always have to be on guard with her. Why does your Paw keep her? Because she's very profitable and a good mother. She's raised five sorrel colts in a row, all but one with a lovely disposition. You always keep this in mind and keep your guard up on one like her. You can get by, if you know her and remember."

Grandma tied off her knot before she continued.

"Now, this Dolly mare out here, was Pete's second colt. Before she was a month old, she ran a staub clear through the frog in the bottom of her front foot and it came out the coronet band at the top of the hoof, right where the hoof joins the leg on the front in the hair. Even though that had to be painful when we doctored her, that filly colt would stretch out that foot for us to clean and pour in medicine. That's been her nature through life, to love, to trust, and be trustworthy. She doesn't seem to know anything else and she's never been mistreated. She stays gentle, never causes any trouble."

"Some people who are supposed to be rough; their roughness is honest. They grew up in a rough and tumble way. You can understand the reason for their roughness." Grandma raised her head and looked away. "Ole Kitty, the mule, was like that. She was reliable, even though she was hard. She'd been used hard, but she didn't bear a grudge, you could depend on her to always do the same things under similar circumstances."

Emma concluded Grandma's comparisons of men to mules were right in some ways. *My brother is a real mule sometimes with his stubbornness.*

"Lee seems mean. When we were young, I remember seeing him pull wings and legs off grasshoppers and flies, and he laughed about it. He pulled some mean tricks on younger children. I'd hate to have to trust him for anything."

Grandma picked up her train of thought, "If Kitty refused to do something, you knew it, she didn't go ahead, then pull a tricky move, or hurt you in the process of gettin' out of somethin'."

Emma wondered where her Grandma's story was leading, but it did bring past memories to her mind.

Grandma finished off another square and tied off her thread. She picked up another threaded needle, knotted her thread and started a new square. Maw kept needles threaded ahead of time, because Grandma's eyes weren't as sharp. It was less embarrassing for her, if Maw stuck a number of needles in the edge of the quilt ready for her.

"Like I said, she was raised rough, but she was good inside."

Emma thought Grandma Logan was certainly taking her ole sweet time getting around to a solution for the *Lees* of the world.

"Granddaughter, do you get what I'm tellin' you? Grandpa would say, if they have a *mean eye,* watch out, they're mean inside. They might look rough, but if they are gentle inside, that's all right. Then there's them that love, no matter what."

"Grandma, I think Grandpa was right, but now how do I get rid of the mean ones I don't want hangin' around?"

"Girl, that ain't always easy. If they're really mean and you make 'em mad, they can do you real harm takin' revenge. Usually they're bullies too. You might be able to bluff them out, if you are stronger emotionally. They like to bring the strong down and they may do it by brute force. If they are stronger mentally than you are, stay away from them kind. Other kinds, it'll be all right to treat them kind, but firm. You'll have to decide when the time arises. I'm sorry I can't do it for you. An ol' Biddy like me, they don't mess with me much."

Maw called the two to lunch. They began to clear away their quilting tools.

"That's one good thing about gettin' old, you just say what you want and you don't care what others think. If you're right with the Lord, you aren't goin' to deliberately say hurtful things to people anyway."

Emma's mind wandered during their prayer.

I find Grandma's presence and thoughts comforting, if not too helpful at the moment.

Aftermath and a Strange Request

Alcott missed his line officer while he was in the field hospital recovering from the hog attack.

JD is a real man. We've trusted him with our lives everyday. I dread going into battle without his cool head. I've never been in much of a battle without JD, even though I was in the Ft. Davidson one when I first joined up. We repulsed the grays three times and then withdrew during the night. I helped blow the magazine when we left. That sure was a big boom!

We didn't have much other action until the Iron Mountain boys were assigned to JD.

I know why JD's not with us. I wonder if'n things are going well for him, or if the hog attack was bad. We might have to face many things without him and that's more than I wanta do.

He sat on the mountain top, he looked to the heavens and spoke to God on JD's behalf.

"Oh, God, please ker fer JD Logan. We need him, he's a good man. You know that, God. He's got a family and they need him as much as we'ens do. Be with him, make him well and bring him back to us. Thank ya Lord for carin' for us this fur, see this country through the next battle and end this th'ng. Amen."

Alcott sat high in the hills and watched the dark gray line of soldiers flow out of a valley cut, as he'd watched the blood flow out of Sarge Jones, before the blood clotted and ceased. He shook his head to clear the picture and came back to the present with a start.

I'd better not think about blood and bodies.

He looked closer, *There's a problem with movement in that mountain cut. There, the enemy's halted.*

For inexplicable reasons, the grayline flowed on, then came down the valley to where the Missouri boys lay in wait; set up for battle at the advantageous site they had chosen.

Their acting commanders knew they would see the opposition arrive, just as they had.

"We're ready."

"Bam!"

"Pshaw, one of our blues had too much time to think on his first shot. He's fired off a round and now they know we'ens are h're," Alcott groaned.

Bedlam broke loose. Alcott remembered how it was when a nervous recruit's finger tightened convulsively and he fired before the order came.

Alcott watched, because he knew the opposition was out of range. A few of the enemy panicked and fell of their own fear. In a few moments they realized they weren't hurt. Sheepishly they crawled back to their retreating, dug-in lines.

Alcott looked upon the few who stayed silent.

Their bodies will soon dissolve away in death, as I've seen others fade into the land.

One side or the other will have to advance or crawl back out. Which side will blink first?

After two hours of silence, with only a few shots, Alcott noted a restlessness among the blurred gray line and saw a man on a black horse ride up, wave and shout a message. There was a flurry of movement.

They retreated!

He felt a stir of cheer go along his own lines. *This is one battle we ain't gonna have ta fight without JD*

"Lord, You must a'ben listenin'. Thanks," he cast to the heavens.

He watched the same mountain cut as the soldiers flowed back out of the valley. His own blues rose to go down the mountain side and march in mass-advance toward the south.

There'll be another battle, another day, but it ain't gonna be today.

JD's leg was finally healing. The surgeons had been too busy to care for, or amputate his leg when it became infected. The well-meaning soldier who poured lye water into the wound and bound it up was *his physician,* but JD didn't remember. The acid-reaction burned out the infected area; cauterized JD's leg; and burned away the necrotic flesh. He then began to recover.

He worked his leg, attempted to recover strength. *I don't have time to pamper myself, my men need me.*

After a short time with a clear mind, he traveled. He struggled along for four days, as he tried to catch up with his men. It was a happy occasion for his boys in blue when JD limped off a supply wagon.

As they slogged along through a wooded area, Alcott noted JD was withdrawn and physically exhausted. He was worried about JD's state of mind. Alcott didn't want to pry into other men's thoughts.

I've gotta know what's eatin' my friend so I can help him.

"Sir, I don't usually butt in if'n I'm not asked— is somethin' wrong?"

JD walked with his head down and his gaze averted for a full ten minutes. Alcott thought JD hadn't heard the question. He seemed far away.

JD finally cleared his throat and began gruffly, "Alcott, I've got an order for you. You are a soldier under my command and you have to obey my orders."

"Sur, I know thet. Ain't I always obeyed like a soldier oughter?"

JD heard the hurt in Alcott's voice and softened.

"I couldn't ask for better, but I have to order you to do something that's against your Christian character. I have made peace with my *Maker* and things are all right with Him and me." They walked a few more steps.

"You remember the hog we killed? Well you fellows are fine, because you cooked him good and hot, but he got me with his old rotten tusk. We talked he might have hydrophobia and be mad?"

"Sure, but I don't think he had it. I think he was just a mean ole hawg that had his own way too long. He may have et on a dead soldier; kinda got the taste for it; maybe gone after it on his own; but I don't think he was mad," Alcott objected.

"Be that as it may, you've got to promise me something," JD silenced Alcott gruffly.

"What's thet, Sir?"

"You've got to promise me if I start actin' strange, you'll see I get killed or you'll kill me yourself."

"But— I cn't do thet Sir! I've never killt a friend! Haven't killt too many enemies for thet matter." Alcott renounced the thought. This was totally foreign to him.

"But this is different! I may already have hydrophobia and I could be a danger to my friends, my men. It is something you *have* to do, whether you want to or not. You have to do what's best for this army!" JD reasoned.

"I know thet, but—please don't ask me thet kinda th'ng."

JD replied almost to himself, "I think I'll know if I'm changing and I'll do it myself. You have to promise me you'll obey my command or see it's done for me, if I can't do it myself. You've got to protect yourselves! Promise me you'll choose five other men—"

Alcott interrupted, "Sir—

"No, hear me out, and *that's an order*! Here's the way I want you to do it, choose five other men. That way someone should be alive and around at all times. Choose men you know can do it. Don't choose someone like Private Tubbs, he hasn't got the stomach for it. I saw that when he tried to butcher the ole hog." JD continued, "Don't tell me who you chose, just have someone at my back all the times. Don't spread it around or none of us will be able to do our job. You've got to protect yourselves and make it look like it happened in battle, or was an accident. Don't make it look deliberate or someone will bring you up on charges, and you'd have a hard time explaining."

"Aw, Sir, I don't think thet's gonna be. . ."

"Alcott, you listen to me! Have you ever seen an animal with hydrophobia? It isn't a pleasant sight, it's horrible. Those poor animals can't drink and they have fits. It's pure misery and it's dangerous for all those around. They don't mean to act that way, it's the symptoms of the disease.

You'd be doing me a favor! If I come down with it, put me out of my misery! I'm not askin', I'm tellin' you. *Understand*?"

Alcott clenched his teeth.

JD continued in a desperate manner, "You have to obey my order. I won't know when it's coming and it won't be painful if you choose the right men. I'll do it myself, if I know. I think my wound would hurt and I'd have a raging fever and a headache, but those symptoms go with many of our camp ailments. You know I wouldn't lay this on you, if I was sure I could handle it myself."

"I'll have to think on et," Alcott groaned.

"What's there to think about? It's got to be done, if I come down with it. You know I won't hold you responsible, because it's something we both know would have to be done," JD was gruff in his emotion.

"I said, I'll th'nk on et!"

I guess that's the best we can do. Think about it, but don't take too long. You have to give me an answer. We'll be talking." He put his arm around Alcott's shoulder and gave him an affectionate shove but his face remained tense.

Both men withdrew into themselves for long miles.

Alcott queried, "Sir? If you got et, how long'd et be? I kinda hav'ta know thet."

" I don't know, I'll try to find out from some of our surgeons," JD spoke hesitantly.

"You gonna ask 'em outrite?"

"No, I'll kind of work around it some way. I'll get back to you soon," He paused in thought for several minutes, "Thanks, Alcott, you're a good man. I'm sorry to have to ask you something like this. No man ought to have to even think about such. You know I'd never ask, if it was under my control?" He paused again, "I'm sorry, but it can't be helped."

Several days passed before JD had the opportunity to make inquiries of another company's Surgeon, William Morris. He brought up the subject of hydrophobia . Casually, he asked about a mad animal, he changed it to a man being bitten by a rabid dog.

"It seems like it can come up anytime after about two weeks," the army surgeon replied, "and could even be as long as several years. We don't really know the full extent of the disease. You know there are two kinds don't you?"

"No, I never heard that. Tell me, what's the first signs?"

"Well, there's the ferocious kind, the animal is thirsty, may foam at the mouth, it becomes vicious, then finally gets paralyzed and dies a horrible death. It can bite someone even before there are signs of it's being sick. Animals or people can take hydrophobia from the bite of a rabid animal." Surgeon Morris sat in thought for a few minutes.

"What about the other kind?" JD reminded.

"It's called *dumb rabies* because the animal seems in a stupor. A night animal may be out in the day, or participate in activities peculiar for species of animal. A wild animal may act tame."

He added, "That's when younguns get bitten by a wild animal, because they think it's a pet."

Surgeon Morris looked searchingly at Captain Jonathan David Logan.

"Say, why are you so interested all of a sudden? Have you seen a rabid animal? If you have, we need to notify everyone to be on the lookout." The surgeon was agitated.

I have to quieten his suspicions. "No, I was just remembering some things I heard about a neighbor once. I got curious."

"You are aware stock animals can get hydrophobia too, aren't you? You gotta be careful of any warm-blooded animal acting unusual—sleepy or has unprovoked viciousness. I've heard of a few cows, horses, hogs, or sheep that were bitten by skunks, coons, or foxes and the owner didn't know *what,* or *when,* but they turned up mad." He cautioned, "You gotta be careful of unusual acting animals."

JD sat passively looking into the fire. Surgeon Morris looked a little uneasy, but didn't pursue the line of thought.

"Sir, do you want more coffee?" Corporal Fike distracted the doctor with his question. Morris dismissed all thought of hydrophobia from his mind. He drifted off into other conversation with mess mates.

JD didn't drift. His mind worked frantically. He hid his thoughts behind the appearance of half-closed eyes and a sleepy, diverted gaze. He kept his coffee cup up to his mouth.

If Surgeon William Morris had looked at JD's face, five minutes after their conversation, he'd have seen agitation racing across the man's features.

JD fought a battle within himself. *I have to go back and confirm what I told Alcott. I have to speed our plan. Time may have almost run out, plans must be in place. We might not have more than a few days to insure all is in order and ready, if the plan is needed.*

I'll let Alcott rest tonight, but tomorrow, I'll make a chance to tell him to get on with choosing the five men and seeing it proceed, if or when necessary.

Alcott worried their situation in his mind. *I am more and more impressed with this man. JD is honest and totally fair, he never raises his voice.*

He had begun to imitate JD's speech and mannerisms. JD was an educated man, and this impressed Alcott.

Someday, I wish to have an education. It isn't that I'm not my own man, or I'm not strong, but I recognize a good thing when I see it. I want to be in on that good thing. I am not only impressed, I admire the man. Actually, I love him!

JD is a father I've never been close to. Sure, I love my Grandpaw, but Grandpaw's a hard man, not given to huggin' or talk. JD's full of both. It makes him easy to ker fer.

Lord, I can't stand it if I've got to kill this man. Have mercy and don't let him go mad.

Matthew to Duty, or Glory?

At home, Matthew had about reached the end of his limits with Maw. He begged to go to war. He had been *ready* when the first shot was fired.

His Paw had given up on eighteen and in desperation, wrote out his permission.

"Matt, your Maw will need you to help her on the farm, you must stay until you're at least seventeen years old." Matt tried to leave earlier, but Maw stuck to her guns, as she tried to farm their own and Granny Logan's farm. She reminded him of his responsibilities, but he'd finally persuaded her.

I am leaving home.

I'm over seventeen. I hardly have peach fuzz on my face, but I'll enlist where the recruiters don't know me well.

Despite his fine bones, and youthful appearance, Matthew had a strength and beauty like an Arabian horse, *small but steel-strong* in bone. He had a gentle, old look about his eyes, even with his obvious lack of years.

At other times his eyes were a devilish blue which looked like deep lake ice on a cold winter day with the sun slanting off.

His sister could tell when he was telling a falsehood. Most took him seriously when he was *pulling their leg,* but Emma could always tell when he wasn't truthful by a certain devilish glint in his eyes.

Matthew's relationship with their neighbor girl, Faith, had grown steadily over the past several years. The difficulty with her dog, revealed his caring side and made him especially protective to her. They spent more and more time, talking and working together. Nothing had been said about their future, but both grew to accept the inevitable. *Our future, is together.*

"Faith, I'm old enough now and the Union needs me. I can't wait any longer. I couldn't live with myself if I don't go," Matthew voiced his plans.

"No!" Faith bowed her head and wouldn't look at him.

"No? Don't say no, I have to go" He took her hand, "Will you wait for me?"

She looked up quickly, to see his face, "You know I'll

always wait for you!"

Matthew had said his *farewells* at home, he planned to leave now, before dawn. He would not her again.

"Please be safe!," she breathed.

"I've got to go." He held her close and kissed her forehead, then pulled away.

"I—love you," she said.

As he released her, she turned and ran away, "Write," was sobbed.

He disappeared from sight. All she heard was the horse's galloping hooves as he faded away from her into the night.

Matthew couldn't have replied, choked as he was by his own feelings. He didn't have the words to convey all he felt for her, his mother, Grandma Logan, and the farm.

He rode past the cut-off and ten miles to the crossroads where one road led southeast toward Louisiana, Missouri. He planned to follow the river until he found Federal Troops.

He dismounted, took his bedroll and gun from the saddle, removed the bridle, tied it by the leather saddle strap to the saddle horn. He gave Dan's nose an extra rub, then threw his arms around the old horse's neck.

"So long, ole Fellow, this may be the last time I see you." He shuddered, released Dan. "Go home." He slapped the old horse on the rump, sending him back north. Dan took off like a colt with the saddle's stirrups flopping.

Matthew had told Maw to watch for old Dan. They often sent him home alone. Dan never failed to make the trip by himself. Matthew knew Maw would need Dan around the place and he was too old to take to war.

It is near dark and he should arrive home by daylight. Sure hope no bushwhackers see him going home and decide they need him.

I finished the crop toward the end of my seventeenth year. The farm is as ready as I can leave it. Mr. Wasson has his instructions and Maw has finally accepted I need to go. The women don't eat much. With me gone, they won't have to work as hard keeping things going.

He mused as he walked through the night, *Where is my Paw? Is he still alive? Will I find him? I hope not in a grave somewhere. Lord, please take care of Paw.*

I can count on Maw to add my name to her prayer list. I can be sure she'll pray for me at each meal, at night, and through the day. No matter what task she is about, I have come upon her with her eyes closed over the wash tub, the ironing board, or the dish pan. She can even weed the garden and pray with her eyes open. Milking time is one of her favorite times to pray. She leans into the cow's flank and sometimes, she talks aloud to the Lord. All kinds of work are times Maw prays. She seems to gain such peace from praying.

Why can't I gain any peace? I can't accept things as they happen. I want to change them. Maw and Paw seem at peace, whatever comes.

I have other things to think about now.

Daylight came slowly over the horizon to the east.

This is a beautiful morning! A layer of clouds hangs, barely touching the earth in the blaze of dawn.

What's that saying? Red Sky in the morning, sailors take warning?

Soldiering

JD didn't know Matthew was already gone from home. He attempted to answer questions his son had written asking about war. Amanda forwarded the letter, unopened, to the St. Louis Post Office, for Matthew.

Dear Matthew,

You asked me how a man becomes a good solider. Here are my thoughts. In battle, I find you never know the answer. We learn as we go.

To become a good soldier, a man must surrender the democratic principle of independent decision for the betterment of the group, or common goal. Do you understand this grand statement? It amounts to the fact most of us want our own way, want to make our own decisions, but we can't, if we're to be good soldiers.

And who is a good leader? We're unable to predict. It is more felt instinctively. A good man cannot always command, may be laughable to his men.

The Germans amongst us, say our soldiers are better than our officers. We haven't been trained in our democracy, to command, or follow. Most good American Officers appear to lead and if the soldiers respect them, they will follow. Most men don't wish to command, or be commanded. We've been independent on our farms, jobs, and in the city. We each wish to continue under our own direction. If the order makes sense to us, we'll do it. Otherwise, don't ask us to do something, because we probably won't. Some say there has probably never been another army where individuals make as many decisions for themselves.

If soldiers don't wish to perform, they straggle on purpose, get lost, fake illness, hide, and some desert rather than obey. No type of punishment appears to make men do what they don't wish to do. Execution, public humiliation, or physical punishment may work on some. None of these work all the time, or any of the time.

I've ridden by pickets who were asleep or didn't ask for a password, and by camps so filthy to realize their loss of at least one man per day to disease, is actually minor considering the conditions.

Men elected from the ranks find it even harder to command old neighbors and friends, and some don't learn by experience. Officers hold clear down the line, a good sergeant steadying a recruit, or on up the line, backing each other.

The best leaders seem to show personal courage; care for their men;, and he must be fair. We cannot do without these traits in our officers.

Son, you may get a good leader and you may get the poorest. Pray he means well, is practical, and open to suggestion. Surely someone among your ranks will have some judgment or knowledge that can get you through, and you know you can always rely upon God, even in the midst of the worst battle. Do your best, no matter what. Keep your head and heart in the right place.

Temptation to steal is strong among the soldiers, because we forage for loose food and it becomes a way of life.

A man's worst battle is always with himself. If he can handle that, he can handle most things.

I'm proud of you and I love you Son. Stay safe and God Bless You.

Paw (Jonathan David Logan)

The letter would not catch Matthew for some time, as he traveled toward Texas.

Matthew rode the railroad to Springfield. He got most of his training, as he, and a troop of green recruits started to march through Oklahoma to South Texas. He marched, and marched, *and marched.* The blue lines swayed ahead and behind him. They marched as they ate. Matthew *thought* they marched as they slept.

They passed through the first part of Indian Territory in Oklahoma. He saw some of the country, if he wasn't too tired to look. Most of the time, he was too tired to think.

The only thing I've seen of interest today, were mud curls on top of a mud slick, when we first hit the road this morning. Toward noon, I saw a flock of saffron butterflies atop another mud slick. They are as thirsty as I am. Probably why I noticed the mud slicks and happened to see the butterflies. We are all so dry. The mud slick curls and the butterflies aren't unusual, but they are something I've always enjoyed.

Toward evening, they camped in some low hills in Oklahoma. Matthew wasn't much interested in anything that evening, but when he arose in the morning and started to march, he was surprised to see occasional Indian houses. The houses were wooden structures, with nothing unusual about them as *poor white homes* go. Mostly the little children and their parents peeped out at the soldiers in fear, but sometimes, they saw an Indian man, or an older child, on horseback, or on foot. They herded cattle or sheep in the distance.

One bright spot in the march was a new friend from Springfield, Missouri. He and Martin talked as they marched.

The young man was about his age, but raised in town. They talked of many things to break the monotony of the march, but didn't dwell on serious topics for long. Both young and full of energy, they looked forward to big adventure.

The Will

JD came upon a deserted campground. They scouted the terrain. An enemy soldier had scrawled on a split log with a piece of charcoal, "Gone to Hell."

The message struck JD a hammer blow.

Oh, Lord, even though he's a declared enemy, I pray that isn't a prophetic statement. Please give him time to put his life in order for this battle, or any other of life's battles. He's in Your hands and we're in Your hands. Thank You Lord.

These thoughts caused JD to consider his mortality. *I'll prepare for any eventuality. I'll write out my will and mail it to my old friend, Mr. Wasson, for safe keeping. I don't wish to frighten Amanda or appear morbid. I never told my family about my injury from the hog, but mentioned I cut my leg and spent several days out of the ranks. I later mentioned I was fully recovered and am in full health. I hope that's true.*

JD went to the chaplain to ask for general information on will-making and was advised by Chaplain Kinkaid as to wording.

JD wrote his will out with his own hand.

I, Jonathan David Logan, of the County of Ralls, State of Missouri, but involved in war, do by these presence, make and publish my last Will and Testament, hereby revoking any disposition statements formerly by me made.

First: I resign my Spirit to my ever kind and merciful God and my body to the grave to be buried. If my death be near home, to be buried in the family plot at Madisonville Cemetery, Missouri, if practical, by my surviving family and friends. If in a distant land, in that area in which I die, and

Second: I wish and direct all my just debts be fully paid, including my burial expenses.

Third: I give and bequeath all the rest and residue of my estate, after said debts, to my beloved wife, Amanda Bowles Logan, for duration of her natural life, to be by her held and used as she may think best promote the comfort and happiness of herself and our children. She hereby authorized to sell or otherwise dispose of any or all my personal property and the crops and products of my entire home farm as she may think best, having full faith and confidence in her that she will do what is best for herself and our children as herewith named and further: Emma Louisa Logan and Matthew David Logan.

In the event my wife Amanda Bowles Logan should precede me in death, I hereby authorize and appoint my son Matthew to receive and manage, and in the event of his failure to act from any cause, then the probate court of Ralls

County shall appoint some fit and proper person therefore who will have due regard for the comfort and welfare of my surviving family, as well as my estate.

Fourth: *After the death of my said wife and the provisions aforementioned, I give and bequeath all and every part and parcel of my estate, real and personal to my two children to wit: Emma Louisa Logan and Matthew David Logan, or in the event of their being deceased, their one half portions, divided equally, to the heirs of each.*

Fifth: *to the end that my estate may be fully settled up and distributed with as little bother and cost as possible, I do hereby authorize and empower my Executor at the proper time, to control and sell any part or all of my real estate and report each and every sale to the probate court of Ralls County. Said court having duly considered and approved such sale, then my Executor shall execute and deliver any and all necessary deeds or either writing necessary to convey the abstract title of such real estate to the purchaser as approved, and will receive the proceeds and distribute the same, according to the fifth clause of this will, and for that purpose, I do hereby appoint and fully authorize my said wife Amanda Bowles Logan as my Executor to execute this will.*

At no time shall my estate be so reduced as to endanger the comfort and happiness of my said wife before her death; witness my hand and seal this 29th day of June AD. 1862, and I hereby request John Rumins, Brille Amyette, Fritz McDaniel and Francis Fridland to witness this as my last Will and Testament.

Jonathan David Logan (signature) *(Seal)*

Amended: *Should I pre-decease my mother Anna Catherine Logan, I wish she be cared for by my executors. She has an estate of her own, however, if she be in need, I would direct my executor meet her needs from my estate.*

JDL. (initialed)

We the undersigned have hereto subscribed our names to the above as the last will of Jonathan David Logan and in his presence and at his request, and in the presence of each other.

The Signatures followed on the document.

These thoughts and deeds tired JD. He was bone-weary when Isaiah 40:31 from his King James Bible came to him.

"But they that wait upon the Lord shall renew their strength; they shall mount up with wings of eagles; they shall run, and not be weary; and they shall walk, and not faint."

Lord, I hope so. Give me strength to bear what will come. Lift me up on those eagle wings and let me rest and be at peace.

Hardship at Home

With fewer farm animals, the women had little access to meat that winter. Their vegetables and fruits would sustain them, but craving for meat was felt by all. Each tried to hide this need. They attempted to make the burdens lighter for the other.

Maybelle invited the three ladies to a beef dinner on Sunday, along with Billy.

The ladies felt they wallowed in luxury when they savored the delicacy. After praise, Maybelle sent the left-over roast home with them for another meal.

Maybelle and Billy shared often. She seemed to understand the family had needs that winter. Amanda's three hens also rested during cold weather.

Fresh milk was the family's main protein food during the difficult winter but Maybelle's contributions of meat made it much easier to last until spring and greater abundance.

Not knowing how many winters of oppression they would have, Amanda dipped into the funds from the gold coin only when absolutely necessary.

Letter From Texas

Matthew assumed his father had been released from the Union Army and addressed his letter to his whole family.

Southeast Texas

Dear Maw, Paw, Emma, and Grandma,

We have only sand and sun here. The wind blows constantly and we have grit in our eyes and mouth all the time.

I can't help but envy the Mexicans and Indians down here. Maybe because they are such a contrast to me. They have darker skin and eyes. The sun and glare doesn't seem to bother them as much. I'm weathered from what I was at home. I keep my hat on, because we've found sun and wind burn can be painful. We're outside day and night.

Whole plantations have transplanted down here. The owners think they can set up a New South in Texas, and one day, they imagine they will return to their southern plantations. Most of them feel Texas will be a slave area, but we think and hope otherwise.

We're really not doing much fighting, just tramping all over and mopping up as they call it. These transplanted southerners are resentful of us, but they attempt to keep themselves and their slaves away from us. Perhaps they think the slaves will join us and leave their plantations. Some do.

We were pleased when we read the Emancipation Proclamation the beginning of January when "all persons once held as slaves in the Confederate States were declared thenceforth and forever free."

We still run across slaves in some areas who haven't

heard about their freedom in the south. Ex slaves who aren't with their former owners, don't seem to know what to do with themselves. They act like sheep without a shepherd. I don't think they are prepared to run their own lives. They seem to be mistreated by almost everyone. Even our soldiers pull tricks on them and they take it all very seriously. I can't help but feel a bit depressed over their attitudes and that of our boys. I guess we've all gotten bored and callused with this rebellion.

My friend named Martin, joined up at Springfield, Missouri. He has been with us most of our time.

We soldier together and have many hours to talk. I'd hate to do without him as a messmate. He makes up for some of our hard times. He's like family and a good person. I wish you could meet him.

Paw should be home by now, his three years should have been up by last winter. I hope he's home safe and rested up by now. I heard from Everett Bond that Paw had camp dysentery. Mr. Bond was with Gen. Scott as they rode by our regiment in December. He had seen Paw at St. Louis as they both passed through there sometime back. Bond went to St. Louis with a group to pick up replacement horses for our artillery and supply wagons. The animals are shipped in from northern Ohio. He said they moved the horses by river barges down the Ohio River and up to St. Louis so as to conserve the horses for further action.

We see a multitude of horses roaming free here in Texas and in some parts of the Indian Territory in Oklahoma when we came across there. It seems strange to bring horses from the north east to the southwestern parts, when there are already herds of free horses roaming here. These Mexican, Indians, and Texicans seem to catch and gentle all they need. The horses are not big tall bays, sorrels, grays, or blacks, like we used at home, but are shaggier and come in sand colored, spotted, blue brown, and all kinds of mixtures of horse colors.

Some of the wealthier Spanish people have beautiful

golden horses with white manes and tails. They use fancy saddles and bridles with silver decorations.

I'd like to bring Faith home a palomino, as the golden horses are called, but I expect I'll be on foot when I arrive, just as when I left. Tell her I wish I could buy her a horse and ride it on all these marches we have to take. We can cover as much as twenty-four miles a day walking, if we have to, but those on horses can cover more and it is easier on those troops.

About all we do is walk, walk, and walk some more. My boots are about gone. I stuffed some rawhide inside the soles and hope I can stay off the rocks.

Your Son, Matthew

Teche Country

Union Gen. Nathaniel P. Banks by-passed Vicksburg by using western navigable waters and captured the productive Teche Country to the west of the Mississippi River. This supplied cotton, salt, lumber, sugar, cattle, horses, and mules to the Union, and robbed these supplies from the Confederates. Foodstuff was again shipped into and through New Orleans. The port city again opened to Union transport. These same efforts forced the movement of the southern capitol and allowed freed Negroes from the Teche Country to enlist in the Union forces, bringing reenforcement's to the river areas.

This event would soon have bearing on JD's next assignment.

Dear Amanda,

I thought of you today, my Sweetheart. You can imagine how I long to see your face and hold you. I can't dwell upon my loneliness or I'd walk away from this war.

Sherman has advanced on Vicksburg and we secure further south daily. I'm on a barge on the Yazoo River. We had hoped to advance on Vicksburg by river and are harassing as we can.

Tell Mother and the rest of the family hello for me. I send my love to you all, even if it isn't a special day.

Love to All, JD

Goin' Home

Amanda looked at Grandma Logan when she was bathed and in her finery. She contemplated the life that was now over.

On the eve of Grandma Logan's burial, Amanda wrote her thoughts to her husband, JD, as she sat near her mother-in-law's body.

Dear JD,

Your mother passed to be with her Lord today. She had been ill for several days and slipped quietly away. She has peace and joy on her face.

In her advanced years, as your mother lays in her pine box, I note her skin and nails are still cared for. She hasn't been ill long enough to gain an unkempt look the old or sick sometimes acquire. I am grateful her final days were not wrought with suffering.

She has spent her life caring for others.

I loved her, but felt relief at her passing peacefully. She had become frail and I knew she didn't have long. She had talked to me about being ready to go meet the Lord face to face and be with Bailey again.

Only her old shell remained, her soul now enjoys the presence of God, and she's with Bailey. I couldn't feel sad for her, only for myself, and for my loss of her presence, and for the loss I know you will feel. I am sad for the loss of her wisdom and presence, especially for our children, and their children.

Grandma Anna Catherine Logan raised me. My mother has been gone so long, I can remember her less than I do your Mother Logan. The important things, I learned from your mother and I thank her for the wonderful way she took me into her home and treated me as her daughter. She included me and my brother in her family when our own parents died while we were only children.

I realize sorrow is a part of living, as is joy. I miss you so much, especially during hard times. Know I love you and pray for you, especially as you get this message about your mother.

Amanda paused to think. *I ceased calling Anna Catherine, Mother or Maw, when Emma and Matthew were born. Then Grandma seemed to be the proper name for Anna.*

A sob rose in her throat and tears burned her eyes when she saw in her memory, things or places through the eyes of Grandma Logan. She resumed her letter to JD.

I see memories as have been described to me in times past by Bailey and Anna. It is their legacy they left for me and our family. I know I have traits from my own father and mother, who people say I favor in disposition and in physical looks and coloring, but I possess more emotional traits I've gained from experiences with Grandma Logan than from my own family.

It is strange when one person dies, all known past lives are called up and taken out for examination. This makes a heavy burden of all deaths piled one upon the other.

How I long for you tonight. We could share this with each other. I need to talk, but I don't wish to burden Emma or your sister, Florence.

She spoke as to Mother Logan, "You were a great mother and example to me. I'll miss you."

After a time of examining the past, Amanda began to pray. She felt the burden lift and joy return in the journey of her mother-in-law to meet her Lord.

"God Speed, Grandma!" She patted Grandma's hand and laid her own head back on her chair. She dozed off into a cozy sleep for the few hours, before dawn.

Florence came at four.

"I couldn't sleep and thought you probably needed me. I need you and to be near Maw a little longer."

The two women hugged.

Amanda brushed a tear from her own face and reached to wipe Florence's cheek.

The two huddled as sisters until time to put bread on for rise.

In the morning before the burial, Amanda finished her letter to JD and posted it. He would know of his mother's passing as soon as possible.

The neighbors arrived early with food and sympathy. She had much to do today. There would be a dinner at noon, after the funeral and burial. The neighbors would stay for a time, applaud Grandma Logan's life, then those living would proceed as normally as possible.

JD's return letter arrived in five weeks.

Dear Amanda, I'm sorry the last time I wrote, I didn't know of Mother's death. My letter asking about her must have added to the burden for you.

As I told you, we didn't receive mail for three months, but then I received five letters from you and others at the same time. I'm glad your latest message wasn't old.

It took me several days to catch up on home, but I had wished for the news as it happened. I know it is hard for you not to be together as a family, as it is for me.

God Bless and keep you all. I pray for you every day and can almost feel your presence at times. You never mention any hardships, except Mother's death, and I know there must be many. Are things going well for you and the community? I pray so.

I guess you noticed my paper? It is not exactly the easiest to write on, or to read. Paper is in short supply as we've been away from necessary supplies. If you see anyone coming to Jefferson City or St. Louis, you might send paper and pencils, if you have any to spare. If not, we should be getting supplies before long.

All my Love to You and the Family,

Paw Jonathan D. Logan

Amanda did have a hard time reading the letter. It was written down the page, then the page was turned and written the second time, vertically. It was crumpled and somewhat soiled. Amanda wondered where JD got the paper.

It didn't matter, the message was the thing she cherished.

I don't possess paper and pencils to send, but I'm hopeful I can acquire some for JD. I'll ask Noah if he can get a supply for me to send to our men.

Vicksburg, Under Attack, May 19-July 4, 1863

JD wrote Amanda a number of letters after the Union Army reached the Vicksburg area. His command joined Grant's forces, to begin attacks on Vicksburg. He could not mail the letters, as the contents would give away battle plans. The strategic ones found their way into the fire each night. This one delegated to the cookfire:

Gen. Grant has been assigned the task of taking Vicksburg and laying siege to the entire Mississippi River to cut the Confederacy in two. This will cut the supplies to the Confederacy in the east and give us a corridor of Union control.

We've spent the past three weeks in and around Vicksburg, taking the surrounding strongholds. We have had nothing but victories. The morale runs very high. Success is wonderful for us and hopefully draws us closer to our goal of this war being ended with the nation intact.

Gen. Sherman attempted to take the heavily fortified Vicksburg five months before but was unsuccessful. Now, Union morale is high from our recent victories in the east. We lost few soldiers, marched 180 miles, took Ports Gibson, Raymond, Jackson, Champion Hill, and now we're ready to cross the Big Black River into Vicksburg. Other Federal troops converge from up and downriver.

We heard, Confederate General Johnston had argued for protection of Tennessee, as the "Shield of the South" and felt these losses were crucial. He preached the defense of Vicksburg and with it control of the Mississippi River, which loss he thought would mean vacating Texas, western Louisiana, Arkansas, and the last hold on Missouri. He had begged for consolidation of the southern forces in both areas, but much to our surprise, President Davis over-ruled him on both counts. Tragic for the south but a real blessing for us. How we come by all this information, I have no idea but thank the Lord for His interest.

Among the scattered sounds of rifle fire and distant cannon, my men were ordered to cross the pontoon bridge as soon as Sherman's men got the India rubber rafts into position. Jockeying the cumbersome air-filled pieces of equipment, the general's men labored to hook the pontoons together securely. We waited impatiently for the signal to advance. All three corps moved across, with my soldiers near the middle. It's a bouncy and unsteady trip across waters on these things.

"Close up, close up! Keep going, come on, come on," I yelled over the bedlam. I had seasoned, well-disciplined soldiers and they hustled across and marched double-time to the base of the ramparts at Vicksburg. Now as the three corps were placed on the heights on the east and looked down on the bottomland, General Sherman was exhilarated. The Big Black had come easily into Union possession.

I looked along the long line of the bluffs on either side of Vicksburg and I could see mortar boats in the river, above and below the town.

Our three generals directed the assault according to the clock. The battles were staged on a time-table. My men and the other corps sprang forward to be met by a surprise, Rebels fired down over the parapets in a cloud of gun powder. I signaled to my men and they held. After twenty minutes, the battering became so severe, I was forced to lead a retreat. We scrambled frantically back to the ravines and ditches to duck down and attempt to protect ourselves.

My men dodged and crouched, as the Rebel bullets mowed down the grass over our heads, helping to cover and hide us, but making our hiding places, blistered dust and debris-laden holes. The Rebels threw 12-inch mortar shells into our havens in a steady stream.

The air was thick with dust and the powder stung our nostrils. No longer could we smell, we could hardly breath. Two hours of continual firing caused heavy casualties. Under cover of darkness, I was able to order my men to retreat quietly back to our first position of the day. Different plans are needed for an attack to prosper.

In exhaustion, JD sank and grieved for the dead and dying who remained where they had fallen, or where they were able to crawl under their own power. No respite came for their rescue.

He continued his thoughts: *Porter's Navy cruised up and down the several rivers, clearing the Rebel steamboats, sawmills, and supply forts from the area. With no reinforcements coming on the river for the Rebels, the Union generals felt more secure in our attempts upon Vicksburg.*

Grant conferred with his subordinates. "We could lay siege without undue fear of retaliation from the rear. The lack of reinforcements and the bombardment from the artillery, will lower the morale of the Rebels, but do little immediate damage to the defenders of Vicksburg. Because of Rebel placement, we'll be in for an extended and difficult battle as long as we continue to attack, but it's necessary. We'll send in artillery bombardment from the river. Prepare to mount your second attack."

"Dismissed, go to your respective places and prepare yourselves."

The second assault was ordered with twenty-four foot scaling ladders.

JD and his men attempted to carry their ladders and advance on the heights again. They met with heavy resistance.

"Fall back, fall back. Use the ditches and ravines for cover. Fire at will," JD yelled at his men. When asked, he had to say, "Leave the wounded where they fall, for now."

They had encountered the same conditions as the day before with heavy casualties. JD was frustrated with his inability to advance, or protect his men.

A third assault occurred during the day, with further poundings on the Union forces.

Night came and with it, another retreat. JD again, dug in and waited through the night. Any unusual noises were greeted with a hail of bullets from the bluff above them.

As the noise quieted slightly, JD heard sounds from those left in front of the lines. There were needy men out there to whose cries he could not close his ears or his heart any longer. He rose slightly. His men turned to look at him.

"Men, pass the word down the line. I'm asking for volunteers to get the wounded under cover of night. You could get shot for helping. Don't feel obligated, but if you choose, go as quietly as possible and any way you can. Every man use his best judgement. Spread out. Let's go."

It was difficult to tell in the dark the number who chose to help, but shadows crawled over the edges of the ridge. Other soldiers stayed in the trenches and offered cover fire to hold the enemy down.

JD found some wounded crawling over the bodies of

fallen comrades, in their attempts to get back to their lines. Several casualties were covered with bodies. The noises led he and his men to move those above to release some. They dragged the wounded behind their lines. Others were willing to help move them back to field hospitals.

JD and his men returned to the wounded. Other exhausted men rose and started to assist in their efforts. By 4 AM, all was quiet on the field. JD and his remaining men lay down in a ravine for a short rest. They'd done all they could and made a tiny dent in the wreck of human casualties in front of their lines. Along other lines of casualties, most were ignored by their comrades.

JD, as a field soldier, did not know the numbers, but Grant had taken one thousand casualties in the first day's advance; three thousand, one hundred and ninety nine on the second day; and had over six hundred soldiers missing. This was more than he'd lost in the three weeks of victorious campaigns, enroute to Vicksburg.

During the third day, in the afternoon of May 25, southern Pemberton, Commander of Vicksburg, could stand the stench and torture of the casualties no longer. He asked for a truce to remove the dead and care for the wounded who lay below the bluffs of his city. At 6 that evening, all firing ceased and the Union dead were buried where they lay. The wounded were removed behind the lines and the firing resumed after dark. JD was thankful for this reprieve. The torture of those laying wounded was more and more on the troops' nerves. They couldn't help but wonder, *If I'm among the wounded, how long will I lay there waiting for assistance?* This thought began to play upon their minds.

"Maybe better not to advance, if the wounded are condemned this torturous end," murmured through the lines.

"I'm leaving," was whispered.

The men were growing weak from the heat, lack of water, and substantial food. Digging round the clock in the intense heat wore on their strength.

"Hardtack, hardtack," the men called, as Grant rode near the ranks. Grant pulled his horse aside to inform the soldiers, hardtack, beans, and coffee supplies were being replenished.

The men were strengthened after their first meals of solid, field food in days. The field trains had finally caught up with the siege troops.

Southern General Johnston had failed in his efforts to cut northern supply lines and keep food from the besiegers.

The next day, General Grant called his generals and their aides together. JD overheard their conference.

"We are going to lay extended siege to Vicksburg. It's impossible under our present circumstances for us to take the city. We'll wait to deplete the Rebel's ammunition and their will to fight further. Take whatever time we need to complete the job. Hand out entrenching shovels and prepare to dig in for a long stay. Throw up as much protection as the men can. Stay behind barriers and fire whenever you see any exposed on the ramparts. The boats will bombard the city and keep on the pressure from a distance."

This met with general agreement. A cheer went up.

After the three defeated assaults, all of us can see no further point in wasting our lives in an effort that is so costly and so futile. Time will take care of Vicksburg. Our job will be to confiscate Rebel stores and prevent outside help from entering the city from any source. JD mulled their situation.

Grant saluted, "Dismissed and get at it!"

In his next dispatch to President Lincoln, the General enumerated their successes thus far at this battle site.

Capture of the Big Black River to the east of Vicksburg and the Haines Bluff to the north, allowed us to take the Yazoo River landings and prevented southern resupply; and furnished the Union a lane of transport. The siege is in place and proceeds. *Gen. U.S. Grant*

JD and the other soldiers worked energetically, because they knew it would be safer to lay siege and further soften Vicksburg, before they assaulted again. As the men dug in the orange clay, JD set Alcott and a number of sharp-shooters to keep the Rebels down and off their backs. The sharpshooters were directed to shoot at any part of a Rebel that appeared over the enemy entrenchments.

Alcott and others were alert and *plunked* away at any movement from the enemy lines. Many shots were thrown in their direction by the enemy above, and the men had to duck frequently. Soon the entrenchments were below the surface of the surrounding terrain, giving them more security. The soldiers packed clay between woven poles and posts to form walls above their trenches.

The trenches branched off and came to within fifty feet of the enemy trenches. Workers' voices could be heard from the enemy lines when the men stopped digging and shelling ceased.

JD found a small clump of brush from which he could occasionally raise his head to view the enemy's position. He thanked the Lord for any cover his men had. He tried to keep enemy attention from those areas, as they blasted to annihilate any possible protection.

JD and his men slept in the trenches at night and the city was bombarded many hours of each day. They grew to expect the noise and awakened when quiet pervaded the area, knowing, even in their sleep, a difference occurred.

Union reinforcements arrived from Tennessee, Miss-ouri, and Kentucky.

By mid-June Grant commanded 71,000 *readies*.

Sherman's troops on the northern flank, were taking a beating from the Confederate gunners. He suspected the defenders were moving artillery from the riverside to pour barrages down upon the siege forces, including JD's.

Grant ordered the Navy's Porter, to check Confederate deployment, by sending the Union ironclad *Cincinnati* to test the fire power from the river side. The Confederates riddled the *Cincinnati* and she sank before she could turn away to safety. JD watched as those left alive swam to safety. This was the third ironclad Porter had lost recently on this section of the Mississippi. Porter renewed the Naval bombardment of the city with a vengeance for many hours each day.

Starvation stared the Confederate states in the face, the troops were demoralized, and talked among themselves of surrendering all the forts along the rivers.

Grant received further reinforcements June 11, from Missouri, with the youngest Major General of the Union, Frank Herron, twenty-five years old, who received his two stars at Prairie Grove, in northern Arkansas.

Grant had only two professional engineers to establish his works, lay bridges across the creeks and bayous, and other construction work, but mid-western farmers were versatile and quickly made up for this lack. With energy and willingness; they were accustomed to *making do* with what they had at hand. There was a youthfulness and creativity in the commanders and among the soldiers which wore down the most difficult problems. Many were good ax men and were put to the backbreaking task of bridging marshy terrain on the western side of the river.

Grant deployed almost half of his troops facing the rear. He thought General Johnston, would eventually, attempt to fight his way into Vicksburg to assist Pemberton. Grant's army alternated in order to allow them respite from continual warfare. JD and his men sometimes faced the guns from Vicksburg and at other times, took the ease of the eastern facing trenches away from Vicksburg's guns, but in the construction of bulwarks to provide rear protection.

During boring times, a favorite game of both sides was the placement of a hat upon a ramrod and betting as to how many bullet holes the hat would receive over a given period of time. During the night, even though forbidden, soldiers talked and exchanged coffee for cigarettes with enemy soldiers or some other item the enemy found in short supply. Most Union soldiers refrained from trading substantial food knowing it would lengthen the siege.

In periods of off-duty, JD and his men examined the Confederate fortifications from a safe distance, as they encircled a three-quarter-moon around the city. They noted the fortifications extended for seven miles, from commanding ridges and anchored at both extremities to sheer bluffs of two hundred feet.

"These southerners hold a very superior position. Our Union forces have to man lines twice as long as the Confederate fortifications, with three times as many men," his surveyor reported to JD when they measured the fortifications with their transom.

The Confederate artillery and guns bristled along the fortifications and commanded overlapping fields of fire. As the northerners backed away, traveled around the fortifications, looked at the effects of the artillery, they were amazed at its power.

"The ground placement of Vicksburg is impossibly rough. The defenders have felled trees that run down to the waterline on the front, making entrance from that direction, almost impossible. Anyone ascending the slopes has to traverse the fallen timber and use his hands for assistance on the steep terrain. These ravines help the siege forces and the defenders. They provide places of protected concealment for one, and added difficulty to an ascending attack," he further disclosed.

Grant had the men dig continuously. They grumbled he planned to go *under* the fortifications, rather than face the enemy head-on. Heat was unbearable as the sun beat down on the Union forces in their wool uniforms. They welcomed the shade from the overhang of the banks, as they tunneled into the earth. Being underground protected them from the *Thunder Barrels,* powder-filled kegs, with fuses in the bong hole, the Rebels lighted and rolled down upon them.

When JD's troops replaced a forward regiment, the officer informed them.

"Watch out on this side, the Rebs are throwing back unexploded Union grenades and un-detonated Naval projectiles they re-fuze and roll from the heights. You may hear them bumping along just before they hit your trench."

JD found hearing or seeing anything coming was almost impossible. The ground continually vibrated around them, dirt sifted down from the ceiling of the tunnels where they crouched. Dust hung in clouds and smoke obscured the heights above them. On occasion, JD's men got bored and shot, but most of the time they couldn't see their targets.

The constant bombardment from the ships on the river kept many of the southern soldiers off the ramparts, but also helped to conserve their ammunition.

JD and his men's hearing became muffled. They had a continual roar in their heads and vibrations in their body. This tormented them when they tried to sleep or in times of quiet. Small sounds escaped them.

"We may not hear the sounds of the woodlands, if we ever get off these mountains," observed Alcott.

When they drew duty on the outer periphery, they talked of the plight of those inside the fortifications at Vicksburg.

"I wish they'd surrender, so no more would be killt or injured. They must be gettin' hungry and tired of this," Alcott muttered.

JD mused more to himself than to Alcott.

"I've never seen inside Vicksburg, but some say it was a beautiful city, almost a hundred years old. Someone said there was a Spanish Fort here before Vicksburg grew up on these bluffs. It's a natural river landing and has protection for this bend with its view in both directions. Someone told me Vicksburg had a civilian population of forty-five hundred people at the beginning of the siege. They've moved to caves carved out in the bluffs below the town, above the river. I wonder how many are still alive? The soldier who came out, said they had taken their most valued possessions to the caves and lived there like moles. It would be safer than those shells bursting over your house or business all day. Wonder if many of the buildings still stand?"

"He said they were gettin' low on food, he'd been eatin' mule beef, killt by our shells," marveled Alcott.

After the main assaults, JD continually lost a trickle of men. They were picked off, one by one, during the siege operation. He was constantly in the forefront and his men felt he was threatened by the enemy.

JD couldn't stand by, not helping when he saw a task that needed another strong back or saw a wounded man who needed retrieval. He was compelled by his own code of values to take on any job he saw. His salvation proved to be, he couldn't see far crouched in the trenches.

"Captain, stay down, let me do that."

JD refused the offers. He felt his responsibility to save as many of his boys as possible. JD's attitude inspired his men to greater bravery.

Bullets plucked at their uniforms and bodies alike. JD's uniform was slowly being ventilated with bullet and shrapnel holes. His hat had one hole and his jacket, shirt and trousers had five holes and one rent. Only the hole at his ankle had drawn noticeable blood.

"Keep your head down. Use it for something besides catching lead," he instructed his men. "Be sensible, don't take risks unless we've got something to gain. We've got several days yet to go. We need you all around when this thing is over." He tried to obey his own rules. He avoided exposure when possible.

JD thought about the wording of a letter, if he were to write one about their attacks and subsequent siege of the town.

We first attempted three attacks all around Vicksburg and have now settled in for a bombardment and plan to wait for Vicksburg's defenses to wear out.

We've tried to dig around, under, and through this place and then tried to go around by Steele's Bayou. We almost got corked in. The boys from the flatboat, had to wade in the water almost to their waists to get to the downed logs placed there by the enemy. They stood on the log barriers, while they chopped a way out. This uncorked the fleet and it took three days for us to maneuver out, after barely scraping our way in. It was harder than backing Ole Dan, hooked to a long-tongued wagon full of hay, down the hallway of the barn.

JD felt no need to censor the rest of his information, *everyone knew Vicksburg was under siege.*

Dear Amanda and Emma,

Vicksburg is marvelously positioned on a high bluff, overlooking the Mississippi River, sticking out into a horse-shoe bend of the river. On either side, it is surrounded by bayou, swamps and generally mountainous, impassable terrain. From below, it is a difficult place to do battle.

I'm very glad Gen. Grant has been assigned this task. He is a real bull dog and once he takes hold, he will not let go, until he succeeds, and we eventually will, unless a new Confederate Army should arise from our rear.

Delegated to the fire:

When some of our boys came in from the riverside, Porter ran the gauntlet of the Vicksburg Battery to meet them south of the city to ferry the army across the river. Porter piled the port sides with bales of cotton, hay, grain and coal barges to float by Vicksburg at night. Vicksburg saw them coming and ignited tar barrel flares and cotton to illuminate the boats. Their artillery bombarded us. Each of our boats was hit repeatedly when we went through singly. All but one made it through, even if they were out of control some of the time.

We sent out two diversionary attacks to confuse the

defenders of Vicksburg. These caused the Confederates to draw first to one side, then the other, and kept them shaken and unsure of our actual attack plans.

Philosophizin'

June 28, JD was off-duty and caught up with his laundry. No matter how busy, they had moments when they had more time to think, than they wanted. No one found a way to turn off his thoughts, unless he was into some physical activity.

JD occupied his mind by placing thoughts in his journal or writing letters.

Outside Vicksburg, Mississippi
June 28, 1863

Dear Amanda,

I'm concerned about this experiment of an American Republic. We have such strong individual freedom, independence of minds, and resources. We are founded on freedom of the individual, where a man can, by the honest sweat of his brow, live as he likes.

In harmony with his neighbors, he can rear his children to be free to pursue their own aspirations in the future, except for the Africans.

I've read Thomas Jefferson was even concerned about the condition and outcome of this nation after the Missouri Compromise, and eventually, the outcome of slavery. Wasn't it a contradiction, he had slaves, and wrote against slavery? I am finding that philosophy a common thing in the southern states. There are good people, who do not believe in slavery, yet possess other human beings. Some of them honestly believe they can't turn the slaves loose, as the slaves can't care for themselves. There is some truth in these thoughts. It has been against the law to educate the slaves. It is ration-

alized into being for the slaves protection to keep them in slavery. I'm unable to see their reasoning.

I've thought about the census in Ralls County for 1860, I still can't imagine nearly one quarter of the county's population were slaves. Where were they? Just outside our boundaries, Hannibal had many, but I didn't see that many in our area. I suppose small numbers count up, but the bigger groups must have been in the larger town areas.

I've contemplated my contradiction: The fact I'm a Democrat; who backs a Republican, Abe Lincoln; and I'm an abolitionist. I guess my Democratic leanings come from the fact I was Kentuckybred. I'm as contradictory as those I'm trying to study.

I guess we can't solve the problems of the world, only work on ourselves.

You are probably tired of my philosophizing and I will get on with telling you I am fine. I have had no more camp problem, for which I had leave. We have many German folk in this group of troops and they are much cleaner than some groups I have served with. Common sense tells you not to drink ground water below a camp. Our hogs aren't as filthy as some of these camps appear.

JD thought, but didn't include in his letter:

I understand there's a problem with the Confederate Prison at Andersonville. There have been very few escapes or parolees, but we have picked up a few. What they tell isn't pleasant, some of their problems arise from the guards living above the prisoners on their main water source.

One escapee told us, our men attempt to dig wells within the prison in order to provide a cleaner water source for themselves. I wish those fellows could be liberated, now!

He added to his letter:

There is nothing very different here, the siege continues and we wait for some break from inside. We don't sit, unfortunately. We move, fire, move again, and again, hoping to dislodge the beseiged enemy.

Take good care of yourself and Emma. We will surely wind this war down before too long and be on our way home. I enjoy looking at the Mississippi as it flows by, wishing and thinking about hopping a steamer going north. I know some of its water comes from out of our little creek, off our farm, or out of Salt River or Spencer Creek. It's much bigger here than the Mississippi close to home. I can't help thinking of all the farms and plantations that contribute to this great river and all those folks are touched by this war in one way or another.

Love, Jonathan David Logan

P.S.

Vicksburg surely can't hold on much longer. I guess I'm a little like that slave owner, I think their surrender will be for their own protection. Isn't that inconsistent? We all know what is best for someone else.

Amanda sighed as she read Jonathan's letter. *We used to so enjoy discussing philosophy and thinking on serious topics. I miss those intellectual talks. It seems all we discuss here at home is, "Has the pig been fed? Let's go to the field, or Have you done the milking?"*

We have to work so hard, we have no time for serious conversation, for conversation's sake. Our minds are all going to be stale by the time this horrible war ends!

Emma came into the house with the evening's milk and Amanda's train of thought shifted.

Perhaps we should try to think a little more deeply and converse about more important and bigger topics.

"Emma, here's a letter from Paw. Would you like to read it? I found it most interesting."

Emma took the letter and settled down to pour over her father's letter.

I vow when Emma finishes the letter, we will have a little talk, on a few deeper subjects.

Outside Vicksburg, Mississippi
Dear Amanda and Emma,

Residents and defenders of Vicksburg must be getting hungry, as they've had nothing going in for almost six weeks.

This one is short enough to send and no vital information is revealed, JD thought, but he'd have to add something more substantial to it. He pocketed it for later additions, and assigned to the fire:

Grant attacked from the circular entrenchments around Vicksburg with eighty-nine artillery positions and two-hundred and twenty guns, with unlimited ammunition. We kept up a relentless fire into the town and the defenders.

We are aware the civilian population of Vicksburg is living in the cliffs below Vicksburg to avoid injury. Some say they go up to the town during the night when there is less danger from the bombardment.

The Confederates are under constant bombardment from the river during daylight by Porter's two-hundred pound shells. We've been six weeks, with our boys shooting from all directions and rotating off to try for rest, between duties. Those inside the city have not had that freedom.

Surrender

Joyously JD mailed this message.

Dear Amanda and Emma, From Inside Vicksburg
Finally, Vicksburg surrendered July 4, when they could no longer maintain a defense or feed their citizens. Grant and Pemberton met on July 3 for discussion of terms.

When the Confederates surrendered Vicksburg, there was no immediate cheering, out of a show of respect for their tenacity and bravery. We paraded from 10 AM till noon. I was so proud when our Gen. Grant rode to the Court House at noon and placed a Union flag. It was high on a hill and visible throughout the heights. He then rode down to the river to commend the fleet.

We carried food into Vicksburg and fed everyone we could find. We have occupied the town and continue to feed as many as come to us. We found the citizens and soldiers had eaten all their mules during the siege and saw the caves where they hid under the bluffs above the river. Their caves were carved out of the soil as were our entrenchments. They were not natural limestone caverns as we have in Missouri. Their caves are as different as a hole in the ground is from a cave. There are no stones in this deep soil.

I'm very sorry for their suffering and we are all glad this part of the war is over.

Surely, this marks the end of the Confederacy, but this war will probably drag on for some time yet. I'm not sure where our next destination will be, and I couldn't write it if I did know.

Here's praying we'll all be together again soon.

I love you, Your Husband and Father, JD Logan.

Amanda saw a newspaper article which quoted Lincoln as having said after the fall of Vicksburg. "The Father of Waters again goes unvexed to the sea."

She took her kitchen shears and cut out the message to send in her next letter to JD, and then another stated: "The day Vicksburg fell, July 4, 1863, was the same day General Lee retreated from Gettysburg, Pennsylvania, after a massive and costly defeat."

I can see JD's prediction of ultimate Confederate defeat has to come true.

JD now had a supply of paper and began to make journal entries for his own amusement:

I'm making more observations on the institution of slavery and of freed slaves. My overall opinion hasn't Chang-

ed much from what I had as a teenager, but I am seeing much of it first hand now and can draw a few conclusions.

We find groups of slaves who feel free when each group of soldiers comes along. They follow us for a time, some return to their work. They seem unsure and lost, once we pass by. Like a horse in a burning barn, they run back into the only place they know and feel security. This loyalty seems to depend on how long they've lived in an area, or if they had been sold from their families. The latter displaced slaves head for family or their last known location, if that is in a free area. Some of these slaves wait for the old masters to tell them they are free, even after we have told them they may go.

We noted some plantation owners have tried to keep control of their slaves by moving them around, away from the armies; keeping the children from the parents, or husbands and wives apart; or giving them feasts and promising land, if they stay.

I think both armies exploit the freed slaves. We don't seem to let them do anything but dig ditches and do hard labor, even though they came to our aid as enlisted soldiers. We've seen the same among the southern ranks. I've noted not too many of the colored men are given guns or do actual fighting. I sometimes think we too, have prejudice and misunderstanding among the northern soldiers and the colored folk. It has the appearance of a fear of the unknown. I have to say I don't know many colored folk and I daresay most other northern boys don't either.

I heard there are colored regiments of freed slaves from Missouri and Arkansas. I think they are called the Kansas First Colored Volunteer Infantry. We witnessed colored soldiers from the Teche Country coming to Vicksburg to assist Union soldiers already there.

I heard of a horrible situation today. When they are captured in battle, Southern armies are executing or selling former slaves who are serving as Union soldiers. This hasn't stopped the colored's desire to fight for their own freedom and help win this war. Everywhere we go colored men come to us and beg to help us fight.

Many of the slaves are afraid to go back to their old homes. They follow along behind the troops.

We have had freed couples flocking into the county seats and to the Justices of the Peace for official marriages. The missionaries with us are requiring ex-slaves traveling with us as husband and wife, be legally married. There has been as many as several thousand at some locations. These freed slaves who follow the army are called contraband which I think means spoils of war. A poor thing to call a human being.

I have to say I am glad they are making their marriages legal. I think they are just as emotionally married as whites, but this puts their marriages on the record books and they take pride in the new records.

We had a colored servant bring in his severely wounded master on the master's horse. Then he ran away as soon as he was sure our surgeons would care for his master.

We see some freed slaves have a great loyalty and love for their white families. They choose to stay and continue in their tasks even when we tell them they are free and may go where they please. We see others with intense hatred and we can only imagine what has brought it on.

We are set to travel again. By JD Logan,

JD Wrote Amanda,

Since mail is very important during the war, for morale purposes, I write with joy, I heard each day, 90,000 letters go through Washington, D.C. and 180,000 through Louisville for the Union Armies in the West. You civilians sure are keeping your pens warm!

Journal Entry:

I sometimes have the task of handing out mail. The men get letters from the north and the south. Some stamps have the Confederate president's picture on their stamps. Kind of a slap to us.

The Union uses stamps with George Washington, eagles, flags, or patriotic symbols. I wonder if I should hand out the mail that arrives from the south? I feel I owe my comrades in arms the courtesy of receiving <u>*all*</u> *mail.*

Some of the soldiers' mail is marked 'postage due.' We aren't always able to buy stamps. Other envelopes have elaborate drawings of battle scenes. With time on our hands, the men enjoy these pictures to send home. Some are comical. Some envelopes are made from wallpaper folded to form note paper on one side and the envelope on the other, usually the fancy side.

I heard two brothers from Missouri fought on opposite sides while we were at Vicksburg. The Confederate soldier sent a roll of bills home to their mother by his Yankee brother.

Another story reminded me of Saul and David's battles during war in the Old Testament. One young man found his father from the opposite side, sleeping in a cave, and left a note on his coat, without awakening the older fellow.

Food is better for us. Recently our cooks scalded and butchered one thousand hogs and baked one thousand loaves of bread for the next day's dinner. That is a great amount of food but there are many hungry mouths amongst us.

<u>More News</u>

The next letter came from Matthew.

I've heard Sherman's troops helped take Vicksburg in the six-week siege where you said Paw fought.

The colored regiments from Missouri who are in Texas with us, took up a collection from their pay to start a

Negro school when they get back home. It is for higher education of the Africans. I chipped in four dollars when I was released to go from the Texas Coast.

We took ships across the Gulf of Mexico to New Orleans. I feel as if I've seen the world. The Gulf was beautiful, the first beauty I've been able to see for a while.

I went from grit and sun to steamy-green. The Spanish moss hangs from the trees like lace curtains. It gives a ghostly appearance, especially on a moonlight night. The moss sways in the breezes and appears like an old woman trailing her hair and long ghostly dress, sadly searching for something.

I think the whole south is searching for something and they haven't found it. I'm not sure we have found all we need, either.

I've written this over the last three months, so it is long and goes on and on. I may be in the city of New Orleans by the time you get this.

With Love From Your Son, Matthew

Two Weeks Later:

We've got to stay here a while and keep martial law in New Orleans. We hope the war will be over and we'll be released. If that should happen, we'd be shipped up the Mississippi River on steamers to St. Louis, when the time comes.

It will be months, maybe even years yet, look for me when you see me, because they don't tell us much. We'll hear more as time passes.

Your Loving Son, Matthew

Campaigns, Fall of 1863

JD, with Grant's army, moved on to Tennessee from Vicksburg and floated down the Tennessee River. They overtook the Confederate troops guarding the river at Chattanooga. Sherman arrived shortly after and took Look Out Mountain within a matter of days, freeing Union General George Thomas' troops. They had been boxed inside Chattanooga for nearly two months. Besieged by southerners under Bragg, they had little to eat but corn and gruel. The men were worn and had lost most of their mules and horses. They need to recuperate before returning to active duty.

JD's command came to protect Chattanooga and help Thomas' men reorganize. The situation reminded JD of Vicksburg, but the shoe was on the other foot this time.

From Look Out Mountain, Tennessee
Dear Ladies,

I'm sending you a sprig of mountain flowers from atop Look Out Mountain above Chattanooga, Tennessee. These little flowers abound here and they make our day more pleasant.

We can overlook several states from our perch atop the mountains. The Tennessee River lays just below us in a bend. When we don't have a fog or rain, we can see our boats going up and down the river.

Last night, I slept out under the stars and the mountain seemed star-high, I thought I might pluck a star to send you, but I found I wasn't as high as I thought.

There are several houses atop these hills and mountains. They have a spectacular view much of the time, as Chattanooga is sprawled before us on the opposite side of the river. If it is clear, they can see into several states.

You might be interested in hearing what one lady has done for the Union. A Mrs. Howe wrote a hymn which is being sung around campfires and during marches. It is called Battle Hymn of the Republic, a stirring hymn about our Lord and His soldiers. The fellows previously sang, John Brown's Body to almost the same tune.

I have to say, I much prefer this hymn over the other song. Whoever heard of a song that spoke of someone's body "moldering in the grave?"

The hymn speaks of seeing the Lord coming, His sword of justice, His being with the soldiers, His Gospel cleaning out the evil in our nation, calling His soldiers to right, and ends with Hallelujahs. It lifts the spirits of the men and takes us away from the unhappy situations in which we find ourselves.

I hope you get to hear it very soon. If I had a copy, I'd send it along, but I'm tired now and I can't think how the first part begins.

Our Chaplain seems to have adopted this hymn and he never fails to use it with each service he holds. I can't fault him, as I find myself singing it <u>in my head</u> *when we move along or work.*

The chorus has come to me: Glory, Glory Hallelujah, Glory, Glory Hallelujah. Glory, Glory Hallelujah, His truth is marching on.

I must stop now. It is nearly midnight and we must arise early in the morning to continue our clean-up work.

Your Loving Husband, JD Logan

Amanda found a copy of the poem in the Hannibal paper, for the *Battle Hymn of the Republic.* The article was copied from *The Atlantic Monthly*, February, 1862.

She read, thinking of JD and the soldiers singing the same words on the battlefields near Chattanooga, Tennessee.

"Battle Hymn of the Republic

She skimmed the words.

I have seen Him in the watch-fires of a hundred circling camps,

She read on tearfully.

As He died to make men holy, let us die to make men free, While God is marching on.

Amanda crushed the paper to her face and cried tears of joy and sadness into its folds.

I feel the message in my soul. It is beautiful and more tragic at the same time. I wish I could hear it set to music.

There is nothing in the paper about the circumstances of the poem's writing, and the paper gives no credit to the author.

The poem haunted Amanda. She vowed to find the circumstances of its writing.

"Mr. Liter if you go to the paper office in Hannibal, when you go for supplies next month would you look for information on the writing of the hymn, *Battle Hymn of the Republic*? I'd certainly appreciate knowing about Mrs. Howe's writing of the poem."

Amanda had almost forgotten her request, when Mr. Liter hailed her at the store on a Friday.

"I bought you something from Hannibal. Here, you'll want to read this."

Mr. Liter handed Amanda a handwritten sheet of paper. She read the notes he had made for her.

"Mrs. Julie Ward Howe was in Washington, D.C. and heard soldiers singing *John Brown's Body*. As she saw the horrors of battle, she observed an undertaking establishment's advertisement, and other sights which horrified her. Mrs. Howe, married to an abolitionist, was especially attuned to the plight of the freed slaves. She declared her "husband was too old to fight and her son too young."

As she lay in bed that night, troubled by the total aspects of the war, words of a verse ran through her mind, she arose to write her thoughts before she could sleep.

The song was first used at a Prison Camp, when President Lincoln heard the song and had it sung twice."

The paper stated Mrs. Howe was quoted as "being happy her poem had bought some help during the Civil War, and hoping it could be used only for peaceful purposes afterwards."

Matthew on Duty

After politically securing New Orleans and the Tech areas, General Banks marched with his three division column up the Red River in a major campaign toward Texas, by way of the Red, Alexandria and Shreveport, Louisiana. When they arrived at the capital city, Banks required several days to establish a Federal Government at Alexandria with the necessary ten percent of loyal citizens. Then the Federal army and escorting naval fleet moved along the Red toward Shreveport and Texas.

Matthew's Texas regiments joined those of Major General Nathaniel P. Banks, as reinforcements in the Red River campaign, along with Sherman's A.J. Smith, who was on short-term loan, but due back very soon to assist Sherman further in his attempt to capture more of the Mississippi River Valley. The Union Navy joined in the effort.

The Red River was lower than usual and once the Federal Navy went upriver, they were stranded by low water. The Confederates advanced from all directions in hopes of capturing the entire Union Fleet, along with many foot soldiers.

Lieutenant Colonel Bailey of the Engineers suggested the building of wing dams to raise the level of the river and float the Union navy to safety.

"This sounds like a fool idea. I've never heard anything so crazy. The water is only four feet deep and we need at least seven feet to float our unloaded vessels. Don't you know the river is 758 feet wide at this point and you'd have to span it at least twice to form a lock and dam system?"

"Yes Sir, but we've done it before," the Lt. Colonel replied.

"Are you certain, have you done it on this big a scale?"

"Not on this wide a span, but ask these men who have been with me. We've done it before successfully, they've witnessed it. Ask them. We've got plenty of men and we're all going to be killed if we hang around here much longer."

"Call up your witnesses."

Several men advanced at Lt. Col. Bailey's signal.

"You've seen this done?"

"Yes Sir. We did it in Wisconsin all the time. It was our job, to build wing dams out of logs and we did it to release trapped steamers on the rivers."

"We've got to do something or we'll lose our entire navy. Lt. Col. Bailey, give the orders," General Banks instructed.

The infantry and artillery guarded the banks against Confederate attack and snipers, while Matthew and Martin worked with 3000 men in the water. Some of these had grown to be dear friends to the pair. They spent time mostly with Alroy from Jefferson City, Missouri; Wakeman from the east; and a disagreeable soldier by the name of Feron clung to them.

They were in the water up to their necks and suffered the exposure of the chill and the softening effect to their skin.

They threw up the wing dam of felled trees and heavy pieces of machinery from local cotton gins and sugar mills. Every building was scavenged for bricks, stones and lumber. Finally, to bridge the central channel, coal barges were loaded with stones and sunk in the last opening.

The first dam gave way before it was of much use. They built a second dam and were finally successful in releasing the Union Naval Vessels. They had lightened the vessels of anything which could be removed and these things were carried downstream by the men on the banks.

The dams were started April 30 and the final remaining Union vessels were released May 13. Several vessels were sunk further up the river by enemy shelling and an explosion.

When they succeeded in finishing the task, the soldiers had trouble marching in retreat from the enemy. They were cornered on the banks of the river and unable to escape. A.J.

Smith, of Sherman's command, was given the task of rear guard, along with Matthew and Martin's regiment.

Again, at the suggestion of Lt. Col. Bailey, twenty-two transports were lashed together side by side and planks were laid across the bows to bridge the water for the passage of the retreating Union army over the swampy Atchafalaya River.

The Texas Confederate Cavalry under Taylor were angry over the firing of local towns and the destruction of the civilian food supplies. They hit the Union rear guard with a vengeance in a final effort to catch and punish the Union as they held the crossing.

Matthew and Martin were deployed in the rear vanguard and under heavy attack. A volley exploded and Martin went down as a piece of shrapnel tore out the side of his chest. They were covered by smoke. Matthew could see no enemy. He picked up Martin in his arms.

Martin gasped, "Go—leave me, I'm too heavy for you. Save yourself—"

Martin convulsed against Matthew's chest. When Matthew turned Martin's face so he could see into his eyes, the spark of life left.

"Martin, Martin, don't die! Stay with me."

But there was no answer. The soul of Martin had flown.

Matthew didn't know how, but he found himself across the water and marching.

"Where is Private Anthony?"

" I left him!" Matthew screamed.

His sergeant shook the young private. "Get hold of yourself boy! We had to hold your hand across the bridge, we ain't got time for this. Snap out of it!"

Matthew trudged on in a daze. He didn't care and he didn't feel.

Three days later, the pain started. He felt it pierce his chest as he lay beside the cook fire. He arose and went to the latrine area, the only place of privacy in his forsaken state. He walked until he fell to the ground, wracked with chills and sobs.

"Oh, God, I never told him. I never asked if he knew You. I feel responsible if he went to hell. We had time—we talked about silly things. Why didn't I ask him if he was saved? Where he'd spend eternity? I'm so guilty—just kill me! I can't stand what I've done.

After hours of torment, Matthew dropped into an exhausted, fitful sleep, not to awaken till rousted by the bugler at daylight.

Matthew was depleted emotionally and physically. The day passed in a fog, but at night, his torment returned by way of dreams.

Martin dies over and over in my arms. I couldn't do anything to save him and I feel guilty every time.

Sherman's troops returned toward Vicksburg, Banks advanced up the Mississippi River toward a court martial for this failure and Matthew's company was sent toward New Orleans.

Matthew missed Martin, more than he could have imagined. His failure to talk seriously with Martin ate at him constantly. It interfered with everything he tried to do.

Today, he sat on the Mississippi River bank at Algiers Landing watching a military ferry transport troops back and forth across the river.

He looked at the city of New Orleans while he wrote a letter home to Maw, Emma and Faith.

New Orleans
Dear Maw, Emma and Faith,

Sherman's troops left soon after Martin died. I sure miss him. It's hard to bear, but I manage the best I can. I'm not sure where A.J. Smith's men went, but I miss some of those old boys too. In war, you get to know someone and they move on or die. It's hard.

This is such a strange city. It is built on very low land and the least little rain, or rise in the water level, raises the water all over the city. The streets are somewhat like wagon wheel spokes, each coming down to the river more narrow than they were on the outer edge. One street is called Canal Street and canal or ditch describes it.

New Orleans is also called the Crescent City . It sits out into the river on a rounded piece of land. In the letter you sent, Paw wrote of Vicksburg sitting on a horseshoe bend high on the river bluffs. This city sits on a gentle curve, lower than the water level.

They usually bury their dead on top of the ground, because the soil is so water-logged. You can imagine the mosquitoes are very bad here and there is much sickness during the summer. No wonder there is illness, as the citizens dump their night-waste and the tides carry it away each day. If the current or tides fail, there is spoilage. This draws flies, other problems to the city, and plain out, smells.

I've read Holland is lower than the sea and surrounded by dikes, maybe that's what New Orleans needs.

They feel the war would have been different, had England continued to buy cotton, been supportive with the south's economic problems; and supplied war material.

I see people here shaking their heads and saying they never thought Yankees would come this far to fight about something which didn't concern them. They won't say it to our faces, but I get the feeling they thought all Yankees were cowards and couldn't face a southern army. They still think their kind of life is the only one in the world.

I look around at the wealth of the plantation houses and lands, and think, For a few, on the backs of others. There are many very poor people in the south, including the slaves. I looked at Nottaway or White Castle Plantation as we steamed to one of the counties with the Provost Marshal.

White Castle is supposed to be the largest, fanciest plantation house on the Mississippi. I couldn't imagine how many hands would have been required to run a place like that. It is a beautiful white house with sweeping lawns going up from the river. It has huge white columns supporting porches and stairs on all levels. It's so large, it looks like a public building. You could get our whole town inside and not be crowded.

I heard it was spared from being burned because one of the soldiers had visited there previously and requested it be spared. I'm glad, it would have been a waste to destroy a beautiful home. There's been too much destruction over the land.

There are many other plantations along the river here close to New Orleans. They call the land road that runs by them, the Great River Road. Much of the traffic is on the river and not on land. I've gone with the government officials to get many of these folks to sign their oaths. I can't help but look around while I'm there. It is a beautiful and disheartening place.

We see some flooding along the river roads. They get so much moisture, the lower portions of some houses are built with cypress wood. Like our cedar, bugs and water won't damage the lumber. Some say the plantation house family members on the Great River Road never sleep on the ground floor due to floods. I could believe it, after seeing the river seems level with the houses. It rains often and is sweltering and damp much of the time. Malaria is prevalent. We use smudge fires at night, but I'm glad we have supplies of quinine pills for those who come down with malaria. Someone told me a Dr. Sappington, from Arrow Rock, discovered quinine's use for malaria. Another Missourian helping us, even if he has southern leanings. His several daughters, one after the other married the Confederate General Marmaduke. The general subsequently married the younger daughter when the older passed on.

I'm glad England didn't come into the battles. This institution of slavery <u>*had*</u> *to end and now that it's gone, I pray it stays gone and I can help finish up this martial law and get on home.*

We have eaten some very strange foods here. Some is spicy and called Cajun, a people descended from the French, whose talk I cannot understand. The food reminds me a little of the Mexican food I ate in Texas, but different somehow. Seafood is eaten and there are shrimp fleets going out every day. We've let them continue to fish, as long as they don't cause any trouble with their coming and going.

There are houseboats on the bayous and those folk hardly ever come into town. We've had to hunt for some of them in order to get oaths of allegiance signed by most of the citizens.

We see alligators in the bayous. The folks trap and fish, they eat all kinds of foods from the water, including alligator and crawdads like we have in the creek at home. I'm trying it all, but I can't say alligator is my favorite. I found it salty and a little grisly.

I guess if I were an animal that could swim that well, I'd have a little muscle too. The alligator fold their hind legs like a frog and glide through the water wiggling their tail like a tadpole. If they are exposed in the water, they look like an old log with rough bark floating quietly along. They sure come alive if they need to.

I hate to say some of our boys like to take target practice on every gator they see, if their officers don't stop them. The local people aren't very happy about this target practice.

Maw, I'm getting an education. I've been where they speak some Spanish and now some French. I've picked up a few words of each, but not enough to do me much good.

I have to apologize to you, Maw. You tried to keep me home and I couldn't wait to get in the army. You were right. <u>*Now I can't wait to get home*</u>*. I hope to see you before long.*

Tell Faith and her family I miss you all.
Love, Matthew

Near New Orleans, Louisiana

Dear Paw, I am writing this to you, but would not wish to convey the same message to the rest of our home folks at Madisonville, Missouri. I know you viewed these same occurrences, so will not be shocked by some of what I write.

I am with the occupation soldiers and participating in keeping the peace here in Louisiana and Mississippi.

I am frustrated by the situation here. The slave who used to be such a valuable piece of property, is now felt to be a menace and many white southerners wish him into extinction. Some participate in attempting to make that come about. The Southern white doesn't accept the freed black has any rights, even when he personally is a man of honor in dealings with other whites. We find white officials afraid to give justice for fear of personal reprisal.

Skulls and parts of Negroes have been displayed as trophies and taken lightly. We found Negroes beaten and crippled from mutilating. In most cases, they were afraid to talk to us. If a Negro attempts reprisal, it often comes back on him. He has to swallow his hurt in an attempt to survive.

They aren't prepared to be responsible for themselves. If he's been a soldier, then he seems more sure of himself, but the whites hate him even more. I suppose his confidence is because he has seen more of the world or gotten a little taste of freedom.

Simple acts are viewed as serious flaunting of the customs. I begin to think we're all insane. We soldiers are taking it and staying here, even though the locals act as they do, both Negro and white.

One old white man told me, "The nigger ain't to

blame." It is a general eruption of hate because of fear and the whole defeat. Nothing is rational about it. Local rangers go about enforcing their form of vigilante justice. We hear about their acts, but never see them or find real, evidence against them.

Black ministers seem to be targets. You always taught us at home, to respect ministers and the Gospel they preach. It is such a twisted view here, I sometimes find it hard to believe these thoughts and actions are coming from human beings.

God's creation? If I were God, I would simply smash the whole bunch and be sorry I had started such creatures.

Whites fear colored, and colored fear whites. It's a vicious cycle of crime, punishing crime. It's like we were as children, "He hit me first!" "No, she hit me first!" and each, thinking he was the wronged party, on and on...

This culture appears to be accustomed to being a law unto itself concerning the former slaves and violence. We hear of white duels in the isolated areas and they dislike interference by us, as soldiers. The colored retaliate on whites more subtly.

Paw, you've always were able to explain things to us, can you help me on this?

There have been examples of friendliness to us and the colored, but the horrors seem to burn out the good memories. The nightmares at night are always of the latest mutilation, rather than something good.

The indifference of those who do not participate in these acts, cause me to feel they may approve.

I can see the mud of our parade ground is trying to grow grass. it gives me a little hope of something clean in this place.

We are having great crowds of colored couples coming to the Army Chaplains to register their marriages. This is a happy time, many of them are not young and accompanied by their families, which we conclude are their children.

Their commitment to each other seems as complete as yours and Maw's. There had been some type of ceremony to mark their marriages, something about <u>*jumpin' the broom*</u>.

We find colored folk obsessed with finding their lost family members. I see much of their seeking as hopeless. There are no records, unless it's the stud book. I've seen pedigrees like we'd keep on animals, on desks in the counties where I accompanied the provost marshals. The owners proudly show us the slave lineage. If it weren't my job to protect the P.M., I'd go outside and be sick.

I didn't know many colored folk before I came here, but there is no doubt they are human and have human feelings as I do. I have to admire them in being able to survive the things I have seen.

Some of the families go to a new location and make a new start. They gather, as a family, in the next town or a nearby plantation. I can't blame them, because these places must be associated with so many bad memories and experiences. I can't wait to get away from the scenes of war and atrocities here.

Paw, I miss Martin. I feel I let him down, not talking to him about Christ. Will I ever be able to forgive myself?

Later, Matthew added to his pages of letter, then he thought, *I can't send this stuff home, my folks would think I'm crazy and would worry about me.* He balled the pages and threw them into the cooking fire. He held the door open and watched the edges catch fire and unroll, then the whole sheet burst into flames, dropped away into leafy pieces. He slammed the door shut, it rebounded and scattered ashes on the floor. He shut it again, more softly. He paced the barracks.

Tomorrow, I'll write something like, "Hello Maw, Paw and Sis, I'm fine, still in Mississippi and Louisiana on occupation duty. The grass is getting green and I know winter will be over for us here, and you, in about two months. I hope you are fine and I hope to see you before long, Love, Matthew.

In my mind, that's safe enough. It will sound dull and safe on paper too. They can't understand if they aren't here and I can't wish this experience on anyone, much less those I love.

When he walked about his duties, there had been some pretty girls, sometimes they were friendly, and other times they spit on the Yankee soldiers. If the soldiers had Negroes with them, the girls would sometimes spit out, "*Nigger Lover*!" or worse.

Matthew thought, *I'd look, and one of them would remind me of Faith, then I'd see something else behind the eyes, a rush of hate.*

I realized for the first time, women can hate. I've seen it in their faces. It took away the beauty and left a twisted mask in it's stead.

Finally, I quit looking, I couldn't stand always being disillusioned about any sweetness or beauty in the women. I feel resentful if they show happiness. What is the matter with them, are they callous? I mistrust gaiety in these circumstances. I won't let them win for losing. Maybe that is my fault, not theirs for feeling this way.

Sometimes if they don't show hatred, they show fear, or greed. Maybe I'd feel the same way if I'd been in their shoes, but it's hard for me to imagine being in their place and feeling their emotions. It's easier to not think about it at all, just do the job, eat, sleep and wait to go home.

People here try to tell us the colored are beasts of burden animals, provided by God for that purpose and they need the whites to take care of them. I don't find the colored to be unintelligent and animals. If they were animals, they would have stayed and been passive in acceptance of anything that came along. They have questioning minds and reasoning powers.

I'm with these children and they learn like any other child. If I shut my eyes, I can't tell the difference from the children at home, except for the southern speech. I've experimented and listened with my head turned or eyes closed. Sometimes I can't tell the difference between white and colored children talking in the south.

He thought about southern Negro speech as he listened to the children talk. I can't understand their talk. When spoken in normal conversation, the sound is soft and pleasant, when uttered in anger, most confusing. Some talk slowly and others fast, depending on the part of the south from which they come. I listen and I'm learning to distinguish most words and understand their meanings.

The colored feel safer and more free in town. In the respect of having sustenance, they are. There isn't enough work to sustain them all in towns. However in town, they live, a dozen, in a hut with only bacon and meal to eat, if that much, and a bunch of rags for clothes and bedding.

Matthew had a headache from the muggy heat and too many thoughts about beliefs. He closed his eyes and attempted to clear his mind of any thought in an effort to sleep. He wasn't successful. Thoughts crept into his subconscious and forced his mind in other directions.

"Martin, where are you? Forgive me, please forgive me!"

"And my buddy Alroy, he's a little better from the wounds in his back and side. He got hit near where Martin died, even said he saw Martin in the burial trenches before that old man saved him. I go by the hospital to see him once in a while. He's walking again but he's sure weak. I still don't know if he's going to make it."

In an effort to sidetrack his wandering thoughts, he began to think of Faith and their childish play when they were children. This led to family members and before he knew it, he had such a wave of homesickness, he thought he'd sob and embarrass himself.

I have to get up and move!

He went out the door and ran across the parade grounds. He startled a brown leghorn rooster and hen scratching in the dirt. He continued around the perimeter of the government buildings, three times, before he thought he'd worked off some of his tension.

He returned quietly, passed the same hen and rooster, now dusting and relaxed in the shade of a building. They looked content. He hunched down to watch them for a few minutes and his mind drifted off to more pleasant thoughts.

I'm getting sleepy. I won't be noticed if I sleep too much. We sleep all times of day.

If I can only sleep, I can forget. I hope. Please, God, let me forget.

Mustering Out, Temporary Answers
At Appomatox Court House

Back in Virginia, southern soldiers cried as General Lee rode by after surrendering at Appomatox Court House, April 9, 1865. About six-hundred and eighteen thousand Americans had died, more from disease than bullets. Both sides had suffered horribly.

JD looked at the bedraggled mobs of men. His mind drifted off to the battles where he might have engaged these very men. *Sometimes I think I've seen every body with my own eyes, and smelled every dead horse with my own nose.*

He and other Union soldiers did not cheer, but watched quietly, as the Confederates stacked arms and prepared to start home. The Union fed the ragged southern army as they straggled by. They looked into the face of shame and depression. Some faces held hatred, however few refused food.

JD learned the general terms Grant gave Lee for the southern army. None of the southern soldiers would ever be prosecuted for treason for the secession activities, provided they obeyed the terms as stated in their oath of allegiance, and obeyed the laws of the state in which they resided. Allowances were made for their horses and their squirrel guns to remain in their possession. Generosity sent them on their way south.

It's a just settlement. Let's all get on with our lives.

The northern army *soldiered* several more weeks and most were discharged.

JD bowed his head and prayed with his men before he dismissed the first group.

"Thank You, Lord, for bringing us through this thing. Bless all these boys as they return to their homes. May we all settle well into normal life. Bless the families who lost members. May *this nation* be united and blessed. Your will be done, Amen."

An Epoch in American history was ended and JD was thankful.

In a few days, JD went to the payroll clerk and mustered out, settling his clothing account for $29.33. This transaction left him with little cash. He had always sent home most of his pay.

Jonathan David Logan, a family man, was shown to have enlisted as a Private, in the spring of 1861, a few months before President Lincoln asked for seventy-five thousand men, got two-hundred thousand, and sent some home because he couldn't arm them.

He had enlisted at New London, Missouri, in Company E, 2nd Missouri State Militia. For the first months, he was listed as furnishing his own equipment and received a larger stipend than most enlistees.

He was a foot soldier, like most of those in the ranks.

On his records, his name was spelled differently by several paymasters, showing the varied educational level in this nation he loved.

I hope educational deficiencies will soon be remedied along with other ills of the nation.

I am listed as being treated at Regimental Hospitals at Bloomfield, St. Louis, and Cape Girardeau, Missouri. I was sent home for twenty days to recover from camp dysentery from Cape Girardeau, Missouri, after I had already spent two months in the hospital. The doctors said I might make a quicker recovery away from the army conditions and army food, in the bosom of my loving family. This was the only leave, I was granted during my four and a half years of service to the United States of America, and the blue uniform of the Union soldier.

JD looked at his hand.

It's strange! I can hold over four years of experiences in one hand. Little shows on the paper record for the sacrifices we all made. My family aren't listed, along with their efforts. I feel a bit futile, but in my heart I know, we have done much more than is written on this handful of paper. He stuffed the papers into his knapsack.

His spirits lifted to elation, as he contemplated the freedom of the slaves, the preservation of the Union of the North American continent contained within that which is labeled, the United States of America!

God Bless America!

He went to gather his meager belongings and part with his remaining men. Many embraced him as they parted. JD was headed home, his last *soldierly* task of this war was over.

Alcott stood back. He waited to speak to his officer Logan. He didn't wish to share this parting with any other. He and JD had shared something important and he meant to make his leave-taking special too.

JD was moved by the parting with his men, but he choked up to a greater degree, when he patted Alcott on the back.

"Son, you know words can't express what I feel for you and what you've done for me. I'll never again ask anyone to do what was required of you. I can't repay you, but if you ever need anything— anything humanly possible, come or send for me. I'll do all I can for you. I've come to realize I can't do everything myself, I'm relying on God, I hope you continue to do the same."

Alcott said, "Sir, you've been like a father to me. I can't thank you enough. Don't ferg't me in your prayers."

"Son, don't call me Sir, anymore! That time is past and it isn't necessary between friends. My name is Jonathan David Logan, but my family calls me JD most of the time. Please call me JD or Jonathan."

With a catch in his voice, Alcott said, "Sir, I mean- I'm sorry. In my part of the state, them's manners. If sir slips out, I don't mean nothin' military by it. Forgive me for slips I make. So long— JD"

From their embrace, the two men clapped each other on the back and parted.

As JD walked away, Alcott's keen eyes saw his hand raise to his face. He knew his captain wiped a tear, as he did.

JD was devastated when he learned President Lincoln had been shot and then died by an assassin's bullet. He mourned with the northern citizens as he read the accounts. The funeral train stopped at every major city between Washington D.C. on the route to Springfield, Illinois. It was draped in black and crept toward Mr. Lincoln's final resting place.

JD didn't know how tired he was, until he'd rested a few days. He still wasn't recovered to full strength.

He now felt free at last to ask the opinion of a surgeon before he left.

For the first time he could remember, the surgeons didn't wear blood on their clothing and could take time to talk at length with a healthy soldier. They now performed more nursing then surgery.

Many of the disabled soldiers would have lifelong wounds and need someone to care for them for the balance of their lives. Some were afraid to go home to their families for fear they would be a burden. Many would remain lost to their families, who assumed they were dead and buried in some battlefield rather than derelict wrecks stashed in some veterans' hospital in some other state. These soldiers felt less then men.

Some surgeons returned home to private practices, much better trained than when the battles began. *Practice does make perfect* and they'd certainly had plenty of practice.

Surgeon Boyd contacted two of his fellow surgeons and they poured over medical texts that had lain in the bottom of their trunks while they were too busy to read. The three men found references on hydrophobia . Two of the three texts stated something like, "Hydrophobia runs its course by three years from the initial contact, it is not possible to contract the disease after that time."

My dangerous time is nearly ended. A few more months and I can go home. Thank you, Lord.

Matthew and Martial Law

Lights were turned out on the steamboats when they ran at night, for the Pilot to see the moon on the water. He must be alert for snags or sandbars. Everyday the mighty river changed. Debris drifted in that hadn't been there the day before.

The first night after lights, Matthew sat against a bale of cotton. He gazed out over the water and the timber.

Tonight, Spanish Moss looks like something from a nightmare, spidery-webbed and grotesque.

I can imagine death's angel floating through the swamps. I wonder if that is really the problem here? Maybe the soul has left the people of the south and Satan rules. Surely these people are unreal and God will right the situation when Satan's reign ends. I smell the dampness of the river. Decay?

Matthew had witnessed some northern steamers, forcing allegiance of the citizenry, as they passed the shores. If the citizens failed to doff their hats or salute, a few shots were fired over their heads. Then, there was a reluctant salutation of some kind. This activity didn't endear northern occupation troops to the local citizens. All made life harder for him.

When they rode the river, occasionally he heard the voices of people, coming over the water. Some sang. Several miles further up the river, he thought he heard an argument, and an occasional hound dog running some animal.

He jerked alert, *some former slave*? He dismissed the thought.

The hound sounds good, more like at home. I wonder if there are 'possums, coon, or wildcats around here? I know there are water moccasins.

He'd walked near the bank the day before. He had seen a huge cottonmouth hanging over the water in the branches of a willow. The snake seemed belligerent and sluggish in moving. It opened its mouth in protest and Matthew saw the white-fluffed wads that gave the snake its name. The snake slid off into the water and swam along on top. It was a heavy, brutish-looking snake, and acted as if it owned the river. It gave Matthew a chill. He withdrew from the brackish water of the marshy bank.

Let the snake claim this putrid stretch of water.

When he walked away, he'd come upon a muddy mound of decaying debris and recognized it as an alligator's nest. The troops had been warned to stay away from those. The females could return at any minute, for a protective check on her incubating eggs.

Matthew beat a hasty retreat. He didn't wish to encounter an angry, mother alligator. He'd heard tales of eight foot monsters walking about or grabbing a swimmer.

The Creole houseboat owner at his wharf told him, in a dialect he could hardly understand, of losing dogs, cats, or even children along the bayous to hungry gators. He didn't intend to check it out to find if it was true on the bank, or in the waters.

This doesn't resemble our swimming hole at home, or any other place I'd ever want to swim.

Dear Family,

I went about with a Provost Marshal in the county to tell the freedmen to work diligently and be patient. The freedmen seemed distrustful of their old masters in matters of pay and treatment. After hearing the P.M. assure them, they fell to and went to work, but I couldn't see any great advantages they gained from when they were slaves. They lived in the same huts, wore the same master's clothing, and had no material belongings, or cash to show for their labor. It was all slavery to me.

This is the second county in which I have been part of the P.M.'s guard. The first man I followed, did a good job for the first month, he started socializing with the former plantation owners, then he seemed no different from them.

The government might as well have appointed one of the planters to do the job and saved themselves the money and time to bring in a person from further north.

In this location, the planters took the oath to the United States Government and went back to working the former slaves on the plantation for wages or on shares.

Some freedmen are skilled, they call them artisans. They receive better compensation and can bargain for payment for their work.

I heard one planter say to a former slave who had leased a piece of farmland, "I won't have you acting an uppity nigger! You get on back to my field, or I'll have your hide."

The sorriest part of it, the former slave looked at him, ducked his head, and went to the field. He looked like a broken man as I watched him walk away. He had no hope and a man needs hope to survive.

I have observed some former slaves retaliating by leaving or messing up on the jobs they are supposed to perform.

The Federal authorities attempt to keep peace and the labor force with a system of labor contracts.

I was on duty as a guard for another Freedman Bureau man, and found him most sincere in attempting to be fair in mediating claims, and keeping the peace. He bucks the local citizenry, but he's doing a good job, and has the respect of some in the community. These men are overworked if they do their job well. They have a wide district and many citizens to administer. His job is to seek work for freedmen, and to relocate them to suitable homes and work places. He finds lost family members, mediates contracts, assures fair treatment, and payment of wages and on, and on. It's an impossible job to do with so few and so little money. He would require the wisdom of Solomon and the experience of a Jethro to get others to help in his decision making. The commissioners require us, as soldiers, to enforce their decisions.

I heard a bureau officer boast with his presence and authority, backed by troops when necessary, he "kept the Negroes at work, and in a good state of discipline."

It did appear some of the ones condemning laziness were the softest and cleanest, with uncalloused hands. It made me wonder who worked and who didn't. The fruits of slave labor were seen in buildings and land that had been cared for, in the past. Most plantations seem to have suffered recently in varying degrees of neglect, but I could see most of it is not long-term. There is a discrepancy between the condition of the main house, the stables, and the slave huts.

Matthew, as a northern soldier, was confused. *All this hypocrisy of the entire system bothers me. The whole world seems false, maybe the only thing real is the colored people. Their starvation looks real, but others appear to have fine clothes. Everything is out of kilter around here.*

I can't wait to get home to see if part of the world is still stable. If it isn't normal at home, I know we are all lost. I feel depressed about the situation of the whole world. Maybe I can get a better perspective if I see my parents and live more normally.

Now, I can't understand my own great dissatisfaction at home to go to war. Then war created more of a void. Martin's death shook me and now I want to be home again.

Will I ever be happy, or is the problem within me? Everyone here seems to not care and be confused; or out to get all they can for themselves.

The season advances toward summer and I have only six more weeks. Surely I can make it.

Matthew continued his letter.

I heard a colored minister preach, if the colored weren't granted the freedom due them, they had several hundreds of thousands of their people trained in warfare, who could prevent the return of slavery if they desired. This brought unrest to the officers and bureau people who heard it. The preacher was reported to their superiors. He was warned about "causing discontent among the freedmen and he would be doing them a grave disservice and be personally punished for inciting a riot."

I could understand his feelings for the working freedmen. I know he speaks the mind of many colored freedmen when he made the statements.

Matthew stopped to think. *This is a dangerous situation and only justice and fairness can be the remedy which could bring about peace between the two factions.*

Matthew wrote, *Earlier, an order was issued to place women in custody for further insults by gesture or word. The Order was published in the paper Times. In my opinion, the General was right. Some soldier would have come to the end of his patience and committed a too harsh act. The General protected the ladies as well as our soldiers. The ladies were like us, as younguns, we teased the bull, but he had a fence or ring between him and us. There are no such constraints here. The people of New Orleans torment the bull.*

Men are not contained by fences. The citizens will find the soldiers are not restrained animals. They may find them wilder and more angry than they expect.

I'm going to remind my family of my upcoming return and end this letter before I write things I shouldn't.

Matthew did not write to his family the commanding General had felt compelled to issue the Order to prevent the retaliation of his soldiers when the civilians emptied chamber pots on the men as they walked patrol. The soldiers were spit upon in the streets and vocally tormented. Common courtesy and decency did not prevail.

"Suffer the Little Children to Come Unto Me"

Matthew attracted little children. He made no effort, but it happened. He was a Pied Piper in New Orleans. Little black and poor white children followed him as he went about his patrol. He was unable to speak to them at length, while on duty, but he was able to do kind deeds for them on his own time.

He found his only peace during the times he was with the children. He fed some, clothed, and befriended others. As he traipsed about with the children, white soldiers and citizens began to take offense to his actions. He began to feel uncomfortable to be seen with the colored children. *Am I prejudiced?* Matthew prayed about his attitude and the needs of the children.

These are God's creations and He cares for them. I would have compassion on any hurt or stray animal, aren't the children of more importance than some stray animal?

This gave Matthew more to fret over.

Homeward Bound

I have my discharge! Finally, my enlistment is up.

Matthew and twenty others were released and put aboard a steamer at New Orleans. They traveled up the Mississippi River toward St. Louis.

The troops were not the only passengers on the steamer. When they passed a burned out section, there were hushed, hate filled conversations in the huddled groups who looked at them angrily.

"Sherman passed through here."

This was a time Matthew was thankful he was in a group with some strength, rather than alone in a northern uniform. Blue was a hated color in these ports.

At Vicksburg, he could see what Paw spoke of in regard to the bluffs and could imagine the difficulty of taking the fortifications.

He'd run into some serious warfare, but he'd never faced anything just like these heights.

He noted Columbus, Tennessee; New Madrid, Missouri; and Island Number Ten. He paid special attention to the names he'd heard and felt some connection. He particularly looked over the swampy area of Cairo, Illinois, where his father had come down the Ohio River as a little boy, with his parents and his mother's families had come before she was born.

"The river looked so wide I couldn't see Missouri," Paw always said. *I see how it might have looked that way to a little boy. It's low and flat over to the hills on the Missouri side.*

They pulled the steamer in at Cairo and *six in blue* departed, two for southern Illinois, the other four headed up the Ohio River to destinations in the northeast.

The steamer, with the remaining soldiers reached Jefferson Barracks at St. Louis. Matthew was astonished at the looks of the place. He'd heard about it, but he didn't expect to see permanent brick buildings. The other army encampments he had visited were always tent cities and temporary. Sometimes they had mounds of earth thrown up for fortifications, but those soon returned to natural-looking grass banks.

The remaining discharged soldiers entered the administration building and were issued pay and vouchers for further travel. They dispersed to go their own ways, while Matthew and six others were transferred to a smaller steamer headed up the Missouri River.

When they advanced north, he felt less tension from the people. They seemed further removed from the actual war. There was more food and shelter available, and fewer Negroes for the whites to fear and argue over; fewer ex-slaves to provide competition for jobs; and slightly fewer jobs which had traditionally been theirs.

The steamer stopped at the German community of Hermann to off-load equipment and supplies. Matthew noted the neatness. Everyone seemed hard at work, the boss or the hired laborer. Even the white women worked outside in the fields and vineyards.

They were in an area of northern sympathy, and the citizens wished to offer appreciation and refreshments to the *boys in blue.* Matthew refused the wine, but accepted the fresh apple cider.

The community storyteller, laughed as he told of General Sterling Price's Confederate raid on Hermann for George Husmann's wine cellar contents.

"They raided other vineries over the state at Cuba, St. James, and Rolla. I vonder, just how the vine helped their var effort? Maybe they raided vith a *happier* mind. Ve trust they treated the folks they raided for horses and var supplies, in a nicer vay."

Matthew's Texas boots had been replaced during his time in Mississippi. He wasn't required to *walk all the way home barefoot,* as he had said he would. He took a stage line from Jefferson City, with stops at Fulton, Mexico, and every little town along the way. He walked across country from Perry, headed almost due east to Madisonville.

My Glory? Did I really think that once? I recall how I kept begging to go to war. I thought I was ready when the first shot was fired!

"Matt, your Maw will need you to help her on the farm, you must stay until you're at least eighteen years old." He could hear his Paw's voice in his head.

I tried, but Maw had finally let me go, even though she was trying to farm the two places. I remember I finished up the crop and left with peach fuzz on my face. Now I have a light honey brown stubble.

I'm still in my nineteenth year when surrender was officially declared, but I had to serve an additional time in New Orleans to get the new government organized. Reconstruction is in full force, I'm almost twenty, and I'm almost home.

I haven't been in the army long, but I experienced too much death and cruelty in a short time. I recall when I shot and wounded an enemy sentry. It tore up my soul and I'm still packing it home, along with the time I held my friend Martin in my arms, as he died on the banks of the Atchafalaya River. I'll never forget I didn't talk to Martin about his feelings toward God. Is he being tormented in hell right now? He may be enduring something much worse than what we went through, but I don't know. He may be in an eternal hell, not a temporary one, like we went through. I'll never know here on earth. I'll never get the chance to tell him what he needed to do in his life.

Martin, I vow, now, right here, I will not neglect to tell someone else about Jesus and His plan for us. Please forgive me! Father, forgive me. . .

In his bedroll, Matthew carried a Spanish shawl for his mother. He'd bought it in Texas, over a year ago.

There Comes a Man

The young sow, looked to Matthew like a smaller version of Nuisance, the pet of their teen years. She was the only living thing that noted his arrival. She raised her little eyes and gave a contented grunt as she turned to flop into her mud hole. Her attitude seemed to say, "This isn't my usual food provider. Why bother to expend any effort in this hot weather." She seemed to prefer to lay cooling, in her mud hole.

Matthew couldn't know the little sow was Nuisance's daughter. Mr. Liter had given her to Emma when Nuisance had too many piglets to feed.

Matthew had missed out on many things. Two years were a long time on a farm. The seasons and the life cycle of the farm had moved without him.

Matthew passed by the swimming hole in the creek where the spring emptied. He could see where Paw had tiled up the spring. He stopped to drink, as he'd craved and dreamed of during the skirmishes in Texas. He took the chipped cup from the nail on the tree and dipped into the bubbling spring. It wasn't enough. He plunged his head under the overflow and came up sputtering.

It is even colder than I remember. If I could only let the spring flow over my body, perhaps it would remove my sense of guilt, depression, or whatever is the load I feel all the time.

Matthew peeled off his smelly, faded uniform and plunged quickly into the swimming hole. He drifted with the flow from the spring, feeling its pull on his whole exhausted soul. He shook the water from his sun bleached hair, his eyes, and his ears, and lay down on the gravel bar to let the sun and breeze bake him dry.

Now he was in a hurry, he pulled on his clothes and moved with resolution, up the hill to the bluff above the creek. He halted to survey the surrounding fields. He saw a patch of morning glory blue in the midst of the green corn rows and with second nature, noted it wasn't the color of Union blue.

I know the color of that bonnet, and it can belong to only one lass, the person I want most to see. I aim to make my presence known to her.

As I moved with the battles of the nation, I found I love her. I always have loved her, even when I was unkind to her when we were young.

In the days since I've been gone to war, when I waited to advance, I recalled many things about our times together. I remember when she got hurt, I always took up for her, but I didn't want her to know I had a soft spot for her. To a young boy, it isn't manly to show your feelings for a girl, especially when you are nine, or twelve, or even fifteen.

After I was fifteen, my feelings became like quick silver, coming and going, fluctuating between brotherly-sisterly feelings and something new.

He ran down the trail, took the rocks in the creek two at a time. He leaped the split rail fence at a low rail and sat his gun down against the persimmon tree at the corner of the field. He ducked into the corn rows and headed in her general direction. He didn't take the easier way down a row, but diagonally crossed with the corn blades slashing his arms like sabers. He felt no physical pain.

He thought as he ran, *This was a day Paw used to say would parboil a fellow, or he could stew in his own juices with this humidity. I ought to be accustomed to it, having just come from Louisiana and the bayous.*

He was a bit disoriented as to her location, but as he plunged across rows of corn, he knew he was nearing her vicinity and turned at a right angle to the corn rows. He came to a row with downed and wilting weeds. The next row, had jimpsin and cotton weeds still standing.

He couldn't see down the row as the young corn was above shoulder height. He dropped to his hands and knees to look down the row below the lush green corn blades. He could see the backs of two bare feet, two dainty ankles and a shapely white calf. When he advanced, he could see a draped and washed out chambray skirt. Faith had hitched the tail of her skirt up through her legs and tucked it into her belt to form baggy trousers.

I've seen maw do this when she needed to move freely or be cooler in her dress. Faith isn't expecting anyone and doesn't know I'm here.

I'll never reach her, my movements seem too slow.

In one over viewing look, he saw one long, thick, strawberry sun-touched braid down the middle of the dampened back of her dress and the ever-present halo framing her head. Her braid swung between her shoulder blades as she raised her hoe and came down on first one weed, then the next.

Her strength has grown. I used to tease her when she had to chop with her hoe more than once, to get a big weed cut through.

He didn't speak, but walked soundlessly toward her. When he stepped to within one yard and started to reach out, she turned in one sweeping movement, with her hoe raised in a defiant manner. She didn't say anything, but he could tell she meant business and would use her hoe as a defense.

"It's me, Faith, it's all right." Matthew managed to speak over his emotion.

I can see she's changed.

It took only a few seconds for her to assess his features and then take a flying step into his arms. He didn't know where her hoe went. Neither cared.

Her bonnet fell from her head, she reached for his face with her hand.

He passed her hand and buried his face in the side of her hair, above her ear. He didn't want her to see his eyes, they were filled with tears and he somehow thought, *men don't cry. I don't want her to think I am weak. Anyone who has been through what I've undergone certainly can't be weak, but she won't know all that. I can't trust myself with all these feelings yet.*

When I left, we were kids. It isn't hard to tell she has become a woman. I thought I loved her when I left, but I doubt we knew what love meant.

She clung to him, with her face buried in his shoulder. He felt her body shudder with a released sob.

We shared plans for our future through letters, but we haven't seen each other for two years. It'ss going to be different talking as two grown people. We will no longer pass the time of day, bending willows over the creek, skipping rocks, or wrestling together as children. We'll have to learn about two new people, ourselves, and we'll have a different relationship.

Jealousy

Kate Towner ran to meet Amanda at church on a hot Sunday the first part of July. She waved a piece of paper and spoke loudly when she came across the yard.

Amanda climbed out of her buggy.

"Will's coming home! I got a letter just yesterday. I can hardly wait. I think he went after JD did. Have you heard from JD? Is he coming home too? Here, do you want to read it?"

She didn't give Amanda time to answer, but Amanda was fairly certain JD wasn't coming home for a bit.

She was saddened, but she shared Kate's happiness, when she read the offered letter.

June 4, 1864
My Dear Wife Kate,

I will complete my three-year enlistment and will be mustered out at St. Louis. I will try to catch a boat up the river and should be home in July at the latest, even if I have to walk. I can't wait to see you. Hug everyone for me and I'll do it for myself next time. The war clean-up isn't quite over and they want some of us to re-enlist. We are so worn and ragged I feel I must rest. I want to spend the winter at home this year. I guess I'm not as young as I once was and my blood just isn't as hot as it was. Dear wife, maybe you will be able to warm me a bit.

My Love,
Preston Towner

Usually Amanda went home from church uplifted and fueled for the next week, but today she went home sadder than when she went to church. She couldn't be envious of Kate, but she did want Jonathan David home.

He's been gone longer than almost anyone. Why can't this separation be over and they all come home?

She felt sorry for herself most of Sunday dinner. Her grown children had chosen to spend the day with their friends and she was alone. She usually enjoyed solitude, but today? She would have to think of something to cheer herself up.

She studied what she wished to do. She didn't have long to contemplate her problem, before she heard footsteps on her back porch. Her nerves jerked, as they had, since the incident with the rough soldiers. She hurried to the door to see who had arrived. It was Billy McIntire and he looked very agitated.

"Matilda's having our baby and I need you to come and help. We didn't think it was quite time and her Maw went to help her Aunt. Mrs. Liter won't be home for a few days. Miss Maybelle says she can't help, she doesn't know anything about laying in."

God has provided again! There's nothing like the excitement of a birth and caring for a new mother and babe to get my mind off myself and my problems. Thank You, Lord.

Dr. Marshall was no longer up to the all-night sessions which often went with the birth of babies and was happy to be relieved of that duty. In this community, women generally assisted in birthing, unless there were unexpected problems, in which case, the doctor was called in. He assured the ladies he had no resentment, if they choose to have Amanda attend them.

Amanda wrote a note and left it on the kitchen table for Matthew and Emma. She knew they would be home in time to do the evening chores. Matthew would probably drop by Billy's house later, to see if they needed anything. She could tell him more then.

Amanda hurried to get her black midwife bag and her basket of sheeting and linens for the impending laying-in. She'd spoken to Matilda recently and had it packed. She took along her own clothing, planning to stay a few days. When she assessed the situation, then she could hurry home for more things.

Amanda rode in the buggy with Billy to their home in Madisonville. She hurried into the house, as Billy unhitched the horse and put it and the buggy away.

Maybelle was wringing her hands. No help.

“She needs to be in bed. Doesn’t she need to be in bed?”

Amanda patted Maybelle’s arm, “Walking is good for her, if she feels like it.”

Matilda was in her nightgown, but walked the floor when Amanda entered through the kitchen.

As Amanda turned to hang up her coat, Matilda grabbed the back of a kitchen chair and doubled over.

Amanda placed her arms around Matilda's shoulders to steady her. "When this contraction passes, we'll get you into bed and see how things are coming along," she soothed.

Matilda didn't answer, occupied. She soon straightened and breathed out.

"Whee, that was a harder one. I am feeling downward pressure. I think it may be time for me to get into bed," Matilda said.

Amanda helped her toward their bedroom. She saw they had prepared the bed with the extra sheeting and had the cradle and other supplies near. She began to wonder if Matilda hadn't been in labor longer than she realized. She seemed to be far along for early labor.

"I'll go wash up, then we'll see how you're doing."

Amanda went to the kitchen.

Maybelle met her at the door. “I think I’ll go home for a little while. This is getting on my nerves and I can’t seem to do a thing about it.”

“That’s fine, we’ll send Billy if we need anything. You get a little rest and you can help in the morning when we get ready for breakfast.”

Maybelle scurried to the door. She hesitated and looked back.

Matilda gave a moan.

Maybelle turned and left quickly.

Amanda took the teakettle from the wood stove, filled the pan and soaped her hands and arms. *I can’t help but think of the births of my own babies.*

Lord, let things go well and this be easy for Matilda and her baby. Give me the patience and knowledge I need to do this with Matilda's and Your help. Thank you Lord, for this little family. Protect them and keep them well. Help Billy as he waits with us. In Jesus' name, Amen.

Amanda rinsed and dried her hands, then went back to Matilda, who was involved with another contraction, this one longer and harder than the last. The contractions were close together and lasted about sixty seconds. Amanda unfolded the clean sheet and placed it over Matilda's body, she raised the lower side and eased up Matilda's gown. She took a clean pan of warm water and bathed Matilda. As she worked, she talked to Matilda soothingly.

"It's not going to be long. How long have you had pains?"

Matilda had to wait for another contraction to answer.

"I've had a really bad backache all day, but I thought my back was tired. The last hour, I've had definite regular pains. I guess I was in labor and didn't know it." Just then another contraction hit, Matilda grunted, and bore down.

"I can tell you, your baby has dark hair. Go easy and give your body time to adjust with this next pain. You'll heal faster if we don't cause a tear."

Between contractions, Amanda unfolded another clean towel and placed it under Matilda. She placed two more unfolded towels beside her, in which to receive the baby.

Billy had come into the kitchen and was peering into the room. He shuffled worriedly.

"Things are coming right along, your baby will be here very soon!" Amanda called out, "You can fill the teakettle and get bath water ready for these two."

Billy hurried to fill the teakettle from the water bucket sitting on a table by the back door. His movements were awkward in his nervousness and he banged the dipper in the pail, then on the teakettle. In his haste, he spilled moderate amounts of water as he filled the teakettle. He placed the kettle back on the wood cook stove. He opened the stove door to add more wood. He wanted the water warm for the baby and Matilda.

"Billy, I'd like for you to come in here," Matilda asked, as he finished.

Amanda felt surprise, not many women wanted their husbands to see them during childbirth. She remembered JD delivering their Emma and it had been a special time, but not many were so involved.

"Are you sure, Matilda?" Billy asked.

"Will it bother you to be in here?" she asked.

"Remember I've been on the battlefield and in hospitals, but I don't want to do anything you don't want." Billy was tentative.

"If you'd like, I *really* want you to be with us in everything," another contraction caught Matilda's last word.

Billy moved in to hold Matilda's hand. She squeezed his one hand so tightly, he felt his fingers give. He leaned into her shoulder.

"Now, Matilda, you can bear down on this next contraction. Your baby's head is ready to be born," Amanda instructed.

Matilda did as told. The baby moved down, rotated, and began to snuffle. Amanda took a piece of clean sheeting, swiped through it's mouth. She used a clean spot for the baby's face.

The baby snuffled more, turned and was fully born. Amanda had a towel ready and wrapped the baby in the towel. She attended to the cord and handed the baby to Billy. He placed the baby next to Matilda. Together they unwrapped the baby enough to see it was a girl. They began to towel her dry.

Amanda was busy, but not so occupied she didn't see the tears in Billy's eyes and his totally enraptured look. He covered the baby and took Matilda into his embrace. Amanda couldn't tell who was crying the most, the baby, or her parents. Amanda stayed quiet. She didn't want to interfere in the couple's happiness.

As midwife, she finished and bathed Matilda, then covered her dry and warm. She took the baby from Billy and bathed her.

The little girl remained amazingly peaceful throughout all her care. After drying, the baby was dressed in a diaper and little shirt, then a gown and swaddled in a blanket Matilda had made.

Amanda handed her back to her parents. She took the soiled linens into the kitchen to soak in the wash tub. She peeped back into the bedroom often to assure herself of the continued good progress of the new baby and mother.

After she washed up, she went back to assist Matilda with the baby's first nursing and preparation for a good rest for both of her patients. Billy made himself scarce. He refilled the water bucket, carried in more wood from outside, and dampened down the fire for the night..

When the baby seemed satisfied, Amanda placed the little girl on her shoulder and patted her back for the first burp.

"This is the way you bring up air to keep her from having a tummy ache. She may spit up a bit, but she's fine, just some milk coming up with the air bubble."

"I remember my baby sister and brothers when we did that for them," Matilda answered.

"You can show Billy later, so he'll know what to do too. Sometimes after babies nurse, they wiggle around. That may be a sign of another bubble and she may need to be burped again. He'll be able to get her for you more easily than you will for a few days."

After the burp, Amanda wrapped her and handed the baby to Billy. He stared into his new daughter's face as she slept on his arm.

"What are you going to name her?" Amanda asked.

"We thought we'd name her Elizabeth Ann and we might call her Lizzie," Matilda looked at Billy.

"I like her name, she looks like an Elizabeth. Lizzie?

I like it." Amanda turned, and after checking Matilda, said, "I think I'll go sit in the rocking chair and read my Bible by the lamplight. I'll look in every little bit. If you need anything, just call me and I'll hear."

"I'll stay here in this chair and rock Lizzie, if it's all right?" Billy looked at Amanda for her consent.

She nodded. "Fine, but don't do it *all* the time in the next few weeks, or you may have a *demanding* little soul on your hands," she cautioned with a smile in her voice.

After an uneventful four hours, with one more feeding, Amanda turned down the lamp in the kitchen and prepared Matilda for sleep. She could still see Matilda and Billy in their lamp's glow, from where she sat. She had told Billy he could lay Lizzie in her cradle and lay down beside Matilda, but he seemed too excited to relax.

Toward morning, Amanda drifted off to sleep in the chair and when she awoke at 5, Lizzie was asleep in her cradle and Billy peacefully slept on top of the quilt, next to Matilda.

Lizzie awoke at 5:30. Matthew dropped by in time to see her before her feeding, but her father slept on, and got no congratulations this trip.

After she changed Lizzie, Amanda gave her to her mother. Matilda nursed Lizzie, Billy slept on, undisturbed.

In the next few days, Amanda observed the sweetest couple she'd ever seen, caring for their baby. She heard Billy call Matilda, *Tildy* often. He couldn't keep his love out of his hand, or his voice, as he cared for her or their baby, Lizzie. She had seen few men who were able to do so many thoughtful things for their family.

Billy seems to have a special appreciation, maybe because of his own handicap. He is such good help, I can drive his buggy home for more supplies. They can be alone for a few hours.

During Amanda's stay with Matilda, she was able to get outside the house and walk about in Madisonville. Billy was there to see after his little family. Amanda found it strange to be in town, where others lived nearby. She visited briefly with most of her town neighbors and many came to see the new baby.

Maybelle considered herself Lizzie's Grandmother. She brought a quilt for the baby. The ladies finished the quilting in the bedroom with Matilda and Lizzie nearby.

Matilda became stronger each day. The Madisonville ladies promised to look in often. On the second weekly birthday for Lizzie, Amanda returned to her own home.

Billy would not open school until mid-October, when the crops were all harvested and in the barns. The pupils would be free to come back to school then.

He proved such a devoted father, Amanda had no qualms about Lizzie or Matilda's care.

Matilda's mother was due back home and could give her assistance too.

When she got home, Amanda was at *loose ends* for a few hours, but then found she was glad to be home in her peaceful kitchen, on her own quiet farm. She could hardly contain herself. Emma had things in order, everything looked wonderful to her.

Town-living is not for me, even though it was a nice change. I am so thankful for the good health of Lizzie and her mommy.

Thank You, Lord, for Billy and Matilda's little family and the friendship they give to me. Thank You I am able to help my friends. You've given me a good work to do and a good way to occupy my time waiting for JD. May Emma have as easy a time, if she ever has children. Bless my family and especially JD, keep him safe and bring him back to us. Your will be done, Amen.

Tumultuous Relationships

Faith and Matthew's relationship continued. They soon left the euphoria of the newly reunited. Their lives settled into dense problems for which they had no understanding, and *no answers.*

They prayed together, and separately. They fussed and fretted together, and separately. Faith was glad Matthew was back. He was glad to be back, and see her every day, but he had a restlessness he couldn't seem to manage. No matter how hard he worked, he was agitated, even as he tried to relax.

I cause Faith pain, because I don't know how to tell her what my problem is. I don't know what it is. My restlessness is not her fault, but it hurts her. She cries in frustration and I don't know how to fix her hurt. I can't protect her from myself.

There is trouble with Maw. She treats me like a kid, and then she wants me to act like the man of the house. I don't know what Maw wants.

Maw is still running the farm and having a hard time fitting back into what I remember as her proper place in our family. It seems we are all at odds and hurt each other at every turn. Ours isn't a peaceful home.

Amanda thought of her son, Matthew when she kneaded the fresh bread dough:

He's so quiet, why can't he talk about it? If he could let it out, he'd be better. What is wrong with him and Faith? Maybe they can't be buddies anymore, their experiences have been very different, maybe they've out-grown their friendship and don't have anything left. They were like two little brothers when they were small, what one did, the other tried to do. She couldn't quite keep up with him because he was a little older and stronger, but they were always together.

They don't have being brothers in common anymore.

Faith is a beautiful young woman. She waited for him while he was gone. Others came around for awhile, but she always made it clear where her interest lay. Her heart's always belonged to Matthew, but maybe she outgrew him, he doesn't seem to know her any longer.

Right now, he doesn't see anythin' that doesn't knock him over.

Amanda started talking softly to her Lord in time to her kneading, "Lord, I can't handle this being the mother of grown children. Can't You bring Jonathan home to us. I need him, his children need him more. We can't get along much longer without some help around here. It's not the work, it's being a...parent... I can't handle . . .all by myself. Lord, You know what I need. Guess I'll give it to You and let You handle it because I sure am not doing a very good job of it. Thank You Lord, I feel a little easier. Your will be done. Amen."

Faith also worried. She thought to herself as she milked. *Matthew works and works, but he can't talk to me. We were so happy when he first got home, but something is wrong and I can't find out what it is. His Maw asked me if he talked to me and I had to tell her, "No." She says he won't talk to her either, he looks far away, or he gets angry and leaves the house.*

He cared too much as a little boy. I remember his folks saying, when we were little, he found the setting hen's nest that she'd hid out in the straw stack. His folks knew about the nest, but they didn't happen to tell us. Matthew saw the eggs. We were supposed to leave eggs alone when we found them in a nest. He wanted to show his Maw or Paw. He was so proud, he found those eggs all by himself. He put those eight eggs in his little gallon feed bucket and ran as fast as he could to show them what he'd found. He tripped on the first step and fell. The eggs splattered all over.

The nest of eggs had been set on by the ole mommy hen for about two weeks and they had little chicks inside.

Several of the eggs were unrecognizable, but two of them landed right there on the step and Matthew was surprised to see all that bloody mess. Those two little half-formed chicks lay there struggling to live, when they were too little. He screamed and his Maw came running.

I remember he cried and cried. He couldn't stand he'd hurt those little babies. His maw tried to quieten him, but he sobbed himself to sleep. While he napped, his Maw washed the steps and got rid of the shells.

When his Paw came in, Matthew woke up and started crying again. He was so ashamed and sad. He couldn't tell his Paw what happened for sobbing. They said, Matthew didn't get over that for weeks.

"I never saw a child take on so," I heard Matthew's Maw say. "He's got the kindest heart. That boy's gonna get hurt a passel in his lifetime, he's too tenderhearted."

Maybe he's afraid to care again. We heard he lost some of those he fought with at the Red River Crossing. By the way he wrote before the battle, we know he cared. Maybe he cared too much and got his tender heart hurt again. Did he think it was his fault somehow? He was just a foot soldier in the battle, how could he have done anything any differently? One soldier can't make much difference.

Faith cried into her pillow that night.

I wish he could talk to somebody, I don't care if it's me, his Maw, the preacher, or who, just talk to somebody! Dear Lord, he's just gotta talk to somebody! Lord, can't You help him? We don't know what to do or say. Please help us, we're getting desperate and he seems less happy everyday. He can't go on like this. Lord, we can't any of us, go on like this. Please Lord, I don't know the answer, please help Matthew and please help his family and I. Lord, I give up, You take over and give him some peace. Thank You Lord for bringing him home, now, take care of him and us. Amen.

Everything added to Matthew's burden of hopelessness.

He peeled off his worn pants and shirt and plunged quickly into the cool waters of the swimming hole. He allowed the flow of the creek to pull on his whole exhausted soul. Matt floated on his back, he felt so unsettled. He thought of allowing himself the blessing of sinking, to rise no more.

It would be easy for me to allow it to happen. Surely the peace of death would lift this burden from me.

Matthew closed his eyes and sank, all the while thinking back to Maw and Paw, Sis, Faith, and his departed Grandma Logan. Before the water could pass fully over his face, he leaped to the surface.

No, I can't do this to them! I can't come clear back home and have them find my body in the creek.

He bowed his face in his hands and sobbed out great wracking sobs.

He thought as he quieted. *If I were somewhere else, far away, I might go through with drowning myself, but I can't do it here. I've seen suicide and the family blames themselves their whole lives. It's the cruelest punishment a person can lay on those he loves. I love them and I can't do this to them!*

He pounded his fists into his thighs. He anguished, *Oh God, help me to be stronger than this. I need strength I don't have. If You can't give it to me, I don't know where to go. My family hasn't been able to give me what I need. Faith has tried. Oh God, she has tried and I just hurt her over and over. Help me know what to do!*

It was a mistake for me to come home. I wanted it so bad. Why can't I be happy? Why can't I settle down with Faith and adjust to life again? It's what I want.

When I returned from war, I was different and Faith is different than when I left.

Faith told me, "I couldn't go, where you went, or see what you endured. We had different things to handle here at home. It changed us, all, but from this time, I wish to be with you and share everything with you."

I turned to her but couldn't speak my mind. "I can't accept you, because I can't accept myself and what I have been forced by war to do. What I did was the only way I could have lived, but maybe I shouldn't have lived. I'll never forget my failure with Martin. I feel emptiness and devastation in my life, I have to have space or I might do something terrible."

I told her, "I don't know about us, because I don't know about me. Now, I have nothing to give anyone. I'm sorry." Tears streamed down Faith's and my face.

I saw the look of hurt, then resignation in her face. How can she fight this kind of rival? There is no defense.

"We both have to go on with our lives as we were, and hope time might restore- hope in my heart."

She asked, "Can you to pray for us?"

"Yes, I can and I will."

We prayed without an answer.

I said, "If I can get this settled, I will come back. Maybe God can give me a solution, I can't find one here. I have to be complete myself before I'm any good to anyone else."

That evening, Matt gathered his family for a talk during their daily Bible time. He knew he was going to hurt them again, but this would be less painful than the alternatives he had thought of.

Here goes, I have to do it. "Mom and Sis, I've got to leave. I need to work some things out in my mind. It isn't your fault and you shouldn't blame yourself. I can't totally blame myself, it's just this whole experience we've *all* had."

They tried to interrupt to argue with him.

"Matt, I'm afraid for you to be alone and away from your family," Amanda said.

"My mind is made up, I have to do this," he said. "Please don't make it harder for me. I'll be back when I get this settled. It's my problem. If I don't go, something awful is going to happen."

Matt looked at his mother. She had a shocked look, but understanding shown in her face.

I've known he wasn't happy and I'm not able to fix it for him like I did when he was a little boy. I don't understand his problem, but I know something is very wrong.

Dear God. Amanda felt God's hand on her heart giving her peace in this decision. *You must accept this. It is MY will for the family.*

She bowed her head in assent.

Matt looked at the top of her head. *Don't cry, please Maw, don't cry.*

Amanda raised her face and looked at her youngest child.

Matt stared at her face. *Maw looks a little relieved. That bothers me, but I know she suffers too. This is for the best. I can't turn back.*

Amanda spoke softly, "Matthew, I feel God's hand in this. Let's pray we can all have peace and God will bless you as you go. He'll help us to bear this and come out on the other side, healed."

The family bowed and prayed silently. Matthew closed the family prayer.

"I'll be going in the morning. I plan to head west. I have to see Faith again. I pray she can accept my decision. Pray for her and me."

The family sat in silence, eyes closed, each caught up in their own thoughts.

"I must go tell Faith when I'm leaving."

He had more difficulty saying farewell to Faith. She was already unhappy, but she didn't know what else she could do. They were unable to fix their relationship and she knew it. She clung to straws as a lifeline.

"Matthew, I'll go with you. Let me go and help you. Let's be together to work this out."

Matthew was struck with a knife of pain. *I am going*

to hurt her again.

"Faith, I can't take you, I can't even emotionally take care of myself. I can't be sure I could take care of you. It's not your problem, you're wonderful. I'm the problem, you can't solve it for me."

"I don't want you to go," she sobbed.

Matthew finally convinced Faith to agree, "I suppose this might be better than hangin' around here, not settlin' anything."

She reached for Matthew and hugged him. She lay her head on his chest and said in a resigned voice, "Do what you have to do. I love you, don't ever forget. Take care of yourself and hurry back, if you ca . . ."

Matthew heard a whisper. The last words were cut off by a sob. He turned away and couldn't look back.

Matthew Takes Leave

Maw insisted Matthew pack food into his saddle-bags. He gathered his belongings, rolled his bedding before dawn, and left with no further conversation. A note sat on the table for his mother, saying he'd leave a note for Faith and be heading west.

From her bed, Amanda heard him shut the door but she couldn't look to see him go.

Oh God, keep him safe and bring him back whole!

She opened the note from the table.

Dear Maw & Emma,

Don't worry if you don't hear for awhile. God is going with me and I'll be fine. Pray for Faith and try to include her in things you do. This will be harder on her than it is on me.

I know railroads need rebuilding. I'll go to the Missouri River counties first

God Bless You All, Matt

For the next several days, he worked a few hours here and there, for a place to stay or food to eat. Work was scarce, due to displaced soldiers.

He didn't sleep much as he traveled. If he slept, he had nightmares.

The third night, he lay back on a log and drifted, he was afraid to sleep. He'd only dream of the war and its horror.

Oh God, help me forget, help me!

At the Missouri River, he hired on with a crew he found working on restoration of the railroads which had been damaged during the war. Swinging a sledge the first day, his hands became so numb he could no longer grip the sledge.

When the sledge slipped from his hand the second time, the foreman took him off that job, afraid he'd hurt someone,

The boss put *the boy* at the end of a spade. This job used Matt's legs more than his arms. He was so exhausted the first night, he couldn't eat his supper of beans and bread, but lay down with a groan in his blanket and coat. It seemed as he hit the ground, they shouted him awake.

Can I ever endure another day? I can't unbend to stand up.

I can't remember half of the second day, the third was better and by the fourth, I am alive again.

Faith found herself unsettled after Matt's departure. She envied the older members of the community, they seemed peaceful in their lives. She envied several of her friends, because they knew what they were going to do with their lives. They had goals and a future. They were getting married, setting up their own homes. Several of her friends had married during the war. They already had babies, some even had their second.

She felt restless when it began to get dark. Young men

came calling, but she gave them little encouragement and they soon went elsewhere. To her friends, she seemed detached. She felt like a sore thumb, totally unnecessary, in the way, and always hurting.

She visited her good friends Matilda and Billy and their little Lizzie often. She tried other things, but her heart wasn't in them.

Down By the Riverside

By the third week of railroad work, Matt was able to laugh at himself and the use of his muscles was feeling good. He was beginning to sleep without dreaming of the gore spread all around him.

Then a fight occurred. Two men of unknown origin, obviously not local, became angry when one slipped and hit a glancing blow on the other's shin with his sledge. The injured, hit before he spoke, catching the careless one under the ribs. Before anyone saw a movement, the careless man had flashed a knife from the back of his belt and plunged it into the neck of the other man. Blood sprayed. The wounded man gurgled and died on the spot.

Martin's wounded. I'm in the midst of war and death. It's flooding back on me.

The crew drew back, murmured, then several rolled the bloodied body into the fill. Others watched without a word. The mules passed over the ditch. The team shied from the smell and the body. When the shovel dumped its load of dirt over the body, it jerked, as if alive.

An eerie silence invaded the group.

Continued passes with the shovel, soon obliterated all traces of the man.

Could a human life be snuffed out, with so little attention from this crew?

Each looked furtively at the dirt fill, but there was no outward sign.

Maybe it never occurred, we imagined it.

The rough and tumble atmosphere was destroyed. Tempers flared all day. Supper was quieter, the crew drifted to their blankets earlier than usual. Matt didn't hear snores till after midnight. The whole crew was affected.

Denial seems to be the cure for the crew.

Everyone was cautious, all had noted where the knife wielder placed his blanket at bedtime. The man stayed on the outer western periphery of the crew, alone.

No one spoke to him, he commented to no one.

Two left during the night. Matt heard them quietly leave. The clomp of their horses' disappeared into the distance to the east.

The knife wielder's bedroll and horse were gone in the morning. No one knew when, or in which direction he went.

I don't know if I would recognize the man, if I met him again. I feel some pity for him and for the dead man, to be valued so lightly and to take a life so easily. This kind of reaction isn't for me. I had hoped I'd never again feel ill toward anyone, much less think of taking someone's life.

Matt worked for another week, then declared himself finished at the end of Saturday's work. The comradeship of this crew had been destroyed.

The crew boss gave Matt a recommendation. He would be able to work on the line outside Kansas City, if he wished.

Matt lazed along the river going west for five days and then reported to another crew.

It's not the same, my mind has begun to work again. The work no longer requires all my energy to complete the day. I can't run away any longer.

I've heard rumors of Quantrell and the James boys. Many are having problems settling back into normal life. What is normal life? Who knows? I can accept I have to face life when it occurs. I can see the war from a greater distance now. Given a bit of time, I think I can at least accept what happened, mentally. The emotional acceptance? Maybe it will never come, but I can get on with my life.

Several months after Matthew left, Faith decided she must find something to occupy herself, or she felt she would go crazy.

Preacher Wilson had chest pains and was giving up some of the work at the school. She might try it, but somehow she couldn't quite picture herself as a school teacher, and it looked as if Matilda might wish to start helping her husband again. Faith often saw her and little Lizzie at the school.

The town had put up a new combined school and church building. With some of the men home, many of the older children were able to leave the chores and go to school as well. The benches were improved and they had built desks for school, which they set aside on Sunday. There were new businesses in town, life was getting progressive around Madisonville.

My mother often helps others who are ill, perhaps I'll try that first. Maw is getting older and she hates to be away from our family for more than a week. I don't have anyone to come home to, I think I could go on some of these missions and care for some of the patients for Maw. Mrs. Logan does this too, so it seems a worthy task. I've helped Maw many times. I think I could handle it.

When there aren't nursing duties, I'll help Maw and Paw do the farming.

Almost There

JD had three months left to complete the three years since the hog slashed his leg.

I'll give myself two extra months to be sure. If I feel well at the end of that time, I'm on my way home!

He purposely hadn't written a definite date to his family, in case signs of illness developed. *When I get down to the last month, I'll start hinting at my ultimate arrival date.*

I dislike missing this crop season, but after five years, it can't be helped and won't make much difference.

JD carried the devastation of President Lincoln's assassination with him.

I've never lost my feeling for Lincoln. He was a savior of the nation, not in a holy sense, but a physical and moral sense. I regretted the harshness of feeling from a part of the nation, people who would reject the one who could have mended broken relationships, those who had no understanding of the actual loss they suffered in the loss of a compassionate leader. I pray for the salvation of the nation, both spiritually and geographically. Help mend the broken trust and make us a family again.

Two months before JD's three years were up, he wrote his family he was completing an assignment. He continued to send money and wrote he'd soon be home.

I dropped a hint I'm in Ohio, but I'll ship my letter by a traveling man. I can't be traced.

I checked out his father's grave when I passed through Kentucky on my way up the Ohio River. I also located relatives on my way further north.

I know it wouldn't do for me to arrive home and then become rabid. I feel safer as time passes and the Lord's assurance life will soon be normal.

I've worked here at Cincinnati, Ohio, ever since I got out of the war. Mr. Brown has a small implement factory. He wasn't able to find enough skilled men who could make the tools necessary for farmers.

I found the north is a bit more prosperous than the south. There isn't much loose cash and the job market is flooded with returned soldiers, so I've been blessed to have paying work.

The war is over, but families have to eat.

The men here accept me. Most of them were in the Union Army and sometimes talk war stories.

I don't like to talk about my experiences and usually I work harder when the subject arises. Many have plenty to say. They don't notice my lack of participation with my past experiences. I had to tell the owner a few details when I signed on, so he'd hire me. I consider my war experiences a closed book which I wish to forget. I only wish to remember friends I've had, or relationships I've formed. Wonder how ole Alcott is doing? I'm close to God and will always carry my faith and the war with me, but the bad experiences, I choose to forget.

I enjoy my employer's children. They remind me of my own when they were small. More and more details of my previous life are coming to mind as the war fades into the background.

I am moving, mentally, back home. Once in a while, I prod myself to note the date, to gain assurance of my health. During the last thirty days, I'll mark off each day on my calendar as it slowly passes.

Fourteen days before he felt his time of danger was up, he called Paul Brown back into the work shed after the crew left their work.

"I'll be leaving for home in fourteen days. I wish to express my gratitude to you and your family. Thank you for your concern and kindness while I've been there. You've made it possible for me to endure some difficult times."

Mr. Brown said, "I've been most pleased with your work. I was having trouble finding men who had your skill and work habits. You've been an asset to my business and a steadying influence on the other men. I'm sorry to see you go, but I can understand you want to see your family after all this time. My thoughts will go with you. If you need a recommendation anytime, let me know. If you are ever in these parts again, you know where we live, look us up. Hope you hit good traveling conditions. Thank you and Godspeed on your way home. I fully understand your desire to be reunited with your family, but I do hate to lose you."

On the last payday in Ohio, Mr. Brown handed JD an envelope with his pay in it. JD stuffed the envelope inside his shirt and shook Mr. Brown's hand.

"So long, I wish you and your family well."

JD picked up his bag of clothes and started down the road on a Saturday evening before dark. When he stopped at a farm house to purchase breakfast the next morning, he found an additional twenty-five dollars in his pay envelope.

One Last Task

JD had one last task before he went home. Drifting along with the current, he traveled down the Ohio River on a flatboat. The only steering the men gave the boat was an occasional poling to keep from hitting driftwood, a sandbar, or the bank. They lazed away the warm afternoons reclining among the stores of equipment.

I remember this is the same route my father's family, including himself, made about forty years before. I vaguely remember the swampy area, called Cairo, Illinois, where the clearer Ohio, meets the Mighty Mississippi River as it flows along. The wide, slow water from the Ohio and the Mississippi flow along separately, spread out over the flat countryside. The two currents flow side by side and then finally roil into an indiscriminate mix.

It isn't quite as I remember. As a boy, I thought the water was so wide we couldn't see across to Missouri, but I can. It is one of the most beautiful sights I've seen. I have thought many times it was a sight I would never see again, Missouri and my home.

He paid his fare for a steamer and traveled across the Mississippi River to New Madrid on the Missouri side. The steamer had to work to get across without drifting south. The Missouri landing area, located south of the Cairo side, wasn't much to look at, but it felt good to him.

I don't have much cash money left or I could take a steamer to St. Louis, or Hannibal, Missouri. I sent most of my pay home and shorted myself, thinking I could work my way along. There are too many drifters with the same idea. Work is scarce.

I've gone through my cash faster than I thought possible, but I have a side trip to make. Hannibal is out for now.

Alcott said he was from near Iron Mountain in Missouri. I'm not sure which town.

Pilot Knob, or Ironton maybe? Surely if he lives almost in sight of the tallest mountain in Missouri and old Fort Davidson, there can't be too many towns around close.

Alcott was the kind of man who traveled and scouted his territory. Surely he'd be well known in his own community.

Iron Mountain men were in on the early attacks of the south toward the Arsenal at St. Louis and Camp Jackson. The Iron Mountain men blew up Fort Davidson and helped chase the Rebels back down toward Springfield and Wilson's Creek, where we northern troops got soundly whipped.

Many fled back toward St. Louis and home, but I know Alcott continued on to Pea Ridge, Arkansas, and kept going from then on.

Alcott was only twenty three years old, three years ago, when he first met me, so he'd be twenty six. I wonder if he has a wife and family back home? Alcott never mentioned a wife, but he didn't seem to be looking at the girls as we fought over the countryside.

I know all I need to know about him. He's a Christian.

He is dependable, he'd never let me down, and he did me one of the biggest favors a man could ever ask of a friend. I will be forever grateful to him. No words or actions can ever repay what I owe, but I know Alcott won't ask, or accept payment.

As JD walked, he mulled over the past and present sights. He cut across rough timbered terrain. It was a slow, but beautiful journey.

Madisonville is in a timbered area of low hills. This area isn't too different, except for the pines here, and the hills are higher and steeper. I've seen so many hills, I'm not sure some aren't blended together. I'm not sure anymore which are home, in Tennessee, Kentucky, Louisiana, or Georgia.

I hope my mind isn't affected. It seems hard to remember details. If I didn't know my time for rabies wasn't more than up, I'd think my memory might be going.

Even yet, fear creeps in, over the possibility of going mad and its horrible symptoms.

He talked aloud with God, because there was no one to hear him, but the birds and the animals.

"We've been through many things together. Thank you for going along beside me. Thank You for keeping my family's bodies and souls together while I've been gone, except for Grandma Logan. I knew she couldn't last forever. Thank You for caring for her and taking her to be with You. I'll miss her. Thank You for her in my life. She was a wonderful mother to me and to Amanda.

I can't wait to get home, but I know You've been there all the time. I know You love them more than I do, so You'd give them the best. I've had to place them in Your hand, because I had no choice in what happened to me or to them. Thank You for handling it for me. Bear with me a little longer, I'll soon get it all together and we can go on with our lives. Dear Father, thank You for the strength You've given me to make it thus far. Your will be done. Amen."

He walked on a few miles further, and came out on the top of a high hill. He looked down and saw the beauty of God's creation spread before him.

"Lord, thank you for this land, may it heal and be knit back together as one nation. Heal all the hurts and restore Your favor over the land. Continue to bless us as one people. Help us to get along with each other. Amen"

He looked at the hills in admiration and reverence.

"I will lift up mine eyes unto the hills, from whence cometh my strength" came to him often, as he walked through the Ozark Plateaus of southeastern Missouri.

He saw a meadow covered with weeds and thorns.

I know it once produced sweet hay. I can close my eyes and smell the new mown grass. No workmen labor here now. Where are they? In some grave in a distant state or disabled?

He passed the abandoned farmstead to which the meadow belonged, he looked inside the worn house and saw the table overturned in the kitchen. No dishes of food graced it's wrinkled and cracked top, no wood was in the firebox beside the rusty stove. He could see blue sky where the roof was weathered and in ill-repair. He sadly turned back to the road. A cemetery on the hill behind the house, caught his eye. He walked up the hill and stood in the shade beneath the trees, his mind wandered:

What family is left and where have they gone? Do they ever come with love and tears to read the stones or kneel here to pray? These are their ancestors, from whence they came. What do they owe to these laying beneath the ground? Did the dead's spirits go to heaven or hell?

JD found himself especially melancholy as he turned to leave the peaceful site on the hillside.

"One day, I'll lay this ole body down and meet a similar fate."

On the lower limb of a bush next to a tombstone, the flicker of a crimson cardinal caught JD's eye.

With renewed thoughts, he breathed, "I know where my spirit will go when this body is laid to rest. Thank You, Jesus."

Several times, farmers offered him short rides in their wagons, but *shank's mare* did most of his carrying. As he walked along, he thought about the old saying *shank's mare*. It was an expression he'd heard the old timers use when they meant walking on your own shanks.

This is a good time for me. I'm working out things between myself and God, getting a clearer picture in my mind of what my life will be henceforth. I've been busy during the war, I didn't have much time to think about my own life.

JD began to feel at peace with himself and with the world.

I'll face one thing at a time, me and God can handle it. I feel more rested than I have for years. The hills, with God as my companion, are the best therapy I could find.

JD inquired and found a small mountain farm which belonged to a John William Alcott. He was informed the man was the soldier's grandfather.

The man stated, "Alcott the younger has no other immediate family living, other than a brother we ain't seen for a long time."

Alcott the *younger* and *older,* welcomed JD to their humble abode.

JD sensed a restlessness in the younger man, and a dissatisfaction in the grandfather.

"I saw the maturity of this fellow when we worked together. I'd never have made it without his friendship. I want to thank whoever raised him, for the kind of man he became," JD praised Alcott to his grandfather.

"Guess you can blame that on me, and his Maw," Alcott's grandfather said. "We didn't have much help for a long time. He is a good boy, he just has big ideas sometimes."

JD and Alcott walked over the fields. The young man talked of the times he'd lived here as a child with his mother and his brother.

The two men discussed the possibilities of work in the area.

Alcott continued in this train of thought. "There ain't no work around here. The saltpeter minin' ain't necessary for ammunition nomore and I pray it'll never be agin. The iron mines are cuttin' back cause we don't need cannon or small arms. I don't know what's gonna happen around here, where I'm gonna work. I been cleanin' up the ole place, but there's not enough work for Grampaw and me here. He's in good health and I think he kind of resents me tryin' to change things. I may go somewheres else. I'll sure think on your askin' me to come see you."

At the end of a two day visit, JD felt the need to move toward home. The men looked into each others' eyes and embraced again. Affection and respect shown on their faces.

"I'm havin' a hard time settlin' down. This place seems smaller than it used ta. I may make a trip your way one of these days," Alcott said.

"You know where I live and I'm leaving you these directions to Madisonville. If you ever want to come see us, you'll be welcome. My home's your home. You've been like a son to me. I release you from the favor I asked, it won't be necessary." JD delivered the final word, "Thank you again."

He turned quickly to keep Alcott from looking into his eyes.

As JD walked north toward home, he happened to think he never knew Alcott's given name.

Strange, how I was so close to the man and never knew his whole name. God knows and Alcott can get to God.

I'll write Alcott and ask him.

That'd be strange, if I write and the letter doesn't reach Alcott because I don't know his given name. I had enough directions to get to his home, so I can write enough description to get a letter to him. Alcott's Grandpa's name is John William Alcott, so surely there aren't too many of those around. I'll put the grandfather's name on the letter, and use Ironton as the town's address.

My mind is finally at peace. Now to get about the job of going home.

He crossed the Missouri River on a ferry above Washington. In conversation with the owner of the ferry, Adam Grantz, JD learned of a steamer loaded with ties and parcels bound for Hannibal.

"I know Captain Wright, who lives at Riverscene across from Boonville, Missouri. If you'd like, I'll put in a word for you when they come by," Mr. Grantz said. "Maybe you could catch a ride, and a job, at the same time."

JD was eager for the chance to work his way toward home. *If I can get the job, it will be a way to go home with a few dollars in my pocket, plus a quicker, easier route.*

He helped Mr. Grantz lever the pulleys on the ferry back and forth across the Missouri River that day.

JD thought about Boonville as he worked. His father had worked out of Franklin, across from Boonville, on the Santa Fe Trail.

"Mr. Grantz, didn't I hear Franklin flooded and the town washed away? "

"Yes, she sure did. About 1827, if I remember correctly. They had some warning and moved most of the buildings before the flood scrubbed off the low area on the north bank of the river. They moved up the hill and started a new town called New Franklin.".

"My father often reminisced of freighting to Santa Fe, then later with a group of fifty wagons going to Ft. Laramie, Wyoming Territory, in about 1834. I remember hearing him say, "Oxen are slower, but they plugged along. It amuses me to think an oxen is kind of like the tortoise in the story of the Tortoise and the Hare I read to our children when they were small," JD added.

Word traveled quickly on the river and Captain Wright's steamer arrived going down river toward St. Louis. on the next day. Mr. Grantz was faithful in passing on JD's request to the Captain when he stopped at the ferry landing to load wood.

"This man's a good worker, he's helped me yesterday and part of today. He needs to hitch a ride to Hannibal. You got room for a good man?"

"Sure, I always need good help loading and unloading freight and wood. I'll take your word for it." He turned toward JD, "Mr., eh?"

"JD Logan, Sir."

"Come aboard, we'll be leaving as soon as we stow these last two bales of freight and load on the wood."

"Here, I'll help."

"No, put your things in the fourth door on the left on the lower deck. I've got an extra bunk in there. You'll be able to tell which one when you see it. Go on and get your gear stowed."

J. D. thanked Mr. Grantz for his kindness and marched aboard.

Homecoming

Captain Wright put JD to work. Being a man accustomed to heavy labor, loading and off-loading the cargo was not as tiring for JD as it might have been for some.

The steamer tied up at many of the smaller docks while going down the Missouri River toward St. Louis. Most of the villages loaded on minor produce or grain, bound for St. Louis, or ports north and south. Cords of wood were loaded for fuel at several stops. Passengers boarded for journeys into St. Louis to conduct business, travel, or for entertainment.

JD found it an enlightening experience, much fraught with excitement and interesting sights. St. Charles had an old river port appearance, and St. Louis was a delight with the land tapering down to the river and a wealth of warehouses and buildings along the landings.

JD knew the founding fathers of St. Louis based much of their exploration and wealth on furs from the Missouri and other river areas. He took the opportunity to explore the old fur and tobacco warehouses and other old businesses which remained on the wharf area.

Captain Wright had told him to be present for reloading at 2 on Wednesday afternoon. JD had a free day on his own in St. Louis.

He meant to acquire gifts for his family. He hadn't seen them for a long while, his *little* girl might not want candy. He got her a lace hankie. He knew what his wife liked. She would be pleased with French chocolates to satisfy her sweet tooth. With the weather cooler, he took the chance of the chocolates lasting to Ralls County. JD picked up other minor purchases for his extended family. Anxious to reach home, he was present two hours before loading time to go aboard. He stowed his purchases and located the Captain to see if there was any tasks for him.

Captain Wright gave him some minor duties, then they loaded heavy bales with winches. The bales were bound. JD wasn't sure what they contained. He and other stevedores levered the cargo aboard and stowed it carefully away from the water spray of the paddle wheel.

The load reminded JD, of the bales of cotton the soldiers had used for protection against enemy fire and other protective barriers they erected when they traveled the rivers of the southern states. He hoped and prayed as he loaded, that these items would never come into use for the military. The items had a peaceful purpose.

So be it.

One pack was labeled Holy Bibles, bound for Zoar Baptist Church, Hannibal, Missouri. That was one packet he'd make sure stayed dry and got delivered safely.

"All aboard, bound for Hannibal, Quincy, Rock Island, Keokuk, Fort Madison, and ports north, returning back south to New Orleans, Louisiana," shouted a voice aboard the steamer.

J.D's blood sang. *I am almost home! If I could get off at the Salt River, it would be a minor walk to our place. I am booked to Hannibal to complete my assignment for Captain Wright. I'll think home when we pass the mouth of the Salt.*

The Mississippi River narrowed slightly, above St. Louis, once the Missouri's influence ended. The river ran through more areas of plains, but river bluffs were always in sight on at least one side of the river. JD's eyes were *glued* to the western shore as they passed the mouth of the Salt River and beyond, then headed on to Hannibal. His excitement grew as he rounded a bend in the bluffs below Hannibal.

I can see the short round lighthouse on a hill above the landing. I have a job to complete, but I'm only a short distance from home.

The stevedores threw in the lines and tied up quickly. Passengers and workmen gathered about, coming and going from the boat. The workmen began to unload and partition out parcels and bales as soon as they had dry footing.

JD laid the Bibles to the left of the parcels and watched out of the corner of his eye for the person who came to claim those.

After most of the load was shifted, he saw the approach of a short, heavily-built man. The man inquired of the steamer's clerk. JD noted the pointing of the clerk's hand to the Bibles. He hurried to catch the man.

As JD approached, he realized the man had a body as hard as nails.

JD introduced himself as being from Madisonville. The hand the preacher presented to JD was hard and callused.

This is a man of toil, accustomed to earning his living with his hands, as well as his mind and voice.

JD had relatives by the name of Self, who had helped found this church. After Reverend Hamilton Jacoby introduced himself fully, JD asked the Reverend if he knew the Stuart Self family. He was pleased to find they were still members of the church.

"They live south west of town," the Reverend Jacoby stated. "I'm traveling near there. I would be happy to give you a ride out that way, if you'd like to wait a few minutes while I load our parcel and send off some mail."

JD helped the Reverend load the Bibles and carried several minor parcels to a horse and buggy hitched to the landing's hitching rail. They loaded mail onto the steamer.

JD shook hands with Captain Wright. He thanked the Captain for his transportation and kind treatment on the river.

JD boarded the buggy while the reverend tied up the lead. He noted the bay horse hitched to the Reverend's buggy, was freshly shod and had a fast look about him.

JD soon found he wasn't wrong, as they pulled away from the hitching rail. Reverend Jacoby kept a steady rein on the animal to keep him from overtaking pedestrians and other horse drawn vehicles.

"Your bay is in a hurry to go somewhere," JD commented.

"I'm a blacksmith on the side and enjoy fine horses," the Reverend stated, as they drove through the dirt streets of Hannibal. " I served as a chaplain in the Union Army. I bought this horse back from a battle in Pennsylvania. He belonged to a friend in the ranks with me, who was killed in the battle. He and I had discussed his horse. This animal has some unusual quirks. Most can't handle him, wouldn't want him around. He makes most people mad but if they get rough on him, he fights back. In talking with my friend, I found this animal had good reason for his quirks, just as I find most people have reasons for their unfriendly behavior. Handled with love and steady discipline, this is the *best* animal I've ever had. He's willing to serve and has what I'd call *heart*. He never quits on me. In one emergency, he trotted seventy-five miles in one day to take a man to see his dying wife. Thanks to the bay, we made it in time too. He's a grand animal."

JD realized the Reverend was almost misty-eyed about his horse

"I understand gratitude to a special friend, be it animal or man. Heart and fortitude are grand gifts from God. The magnificence of your horsel is impressive as he moves along. He accomplishes his task with apparent ease and efficiency of motion, he moves ahead without complaint and seems to get the job done," JD said.

"Twenty-four hours after that seventy-five mile drive, I couldn't tell he'd worked at all. He came out of the barn with spirit as usual, and we went on about our business. I take good care of him and he takes good care of me. He is a once in a lifetime gift from a friend," the minister commented.

The two men discussed religion, their faith in the Lord and His providence toward them. When conversation slacked, they rode in companionable silence, breaking in when either had some comment. They admired the countryside as they drove along and Reverend Jacoby told JD a little about his congregation. He had families and one single colored woman named Miss Molly.

He commented, "In Missouri river towns, there have been slave members who sat in the back of some of the churches, but it is unusual for a church to have a full-fledged member who sits among the white folk of the congregation. *Miss Molly* is a fixture of my congregation and has been in Hannibal longer than any of my people could remember. She was on the charter membership roll and a most-accepted and loved member of the congregation. Miss Molly is very old and I don't know her beginnings. To my knowledge, she has no other name."

"I'm glad she's accepted," JD stated, "That's the reason

I've been away from home for the last five years. I'd hate to come home and find it for naught. That would disappoint me in the human race. I pray it can be the same over the entire nation. I've seen bigotry and hatred enough for several lifetimes. Let's hope it has ended."

The Reverend interrupted as he turned into the gate of a stately, three-story house of slate-green with cream trim.

JD couldn't help but be impressed. The place bore a well-cared for and much-loved look. Three dormers trimmed with cream clapboard siding adorned the roof.

It was an interesting place. JD noted the speckled black and white Dominicker hens and roosters in the chicken yard; a couple of red roan cows and a bull in the pasture; and several light saddle horses; also a driving horse in the pasture. He noted no draft stock, but imagined those that remained after the war, were at work in the fields, or resting between farm work in some distant shady pasture.

"They have livestock? I thought many of the farmers were raided during the war." JD asked.

"Some were. Other areas avoided the raids. Don't know what caused the difference, other than some raids were grudges or maybe the opportunity presented itself. Hard to say," Rev. Jacoby commented.

JD noted a rick of freshly split wood, near the rear of the house and best of all, *no slaves* working the yards or fields, and no slave huts out back.

This is a more prosperous place than most and much grander than our own. I hope ours looks as well-loved.

A tall, handsome, silver-haired man approached from the barn with a bucket of milk in his left hand. He hailed the Reverend.

"Welcome. Come on in for a piece of freshly baked bread and a glass of cold milk."

The Reverend drew JD forward, "I've bought one of your relatives with me. Do you recognize Jonathan David Logan? JD, this is Mr. Stuart Self."

Mr. Self looked JD over. He hadn't known his cousin, but he recognized the family look about JD, as a resemblance to Bailey Logan and Stuart's own father. He had known Bailey from many years ago.

Self noted that he, and JD both had an exceptionally long-legged look, black hair, and finer features than many men of their size.

"My hair has silvered at an early age, but I see you mirror how I thought I looked," Self commented.

He smiled at his own thoughts, *I wonder if JD has the long toe?*

"JD, I apologize for my smile which doesn't relate to our meeting. I couldn't help but think you look like my father and your father. I was wondering in my mind if you had a long second toe? It's been a source of amusement and distinction in the family for years."

"As a matter of fact, I do have a long second toe! I didn't know it was a family trait however, but now that you mention it, I think perhaps you are right," JD looked surprised. "My son has the same toe and my wife, Amanda definitely doesn't carry that trait, as her feet are short and plump, as are her hands." JD flushed and added, "She's a slim woman otherwise, I wouldn't wish to offend her by a description which makes her appear that she isn't beautiful."

"I don't wish to impose on your hospitality, Mr. Self," JD quickly stated, "but I wished to look up a family member while I was close by. I haven't been home to Ralls County in almost five years while I was off at war. As you can imagine, I'm anxious to get on the road."

"Well, you and the Reverend come on in for some fresh bread, butter, strawberry jam, and cold milk and call me Stuart, this Mr. Self stuff makes me feel too old," he hurried to say. "You'll feel much better to get on the road home. I wouldn't feel right sending you home hungry. Spend the night and get on the road in the morning after breakfast, if you like. We appreciate what you've done for the country and we are beholden to you men in blue."

"Come in and meet the Missus and our daughter, Nancy. The other children are in school, or at Hannibal today."

They walked toward the back door as Mr. Self commented, "I'm sorry you can't meet all your cousins."

Even though it was nearing dusk, refreshed by the Self family's courtesy, JD started for home. He waved to the Selfs.

"Thank you for your hospitality. I wish you the best and hope to see both of you again. Come see us if you get down Madisonville way," he invited.

Rev. Jacoby left for a pastoral visit to an ill member.

As JD walked, the moon rose high and bright in the sky. JD imagined himself in the milky way.

I feel light, joyful.

I would like to be home by daylight, but being almost twenty miles, I know that's probably impossible.

The sky began to lighten at 6 AM. JD looked for changes as he passed by familiar places.

I passed by Old Colonel Ralls' home near New London during the night. Our county was named for Ralls. He died while at the old state capital in St. Charles shortly after they carried him down in his bed to cast his last vote.

By noon he was at Center, where he caught a ride on a farm wagon carrying feed from the mill to a neighbor's. JD didn't recognize the youngster driving the wagon, but he did recognize the name on the wagon and the destination of the delivery.

JD visited with the youngster as they rode along behind a young team of fine sorrel Belgians with flaxen manes and tails. He enjoyed watching the rise and fall of those massive haunches as the Belgians smartly trotted along home. This wasn't a heavy load and they appeared to be enjoying the excursion.

The young man filled him in on local marriages and

deaths, another preacher in the community, and recent gossip. JD was saddened to learn several of his neighbors and friends had not returned from the war, while several others had lasting injuries which had changed their lives.

The young man accounted for the neighbors.

" Maybelle Warner is still alive and still talking. She helps the McIntire man who came back from the war. He's married now and has a new baby."

"That's good to hear. I was with him when he was wounded. At first, we weren't sure he was going to make it. Sure glad to hear he's at home and doing well," JD commented. "Who did he marry?"

"The storekeeper's daughter, forgot which one. Say, I think it's your son, Matthew? He got back from the war, then went west."

JD was shocked by this new bit of news.

"Was there a reason for him going West?" he asked.

"Not that I know of," the young boy said.

JD grew quiet.

I can't imagine why Matthew would leave so quickly after coming home. I'll find out about that soon.

"This land needs care."

"There ain't been many able-bodied men left around here, but some have come home and they're gettin' a little work done. There's some ain't comin' back and some who ain't too healthy yet," the boy replied.

Some fields had not been worked in several years, roads needed grading and holes needed to be filled. Second growth was coming back on some of the pastureland. JD expected to see the same on his own farm. There weren't many animals in any of the pastures.

They rounded the bend in the trail west of Madisonville.

"Thank you, I can get home from here. I'll cut across."

JD alighted, stepped over his boundary fence, and ran across his field toward his own home.

I didn't write my family while I journeyed from Iron Mountain. They won't be sure of my arrival time.

Things look wonderful, the fields are planted and growing, the pastures and fence rows look well-cared for and the house shows red and white checked gingham curtains blowing out at the windows. When I left there were faded yellow curtains in the front windows.

He rounded the corner of the house and heard the back door open. Amanda shook her mop off the back porch.

"You dusting a man because he's isn't dirty enough?" JD asked.

Startled, Amanda dropped the mop and sailed down the steps into his arms. They couldn't get enough of each other, they hugged and held on tightly, laughing as he whirled her around. Finally, dizzy, they stopped to look into each other's faces.

He noticed a few fine wrinkles and a freckled golden face, but *nothing,* that wasn't beautiful in his Amanda's face.

Amanda looked into a leaner and harder face and deeper cheek creases.

He's always been in the sun. He still has his beautiful smile and eyes full of twinkle. Oh, I have to feel him close again. She clutched him desperately.

Breathlessly they broke apart and Amanda called into the house.

"Emma, your Poppa's home! Come out and see him."

JD heard a squeal that sounded like a child, but a woman appeared right behind the squeal.

I can't believe this beautiful woman is my little Emma. Now she has smooth, shining black hair, where I left a brown-haired imp. Her eyes are still robin's egg blue, with the snowflake pattern of lighter blue, fringed with dark lashes. She looks—dignified, even though she's barefoot and in a faded dress. I can't get over her healthy-looking vitality, and—face!

Are there young men is standing in the wings waiting

for her? I've prayed for the right man for her, if she wants to marry, but I don't know anything about her life. I'm not in any hurry for that other fellow to come along either.

JD looked at the two women again. *Their dresses are old and worn. Both of them. Maybe the look of this place is the product of hard work, rather than prosperity, as I first thought.*

"I'm so proud of you both. I know you've made all kinds of sacrifices in physical labor and lack of the niceties women enjoy—"

The women both gave a negative reaction to their sacrifices.

I'll have to check that out, JD thought.

"I'm home and we'll remedy that. As soon as I can, you'll enjoy a softer life with me taking up the heavy work. I'm in good health and I'll enjoy working for my family again."

"Have you heard from Matthew?" he asked.

"Not for a couple of months, but his last letter sounded better," Amanda said.

"Why did he leave?"

"I think he saw too much war and he couldn't get it out of his heart. He said he needed to have some time away. It was hard to understand after he'd already been gone, but we had to accept what he thought would help him. As much as I hate to say it, he wasn't getting better here. Somehow I had a peace about his leaving, even though it wasn't my first choice," Amanda said.

Emma shifted. "He wasn't happy here. Faith hears from him oftener than we do. She thinks he's better. In his letters, he said he'd soon come home."

"I hope so," JD said.

JD settled back into a normal routine, life was simpler than before, but very rich to him, after the deprivation of camp life. He soon began to see the women didn't miss some of the things he had assumed were necessary for them in their previous life.

There's less livestock, but we have meat, produce, plenty to eat, and we have each other, our love, and we have our health. The only ones missing are Matthew and Grandma Logan. Maybe one of those problems will soon be remedied.

A Visitor

Six months after JD arrived home, he saw a tall young man coming down his lane.

There's something familiar about his movements. It isn't Matthew, as he has a family-type movement, which I'd recognize from my own father's body build and walk. The sun is shining behind the man. I can't make out features.

JD went to the front yard to meet their visitor and greet him.

When the young man cleared the path of the sun, he shouted to JD.

"Howdy Sir!"

Alcott had come to pay his promised visit.

"You came!" JD let out a shout and ran to meet him.

The family cleared the house, thinking something terrible had occurred. Amanda soon realized this was a joyous meeting. Emma hung back, suddenly shy.

JD released Alcott and grabbed Amanda to bring her forward to introduce to his friend.

"This is Alcott who saved my bacon many a time!"

"He's just bein' modest, we'ens were all in it together," Alcott said.

Amanda immediately liked this young man. He had a modest air, a friendly face, curly hair touched by the sun, and chocolate brown eyes. He possessed an open smile and had the laugh wrinkles of pleasant disposition.

JD turned to find his daughter and found her staring at Alcott. He started to introduce Alcott and realized the young man was struck dumb. There was a charge in the air and even he, an unromantic old father felt something. Amanda looked from one to the other and smiled that knowing motherly smile of a woman with great intuitive instincts..

Amanda immediately felt in her heart, *God will provide.* She amended it to, *God has provided, but Your will be done.*

JD continued with introductions, even though neither of the young people heard what he said.

Amanda and JD murmured a few words and finally gave up. They went about their own business, leaving the young people, one in the porch swing, and another on the front steps.

Each of the two young adults knew many things about the other, because JD had talked of them both. Emma picked up on the story of the hog and Alcott told details from his viewpoint. JD noted Emma had never been quite so enthralled by his account.

The couple went from there to when the bushwhackers came to prey upon Amanda and JD's family. Alcott took his turn to hang on every word Emma spoke.

JD felt a pang. *No longer is Emma my little girl and mine alone. She's a grown woman with her own mind and heart.*

When they passed, Amanda and JD murmured their excuses and went on with their work, Amanda into the house to prepare supper and JD back to the barn to finish the evening chores.

The young adults didn't realize they'd been deserted by their elders. If anyone had asked them, they might have said, "We don't care."

JD took the milk to the house and strained it into the crock. When he passed by Amanda, she had a smug, *cat who swallowed the cream,* look on her face.

I wonder what she is into?

The next time he saw the two young people, Emma was showing Alcott the buckskin horse she often rode into the creek for an afternoon dip; a gallop over the pasture and trails; or into town for supplies. Alcott appeared supremely interested in Emma's horse.

JD went in to wash up for supper. He called the two in to supper. They were both in the swing rocking gently and deep in conversation.

Why didn't I think of it? I can see they are perfectly suited for each other. God willing, they just might be the answer to my prayers.

When Amanda climbed into bed, she said, "Why didn't you think of those two? I noticed it in about ten seconds."

"It took me about two hours, guess I'm just slow. We'll have to be careful to stay out of it. If God has a plan for their lives, let Him reveal it, let's not push them into anything," JD said.

Amanda agreed as they prayed asking God's will in all their lives.

A New Life

Emma had never felt this emptiness in her life before. She grew more and more restless. She rode her buckskin horse at night, going to the creek.

I look at the eyes of the cattle shining red in the dark, or the stars, and listen to the night sounds.

She communed with God, asking relief from her misery.

There is a constant lump in my throat. I feel at loose ends and so lonely. What does it mean? Where am I headed and what am I to do next? How am I to fill this void? What am I seeking?

My parents are no longer my entire life and I feel out of place. I'm not my daddy's buddy any longer. He's been gone too long and I've gotten into other habits.

I felt I belonged, familiar, and now this isn't my home, it is strange and unfamiliar, yet the same. I'm not the same. I thought my life would always be the same. As I grew, this was my home. I love this land, now- I'm on the brink of something, but I don't know what. God, please help me.

Tonight, she went outside and bridled her horse. As she rode away, she saw the lamp burning in the tack room where Alcott slept. Her heart lurched as she thought about him.

He's so handsome. He effects me in a strange way. He has such gentleness and kindness beneath his rough edges. I would trust him with my life and I know he'd never let me down, as a friend.

I don't want my feelings for him to go beyond friendship, because he isn't polished. He isn't what I've always pictured for my husband. Husband? Where did that come from? Is that what I have on my mind?

She argued with herself.

I don't wish to spend my life without him. His wonderful traits, much outweigh his lesser ones.

Tonight, for the first time, I have to consider telling him I'm growing fond of him. I've fought against it, but the draw is there. Could he care for me, as I do for him? I'm not sure how he feels. Actually, he seems to avoid me. When he first came he was so friendly and we talked. I really enjoyed our time together, then he stayed away. There's something wrong, he doesn't like me.

A tear trickled down her cheek. She turned toward home, more lonely and sad than she'd been when she rode out.

Alcott had restrained himself, feeling guilty over the feelings Emma provoked in him. At night, he dreamed of her.

His feelings and dreams agitated him.

I am alive in Emma's presence. She opens something in my heart.

I don't know what I'm doin' when she's around. What is different about her? She is purty. No, beautiful! That long hair ripplin' down her back or over her shoulder. Curls float around her face when she gets busy. I've seen her at her worst, and best, but mostly best. I love her both ways. Love? Yes, I love her and I'd die for her. I want to be with her the rest of my life and I want her to be the mother of my children. But most of all, I'd like to take care of her like a special treasure from God.

Dear Father, I'm afraid to ask her. I don't come up to her family, they're smart—know so much about the world, that I don't. They read books thet I never he'red of. They talk about things I don't know. Give me the answer God, help me go to her, or give me the strength and help me to put her out of my mind. I can't stand this torment. It's gettin' to me. I'll leave this place, if you let me know this ain't rit.

Alcott was in pain. He bowed his head in his hands and sat rocking for a few minutes.

"Oh, God, help me accept Your plan for me. Amen."

He arose to get busy at some task, *any task*, to give his mind a rest. During the day, he worked hard to keep his mind off her and asked the Lord to forgive his thoughts.

Emma's old nemesis, Lee had despaired waiting to find Emma alone. Years had slipped by since the threshing argument he had with her. He'd let the whole Civil War go by without getting back at her, waited longer than he wanted to, longer than he ever had for anyone else who had done him wrong. There hadn't been the opportunity he sought.

Now, time is runnin' out, I have to make it happen! She shamed me at the threshing, I've had to wait to get back at her. She's avoided me since Matthew left, and when I see her, she's always with other women or in the presence of those pansies, the store keeper, the school teacher, the doctor, or the preacher. I've gone to that farm time and again, to catch her out alone, but she always works with her maw or that old man Wasson. Now her father is home, along with the other men of the community. Gotta be more careful. I see Emma going out by herself. Guess she thinks she can stay away from me. I'll show her!

Lee talked himself into a state of rage, as he built up his courage and made his plans.

I've seen her ridin' her buckskin horse down by the creek and I watched her as she waded with her skirt up to her knees.

He mauled plans in his head, *I'll turn loose her horse, cut her off from the house, then I'll have her, she don't know what she wants, but she will. She'll like me when she knows me as a man and I'm finished with her.*

There's a stranger, working in the field across from the creek, too close—be certain to hear her, if she fights. He don't seem to pay her no mind, he don't matter. Wish I knew who he is. *Since he's made no moves on Emma, that don't matter. He'll stay out of the way because he don't have no interest and no reason to interfere between me and my girl. He don't know us. He's a stranger, don't have no friends here.*

Tonight, Lee watched the house all evening. He saw Emma go to the barn lot, she put the bridle on the buckskin and climbed on the fence to straddle the horse's bare back. She turned the horse toward the hillside and rode quietly out of the lights from the house and by the barn.

In the bunkhouse, Alcott sensed his feelings were acceptable, this was God's way of assuring men and women to get together. He read his Bible and it said, 'God looked and His whole creation was good.'

God made it, it's good. Thank you Lord, for giving me direction. Marriage is honorable, and if you will it, we'll be assured of doin' the rit thing. I stayed away from Emma as long as I can and she looks confused. I hate to hurt her. I'll go to her and beg her pardon, for my confusion over what I've felt for her. She may never want me, but she'll know I ker fer her. Then it'll be her choice. Thank you, Lord.

Alcott heard Buck, as Emma went by the barn. He knew she went to the hill above the creek at night to watch the stars and to be alone to think.

"Tonight, I'll go beg her pardon fer the way I treated her and explain my feelin's and confusion."

He put out the coal-oil lamp, opened the door to his bunkhouse and went out into the balmy summer air. He heard Buck blow, as he drank at the crossing. He lost Emma and Buck as they ascended the hill above the creek, but occasionally he caught the sound of a hoof, or a night bird, as it startled. He moved with the sounds she created. He was careful not to frighten her, until he was near enough to call her name and alert her to his presence. He started to call out, but he heard a quick intake of breath.

"Who's there?" Emma spoke tentatively.

Alcott heard Emma's muffled voice, he was surprised she had heard him. He stepped into the opening in the trees and saw Emma in the moonlight. She was not looking at him, but away.

"It's me Emma, I know you missed me," a gruff male voice answered her, turned syrupy, "I haven't seen you in a long time. Sure glad you came to see me."

Alcott was stunned. *I didn't know she had a lover! How could she have hidden someone else from me these past few months? She must have been coming up here to meet him all these nights.* He turned to go. *No, what was it the man said? He hadn't seen her for a long time?* Alcott hesitated for a moment, *There is something about his voice, it sounds mocking.*

"Is that you, Lee?

"Yeah, Sweetheart, I been lookin' for you for a long time," the possessor of the voice said as he grabbed her arm and twisted her from her horse's back. Emma fell heavily against him.

The buckskin shied away from the pair and turned toward the barn.

"You won't get away from me this time," snarled Lee against her ear. His breath in her ear, revived her and she started fighting him.

Alcott heard the smack of the man's hand as it struck flesh.

Emma squealed.

Alcott lunged across the clearing, he caught the man from the rear, and clinched down with his forearm locked across the man's throat. The attacker released Emma and gasped in shock. He lost his footing and fell toward Alcott's feet. The reaction threw Alcott off balance, but took the pair away from Emma. She lunged away and turned to defend herself against this new threat.

Hardened from battle experience and fast on his feet, Alcott recovered quickly.

It didn't take long to know the man Lee was a dirty fighter, and in poor condition. Alcott didn't know Lee had been sucking up easy living, with plenty of liquor.

I don't want to hurt anyone again. Maybe I can hold him long enough to find justice.

"I've had enough fightin', I vowed I'd never fight again, give up, it's time for legal means, rather than fightin'."

The attacker sneered.

"Haw, give myself up, I'll see you in h___ first," he said as he jerked a knife and passed it back and forth in front of Alcott's face. Alcott stepped back to take a new direction, slipped on an exposed root and sprawled.

Lee advanced on him and lunged to bring down his arm. Alcott rolled, and heard a crack and scream. He looked back to see the moonlight reflected off Emma. In her hands was a broken tree branch and the attacker bent over his distorted arm.

Alcott and Emma had no further trouble with their attacker, but marched him unceremoniously, back toward the house.

The black hound barked.

JD heard the commotion and came from the house with a lantern. He raised it to see a man stagger in front of Alcott and Emma. The man was in obvious pain. JD advanced to give assistance, but was held off by Alcott's voice.

"This man attacked Emma and we're takin' him to the law. Do yah know him?"

JD raised the lantern until it shown into Lee's face.

"Yes, I do know this man, he's been a bully all his life. Emma, are you all right?"

She nodded, tight lipped and pale in the lantern light.

"I'm glad someone finally caught him. Now the law will take care of him at last. I'll hitch up the team and we can take him to New London to the sheriff," JD directed.

Alcott and JD helped Amanda place a sling on Lee's arm, providing stability, until they could deliver him, first at Doctor Marshall's, then to the Sheriff in New London.

The men did not return home until dawn the next day.

Neither, Emma nor Alcott could wait to talk to each other. He wished to tell her of his decision about what the Lord wished for him; she to reveal her gratitude and feelings for him. All day they waited, finding no opportunity.

Amanda noted Emma's agitation as the day wore on. "Emma do you want to go see Alcott now?" Amanda asked, "I know your father would let him off for a little while, if you need to talk to him."

"How did you know I was thinking about Alcott?" Emma whirled to look at her mother's face.

"That's not too hard, looking at your face and watching you today as you fumble around trying to keep your hands busy. Go out and catch your father. Ask him if you can have a little of Alcott's time. Your father understands more than you realize." Amanda gave her approval to her daughter.

"Oh, thanks Maw. I think I will go for a walk, but I don't know if I'm ready to talk yet."

JD noted the same unrest as he worked at farm chores, alongside Alcott.

"Alcott, do you want to talk?"

"Uuh, Yes Sir, I love your daughter Emma, and I wanta ask you if'n I can court her. That is if'n she'll have me," blurted out Alcott.

JD was not surprised in the question, but he considered his answer carefully.

"Emma's family loves her dearly, if you were to ask her later to marry you, it's for life, no fooling around."

"You know me. Sir, I've waited fer someone like Emma all my life and it'll be forever when I tell someone I love them. I've already talked it over with God."

In assent, JD threw his arms around Alcott and hugged the young man to himself. *I love this young fellow.*

After supper, as dusk fell, Alcott spoke to Emma.

"Will you walk with me? I have somethin' I need ta tell you."

Emma was unsure if he was going to tell something about the delivery of Lee to the Sheriff, or something else.

"Emma, I had thoughts 'bout you that made me unsure. The Lord let me know these were the feelin's he intended for a man to have for a woman that he loved. Now, I know these are good feelin's and I want to know if you think you could ever ker for me in the same way? If you can't, I can accept it and I won't hold it agin you." Alcott spoke first and was now out of breath.

A tenderness overwhelmed her at the sight of his doubt. Even though things were going faster than she planned, she felt free in her heart to reveal her love for him.

"I love you too," she whispered. Looking into his eyes, she could see his doubts and his love shining there.

"I've waited fer you to say that so long, but I was so afeerd you didn't love me like I love you," he enfolded her in his arms and said, "I'm not polished. You'll hav'ta help me, but I'll do the best I kin. I don't want ya to be ashamed of me."

His humility and sincerity made Emma ashamed for the way she had felt about his lack of polish. *Here is a treasure of a Godly man and I only looked on the surface of his speech.*

"Alcott, you have what really matters to me. We can handle the rest." She moved in his arms for their first shy kiss.

He and Emma began their courting. Alcott needed to earn a few dollars. They spent little on their courtship. They saw each other everyday around the farm.

Emma saw his kindness to the animals; his concern for her father and mother; and he worked harder than anyone. Pride and love bubbled together in her heart. She felt cherished.

My restlessness has ended, I'm at home at last.

Alcott seemed a little in awe of her. He hadn't had sisters to grow up with and young females were a new experience for him. He did the right things, because his heart was right and he did the right things for everyone. Both accepted the ideal of marriage as the ultimate outcome of their time together.

"What we have'll grow into somethin' special worth waitin' fer. I've waited twenty-six years, what's a few more months?"

Emma realized, the loneliness she had felt was the

desire within her heart for her own home and family.

Their relationship grew with easy trust. They worked together and played together. They both rode Buck to the creek and waded. They splashed each other.

"Maybe you oughta know my real name, since we plan to be married someday," Alcott teased on one of their outings.

"Do you have more of a name? I may always call you *Alcott,* because your name is already branded in my heart."

"My full official name is Thomas Jefferson Alcott, but I like Thomas, or Tom best, if you *havta* call me by my first name," he said shyly.

"Oh, I think I can come up with something you'll like even better than Tom or Thomas," Emma bantered back. "Let me think on it for a bit."

After a pause, she said, "How would Darlin' or Sweetheart be? Or would you like something even more demonstrative?"

"I like the sound of them," and he kissed her tenderly on the lips.

He held her clasped in his arms. He whispered, "And who knows, we'ns might come up with better ones, maybe we'd better save those for when no one else is around."

Alcott watched Emma come toward him.

I can hardly keep from crying. He swallowed the lump in his throat. *I can't breath with Emma coming toward me in her wedding gown. Her cornflowers match her eyes and she looks scared and happy at the same time.*

He took her hand and the scared look vanished.

I could dive into her eyes. They hold the deepest love. I've never seen anything so beautiful. She will be mine forever. Thank you, Lord.

He was overwhelmed.

If in a dream, I hope I never wake up. She is more than I ever expected. God has given me a wonderful gift in

Emma, may I be worthy of all she is.

Emma looked at her smooth gold band.

It is Saturday, June 5, 1866. I am proud to become Mrs. Thomas Jefferson Alcott and I know in my heart Thomas J. Alcott is my life partner given to me by God, to live together till only death shall part us. Then we'll walk together into eternity. Thank you, Jesus.

Grandpa William Alcott didn't make the long journey to Madisonville for the ceremony, but sent his regards. He had met JD and knew his grandson was marrying into a family, of which he could approve.

JD and Amanda watched as *their* children pledged their vows. JD had long ago come to see Alcott as *his* son.

Amanda squeezed JD's hand.

"I feel I've always known that young man. Alcott's *family is in attendance*," Amanda commented.

"I couldn't be more pleased with Emma and Alcott's choices," JD said. "God bless His children."

And He did.

New Arrival

In Kansas, Matthew worked through a growing season, His labors away from home gave him time to spend time with his Lord. He agonized. Prompted by his Lord and a wise old friend amongst the laborers, he came to know peace in his own heart. He would never forget he hadn't told Martin about Jesus, but he finally laid it at the feet of Jesus and left it there to rest.

He drew his pay and prepared to head toward Madisonville. He had saved most of his money the past months.

He stopped at a horse ranch and picked out a filly with a coat as bright as a newly minted gold piece. She had a white mane and tail that flowed in the Kansas wind. He led her along behind his saddle horse. He placed a light blanket around her middle to accustom her to carrying something on her back. Thus began the process of training her to saddle as they moved toward home.

He had written, while in Texas, he wished he could bring Faith home a *golden* horse and he meant to accomplish his purpose.

I vow in my heart to never again give Faith such emotional pain as I have in the past.

I am exhilarated and free. I never cease to regret Martin's death, but I'm convinced God has forgiven me. I'll not fail the next time to tell others of my Savior.

I feel light, my feet have wings as we travel from Kansas toward home. Now, I can't wait to get home.

Thoughts went through his mind.

I've seen God's world, He's still in control, even though I saw man's horrible acts to other men. I'm ready to go home and let God handle my life and the future. I can't control everything, but that's fine. I don't know what is going to happen, but He knows. I can't change anything that's happened, but I've learned to live with myself, wherever I am.

He looked over the last rise and saw the farmhouse and barns below. A bubble of anticipation started to grow inside him. He dug his heels into his horse's side and they burst forward, together. The horses leaped ahead toward the homestead, with his heart going home to Faith. He could picture her in a blue dress. He looked and there she was in the field of cut corn.

He tied his horse to the oak limbs hanging over the swimming hole. He left the filly free, depending on his saddle horse to keep her there. He leaped the rail fence and found Faith in the corn field, dragging a bag of ear corn. She shucked the dry stalks.

Her father, with a bag of ear corn, was near the far end of the field. Matt picked ears as he walked, then stood in the row in front of her and watched, as she picked almost to him.

She seemed preoccupied, then she saw his boot and her eyes flew in alarm to his face. The sun broke from her smile, but there was hesitation and question in her eyes.

He stepped forward and took her damp, flushed face between his hands and looked deeply into her eyes.

"It's all right, I'm back to stay. God has settled it for me, and I've accepted His direction."

They enfolded each other in an embrace that promised to span all human wars and experiences together. Unashamed tears streamed down both their faces and they dried each others tears with their hungry kisses.

Celebration

The community was returning to normal. The citizens could forget the war at times, however tempers could be easily stirred, as injustices had been committed on either side.

Several years after the war, at a picnic on Lick Creek, some women still wore black, in remembrance of those lost in the war. Those like Billy McIntire had permanent physical changes in their lives, due to battle wounds. Others had emotional scars.

In the bright sun of mid-October, quietness reigned after the sumptuous dinner on the grounds. Farm folks finally had plenty of food, after some lean war years. They were rebuilding.

Two young men rose with flushed faces. There was jealousy over little Miss Evans, who was enjoying the attention of all eligible men. She was taking advantage of her full-blown feminine beauty for all the attention she could garner.

Others joined the argument and slurs passed freely. The argument escalated and open battle was threatened with men falling in, on the side for which they fought in the war, or for the side their family or friends favored. Weapons appeared and it seemed as if blood would surely flow.

"Is the war to never end?" Amanda asked JD

"Further bloodshed will not enhance community feelings," JD looked toward the noise. He started toward the combatants. "We must live peaceably side by side."

He shouted above the uproar.

"Men of the Missouri State Militia, front and Center! Fall in behind me." He stepped to the front of the fray with a shout.

In blind obedience, his troops fell in and his bark echoed. "About Face," and they marched from the *field of battle,* behind their old captain and out of respect for his leadership. Military discipline won out over their independence, during their service in the war, and again at the picnic.

Silence reigned for a few moments as the milling crowd realized what had happened. A collective, surprised sigh escaped the lips of the women.

Surely this is a miracle of fast thinking.

The crowd, ashamed of their actions, quietly dispersed. A few, who left in a huff, had celebrated a bit too much by the whiskey barrel.

JD was credited with saving the day. The respect of his men and that of the community was spoken of as the families departed the picnic grounds.

Later that afternoon, John Dickerson argued with several of the men from the picnic.

He and his group retired to the Madisonville store to discuss the day. A shot rang out and John fell dying on the floor of the store.

"Hit the floor, they're after us."

Some men leaped out the back window. Others huddled behind the counter.

"Duck!" was shouted by the gathering.

Men thought they heard a horse galloping away, but vision was obscured by the underbrush. Friend and foe came from all directions at the sound of the shot. Dr. Marshall was in the fore of those approaching.

Some of the men gathered the dying John, and laid him on the store counter for Dr. Marshall's attempt to administer medical aid.

The doctor shook his head to those gathered when he inspected John's wound. He was unable to help John, as he lay bleeding from a mortal wound. The doctor applied a damp compress to John's head and dry bandage over his chest wound. The wise man applied pressure.

"This is all that is humanly possible," he whispered.

Each man was quiet, everyone's attention was riveted on Dr. Marshall and John. The men were in stunned shock, those who recovered most quickly, murmured comforting thoughts to John.

John gasped, "Mr. Logan, can I see Mr. Logan?"

JD was not long in arriving at the store. He went to John and leaned over him to listen to John's desperate whisper.

"Please, forgive my sins," he pled.

"I can't forgive your sins, but Jesus can. Believe in Jesus as your Lord and Savior. He came to die for your sins, ask Him to forgive you and He will," JD said.

"Yes, Jesus forgive me—I'm sorry, I've caused trouble around here—Please forgive me," John mumbled.

"He hears son, do you feel Him in your heart?"

John took a stumbling breath.

"Yes—Please? Let there be peace here."

John lay peacefully on the counter, bleeding into the wood and down the front. He felt weighted and cold, as if leaden water bore down on his body. He began to whirl through a lighted tunnel. Jesus extended His hand. John reached, welcomed.

"I see Jesus, He's reaching for me," he said and died. A beautiful smile lit his face.

John's brother arrived just before John died. He heard the last statements. James reached out to John and drew his brother's body to his own.

"John, I'm sorry, please forgive me. John, John?" He looked and saw, not a dead man, but joy upon John's face.

Grown men turned their heads to prevent the sight of tears on their downcast faces. After a few minutes, the strangely sobered men began to drift away.

James William Dickerson took the body of his brother on his own horse. He walked along beside the horse for the four miles to their old residence, thinking deeply. He examined his own thoughts. He felt condemned.

I've been wrong to go along with the group who do not want peace.

John was buried in the family plot with little ceremony.

Later, JD noticed John Dickerson had no tombstone in the Madisonville Cemetery and felt it would be a binding experience for the community to place a tombstone on the graves of John Dickerson and Anthony Suttons. With the leadership of the church, the community came together to purchase and place the tombstones.

Regardless of their previous feelings toward one another, the men worked together to dig the foundation and set the stones.

Lucy Coleman never knew why someone killed her husband during the war, but she remarried to a man who needed a mother for his small children. They found the unexpected blessing of love. Their marriage was no longer one of convenience but one which God had ordained. Their daily association and efforts brought them closer and closer together. Necessity no longer dictated the respect and care they showed for each other. Love won their hearts.

"JD I prayed for a man who could love my children, or a way to hold on to our home. I got a *Yes* answer to both prayers and the bonus of love."

The war was *finally* put to rest for one family.

Mind poisoning hatred lingered to cause someone to fire bullets through the two tombstones, causing desecration. *Every* wound was not healed by a community effort, but not every person had the poison left in their system to continue to taint relationships in the future.

JD drew closer and closer to his God with each experience. He surrendered to his Lord's call to preach the Gospel of Jesus Christ. With the gradual retirement of Pastor Wilson, JD was selected by the local body of believers to fill their pulpit and be their pastor. Reverend Wilson continued as Pastor Emeritus, mostly an honorary position, with JD serving as legs and voice. They offered teamwork in administering Gospel-balm for the healing of their community.

Reconciliation

A few weeks after the tombstones were shattered, James Dickerson, journeyed to the cemetery, to level and sow grass seed on the two graves. He mortared and replaced the broken stones, then knelt and prayed. He turned his face up to God and cried aloud.

"Let this be the last skirmish of the war here at the Madisonville community. Please end the animosity someone felt toward two dead southern boys. I'm empty, I have no hatred left, I don't want to punish them. Help me be man enough to make it up to my folks and others, for John's death and bring reconciliation to the community. I'm sorry I have

About the Author

Anita L. Allee resides on a small farm at the edge of a small town in the Missouri Ozarks.

Two of her great grandfathers and one great grandmother grew up in the vicinity of the *real* small town of Madisonville, Missouri. Despite serving on both sides during the War Between the States, the families appeared to bear no animosity toward each other during the latter years of their lives. Their children married across former loyalty lines.

Like many of the early small towns of the midwest, Madisonville, boasted thriving businesses and energetic citizens. When the railroads came through at other points in the county, these small towns faded into the books of history.

Now the community serves as wooded homesites and bedroom community for those who still prefer the country life of Ralls County, but modern times require them to go elsewhere to earn their living.

I may be reached at:
Anita L. Allee, 13216 Church Road, Versailles, MO 65084
e-mail address: anviallee@earthlink.net

I pray you enjoy reading this book as much as I enjoyed writing it.

Thank you, Anita L. Allee

A Letter to Readers

Dear Reader,

If you would like to reorder or correspond with the author, please fill out the following coupon and relay to Anita.

Please include any review thoughts you might have.

Tell us what you did and didn't like about this book: Hero, heroine, other characters, setting, plot, and inspirational thoughts.

Thank you.

Send to:
Anita L. Allee, 13216 Church Road, Versailles, MO 65084-4722 Or e-mail me at anviallee@earthlink.net
with the following information:

Your Name:________________________________

Address:________________________________

City:__________________________ State:_______

Zip:________________________________